MONSTERS OF CREATION

J.R. GAGNE

WE MAKE WORLDS LLC.

COPYRIGHT

ISBN: 978-1-7371216-3-3 E-Book

ISBN: 978-1-7371216-4-0 Print

CONTENTS

PREFACE

Welcome back as we continue our journey through the ever changing world of Tauro. The stakes are much higher this time around as Arain and Lucious grow stronger, creating even more ferocious beasts than before. Love, loss, and the darker parts of humanity will come to light. So find a comfy place to read, grab an ice cold beverage, and let's not waste another second. Monsters Of Creation awaits!

CHAPTER ONE

STEPPING STONES

General Hortus crested the hill, surveying the road south towards the city of Angor. At least a whole days march still lay ahead of the enormous military force he commanded. Like a dark blue wave, the soldiers marched in cadence, ten across and a thousand soldiers deep. The sound of armor clad boots pounding the road rang out a considerable distance. Corwin pulled his horse beside Hortus. The sight of the two generals sitting on horseback next to each other was almost comical to view, as Hortus was twice the size of Corwin.

Hortus looked over to the mage. "There doesn't appear to be much cover ahead for an ambush, but send out your wisps just in case." He wasn't about to chance anything with Arain Drake.

Corwin nodded in agreement that caution was the best strategy. "Elzeem, spizem," the words hissed from his lips and with a gesture of his scepter three crackling white orbs appeared. All of them floated before the two generals. The only noise they made was the snap and crackle of electrical arcs shooting across their surfaces. "Go forth and secure the road ahead," he commanded. The three wisps bobbed and weaved their way down the hillside and out into the distance. Occasionally one of the wisps would surge with electricity as it fried some poor unsuspecting animal.

"It looks like the road ahead is clear Hortus, shall we continue on?" The massive warrior sat atop his horse silently for just a moment longer before finally signaling his troops to carry onward. The tension built little by little as they marched closer to Angor. Word of Arain's powers spread like a sickness throughout the ranks, lowering morale. Only a fraction of the soldiers had ever been in actual battle, but none of them ever fought against something that wasn't human.

The day dragged on under the unforgiving heat of the sun as they continued marching on. Finally, the sun began to set and the twin moons were on the rise to take its place. Hortus stopped in a wide, open clearing on all sides. "This looks like a highly defensible position to set up camp for the night, wouldn't you agree Corwin?"

Corwin surveyed the location before voicing his opinion. "This spot will work just fine, general." Without a moment to lose, the mage began shouting orders to the other officers who in turn relayed the commands to the various lower ranking soldiers. Patrols were sent out in all directions to scout the area for threats and to lay down a plethora of different traps and warning signals. Tents and barracks were setup along with a slew of fire pits that were dotted around the site. Supplies were unloaded so the cooks could get started on making dinner for the ten thousand hungry stomachs on site, many knew it could very well be their last. Tomorrow would be the day they reached Angor.

Hortus dismounted his horse and handed the reins to a young man who couldn't be more than seventeen. "Take care of this horse like your life depended on it."

The young man was terrified of what Hortus might do to him. "As you wish general, I will not let you down."

Hortus took one last look at the young man, "Dismissed." This was the only command he gave before heading over to where they were erecting his quarters.

Corwin walked the camps perimeter as he laid down barrier and protection spells. *That should just about do it, no sneak attacks to worry about tonight.* Satisfied, he dusted off his robes and headed back into camp to continue supervising the troops. In this campaign, Hortus was given operational control which meant Corwin handled all second in command duties. It bothered him little, he liked serving with Hortus.

Within a relatively short time, they finished setting up camp. Daylight slowly faded as darkness crept in and the days unforgiving heat gave way to a cool breeze from the north.

It was eerily quiet in camp this night. No pre-battle frolicking, no drunken fights, no excitement. Every soul realized that tomorrow they would be fighting against all manner of monsters and men. Not to mention their leader Arain, who they all believed to be un-killable. No good sleep would be had this night.

The night dragged on, watch fires crackled away as soldiers patrolled the camps perimeter. At the center of camp however, no guards patrolled and that is what Arain was banking on.

The dirt slowly and silently sank away in a six foot diameter circle. One by one werewolves spewed forth from the hole and dispersed into the camp. The battle had begun...

With precision, the werewolves entered tent after tent spreading their affliction and swelling their ranks. By the time they were discovered, it was too late. Thousands of soldiers were either dead or turned.

"General Hortus, we're under attack," screamed a blood covered soldier as he burst into his tent and collapsed on the ground dead. Hortus donned his armor and prepared for battle with amazing speed for a man his size.

The body of the soldier on his floor began convulsing violently. "What manner of witchcraft is this?" Drawing his two handed sword, Hortus stood ready. With the utmost caution he approached the body, ready to strike. The quivering stopped when Hortus was within swords reach, then it exploded sending flesh and sticky black fluid everywhere. Hortus was quick enough to shield his face but the front of his plate mail was covered.

"What in the fuck!" Now he was thoroughly pissed off as he burst out of his tent looking for someone to focus his rage on. What he found was a werewolf barreling towards him. Its muzzle glistened red from the fresh blood reflecting off of the campfire light.

Instinct took over, Hortus swung his massive sword in an upward arc so fast it couldn't be seen as it split the werewolf in two. The sections fell on the ground in a twitching heap of fur and blood. Hortus grinned with satisfaction, followed by complete shock as the two halves began slowly mending back together right in front of him.

Little time was given to assess this situation however, Hortus knew he needed to alert everyone of the attack. He began running towards Corwin's tent. One after another, werewolves sprang forth from all sides trying to kill him and all ended the same way as the first, momentarily dead corpses in pools of their own blood. "There it is," forty feet ahead sat the mages tent.

An explosion of white hot light followed by an enormous BOOM erupted through the side of the mage's tent. Standing in its opening was Corwin.

Hortus kept running as he yelled, "Get everyone up now and regroup back to the north!" With an outstretched arm and a flick of the wrist, all of the previously placed warning measures went off around the camp. Giant plumes of bursting light raced skyward illuminating the city of tents below, while horns sounded signaling an attack. From above, werewolves could be seen racing through the camp spreading their disease as quickly as they could. Arain Drakes numbers swelled by the second.

Hortus ran until he reached the officers barracks. His captains were already assembled out front fending off one werewolf after another. His orders rang out with every slash of his sword. "Gather everyone you can and regroup at the north end of camp, also spread the word these beasts do not stay dead!" A volley of, "Yes, general," came from his officers before Hortus continued on northward.

These creatures seem to be getting more frequent the farther I go. When he reached the center of camp he knew why. Before Hortus, the gaping hole spewing creature after creature lay like a gateway to hell itself. "You bastards will pay for this." Raising his sword he placed both hands on the hilt. "Focused destruction" he shouted aloud as he drove the blade into the ground in front of him. A shockwave ripped through the soil causing the hole and the tunnel below to collapse in on itself. Dirt and debris shot out of the hole as it closed making it hard to see. "Dig through that you mangy dogs!" With a forceful heave, Hortus pulled his sword from the ground.

As the dust and dirt began to settle, a massive shape stood where the portal once was. Hortus had only a second to defend himself as Timber burst through the haze to attack. The size of this werewolf made Hortus look small in comparison. A flurry of razor sharp claws and teeth came at him with a speed and strength the likes of which the general had never witnessed. It took every bit of skill Hortus had to keep from being eviscerated. One swipe of Timber's right hand did happen to get through, leaving four deep gashes across the left side of his face. His forehead to his jaw immediately gushed large amounts of blood, which temporarily blinded his left eye. Timber used this to his advantage and followed up with another attack to Hortus' left. His claws pierced the generals breast plate sending him flying to the ground. The force of the impact jarred his sword from his hand. Before Hortus could get back up, Timber pounced on his back, driving him face first into the ground. It almost knocked the general out but his fortitude kept him conscience. Time seemed to slow as he waited for the killing blow from Timber.

It never came. Neither Hortus nor Timber noticed that Corwin had arrived and that gave him the few seconds he needed to cast a powerful spell. "Nathule, invicto, externum!" With the last word uttered, a six foot lance of ice materialized in front of Corwin. It shot forth entering Timber's mouth, traveling through his chest and finally stopping as it stuck out of his right leg. Next came a loud pop as the spell finished by exploding the lance inside the werewolf's body sending tiny razor, sharp ice shards through his internals. Hortus righted himself only to come face to face with his bloated, dead attacker slumped down behind him.

"Serves you right you filthy dog!" Hortus followed his insult with a plate mail boot to the monster's head. Timber's motionless body fell over from its kneeling position and proceeded to ooze fluids from multiple points throughout his body.

"Don't think you'll be coming back from that, will you?" No sooner did the last word leave his lips when he noticed the blood and juices no longer flowing from the beast. Timber's wounds began closing right before the two stunned generals. "Hortus, I think it best we leave right now." The master at arms needed no convincing that staying there would be bad for their survival. Without hesitation, they continued heading north to the rally point.

Blood continued to flow down Hortus' face making it look like some form of war paint, but the wound was all to real. Every step was agony as he let out the occasional grunt and groan. "I'm sure that beast broke a few of my ribs, and my face is burning like someone splashed me with boiling water."

Corwin looked like his head was connected to his body on a swivel as he scanned in all directions for more of those monsters. For now it seemed clear ahead as the werewolves concentrated on the remaining human forces to the south. He surmised that many were probably trying to dig out their brethren as well. "Come on Hortus just a bit further, then we can get you to the healers." The injured warrior looked terrible as he struggled to keep up with the mage. "Look up ahead, Hortus." There some fifty yards away, almost half of his remaining forces waited ready for battle. Large bonfires roared providing much needed light and protection. The heat could be felt quite a distance away and only intensified the closer they came. Corwin with a hand gesture raised a minor barrier spell to protect both of them from the flames.

The moment they passed the flaming barricade, Hortus collapsed to his knees desperately trying to catch his breath. Each inhale felt like daggers were being pushed through his chest. Soldiers rushed forward to aid their wounded leader hoisting him up and carrying him to the makeshift triage tent. Inside looked like a slaughterhouse. Blood covered much of the ground and the handful of cots didn't look much cleaner. At least eight clerics were inside chanting various healing spells to aid all of the injured. Those that help was too late for were carried out and disposed of to make room. Four soldiers hoisted Hortus up onto the best looking cot and quickly began removing the severely damaged breast plate. One cleric brought over a green concoction in a flask and proceeded to pour it into Hortus' mouth. Off the man went while another one arrived and began the process of casting a powerful spell to mend the broken ribs. "Ahhh," through clenched teeth as an audible snapping was heard when the bones cracked back into their proper place. Once they were mended, he moved on to begin working on the facial wounds. The cleric was starting to show signs of fatigue as each spell sapped a little more of their magical reserves. Healer after healer attempted to repair his face with less than satisfactory results. The last one that attempted hung his head in shame. "I apologize general, this wound is unlike anything we have ever treated. The bleeding has stopped but that is all we could do."

Hortus sat up not saying a word, he just grabbed his damaged armor and headed out of the infirmary, towards the makeshift barricades. The mass of his soldiers watched as their leader joined back in the fight when most other warriors would have been finished. Hortus stopped for only a moment when he passed a soldier with a warhammer. He outstretched his hand and only said one word, "Weapon."

The hammer was passed over to Hortus. With one swing and a loud clang, the dent in his breast plate was gone and the hammer was tossed back to its owner. Hortus carried on to the front lines donning his armor while he walked.

CHAPTER TWO

PARTING WAYS

In the great hall of Westlin castle, a massive feast is being prepared for the newly assembled guests. It surprised everyone that the day had breezed by them and now the time to get ready for more serious discussions was upon them. King Elrick and Queen Victoria had returned from their previous duties to start the planning over dinner. The long rectangular table now had beautiful multi-tiered candles placed down the center with fine linen placemats in front of each chair. Magnificent black and white marble plates sat on top of each mat with accompanying gold utensils and a cloth napkin. The initials E-V were embroidered in golden silk thread on each one to signify Elrick and Victoria.

A few minutes later two guards opened the tall wooden doors at the northern end of the great hall. Everyone inside quieted down and stood in orderly fashion to accept the arrival of the king and queen. Almost as if on que, Elrick and Victoria walked hand in hand when they entered. Lucious and his companions all bowed their heads in respect. All except the gryphon who upon seeing Elrick let out an ear piercing screech. The room erupted in laughter at the outburst.

Victoria stepped up to the table, "Come everyone and be seated so we may enjoy the first dinner together between our races." Her voice, so warm and inviting made everyone feel welcome. One by one those in attendance picked their seats. Elrick and Victoria as expected, sat at the head of the table with Lucious and Morgan to their left. Ulandra and Selim sat to the king and queen's right. Ezra took the end of the table so he could see everyone. Bibble and Bobble sat to his left and right. Stormy and the gryphon although not at the table sat close by.

The lead server clapped his hands twice to signal the others to begin bringing in the almost endless line of food. Like a synchronized machine, each server knew their exact role. First the goblets were placed in front of each guest and filled with one of multiple choices of drink. When they finished, the next set of servers came in and placed steaming hot rolls and butter. After that the meats, greens, and vegetables were placed neatly on each plate. When they had finished, one server stood three feet behind each person in attendance to take care of any refilling or whatever need arose. Last were the meals for the gryphon and Stormy. A heaping serving of assorted meats for the massive gryphon and a full bowl of assorted greens and vegetables for Stormy.

Victoria looked around at everyone. "I would like us all now to hold the hand of the person next to you so we may share a prayer." This was the first time all day that the great hall was completely silent. Human held Draconian hand who in turn held a Veassel hand until they were all united. "I humbly ask you mother nature and father sun, to guide us down the safest paths through these dark and troublesome times. But if we should falter, please father, let your light shine. No matter how difficult and dangerous things may be, please let us all return here, safely. Blessed be all."

With her prayer finished, they all silently wished for the safety of everyone Arain Drake's evil would touch. King Elrick looked to Victoria, "Thank you for such a beautiful prayer, my love." She smiled back with pure love in her eyes. All the seated attendees thanked the queen as well for the prayer. Elrick looked back at his guests. "Let us now enjoy this wonderful meal." The silence of the hall had now been replaced with sounds more related to a holiday feast with friends and family. Utensils cutting meat on the marble plates while goblets were emptied and filled repeatedly. Talks erupted around the table as everyone focused on good times of the past. Course after course was brought out from the kitchen until every man, woman, and creature were stuffed. Bibble sat slouched in his chair with his mouth open like he had a hard time breathing. Bobble wasn't much better sitting in a food induced coma. Even the gryphon and Stormy had over eaten. The majestic beast lay curled in a circle falling asleep. Stormy was nestled up close, using the gryphon's soft feathers for a bed. He was slowly drifting off as well.

Lucious sat back and did a sort of half stretch to try and situate his bulging belly. "I must say that was the most wonderous meal I have ever had. We thank you again for your hospitality, King Elrick and Queen Victoria."

"You all are quite welcome, and please feel free to address us plainly. Elrick and Victoria are just fine," remarked the king.

Lucious gave a nod in response, "As you wish, Elrick."

The head server approached Elrick and bent down. "Your majesty, will there be anything else?"

"No I think we have had quite enough. You may clear the table now."

"As you wish, your majesty." Stepping away from the nobles, the head server gave two loud and quick claps which signaled the dinner was finished. The table was cleared and cleaned in no time at all. The only thing remaining were clean goblets and a few pitchers of wine.

Elrick gestured for the easel with the maps on it be brought over beside himself and the queen. "If everyone is ready, I think it's time we begin planning how we are going to stop Arain Drake." Hearing her name gave Lucious a very uneasy feeling. Even Morgan who was holding his hand noticed. A reassuring smile from her eased the unpleasantness.

Clearing his throat Lucious responded, "We are ready."

The hours passed by quickly as idea after idea was cast forth and vetted by the group. Everyone had input and different points of view on the situation. It was just past eleven at night when all of the plans were finalized and documented by Victoria. She went over them for the final time with everyone. "Ezra and Ulandra will travel south by gryphon to the homeland of the Draconians. Once there, they will gather as many able bodied warriors as they can. Ezra, Ulandra and the Draconian army will then travel northwest until they reach the City of Knowledge. Once they arrive, they will rejoin Elrick, Lucious, and Morgan along with fifty thousand soldiers. The City of Knowledge will be where we make our first and hopefully only stand. Elrick has already sent a small group ahead to inform the council of the approaching threat so hopefully we can add their forces to our own. Bibble and Bobble, you will go with Selim and Robert to the Veassel homeland and gather as many of them as you can. You four, plus the Veassel forces, will return to Tellium and join up with General Erin and her forces of about thirty thousand. There you will set up our second line of defense in case the first line in the City of Knowledge fails. Myself and General

Cappell, will setup the last line of defense here at Westlin castle. If for any reason the first and second defensive lines fail, they are to retreat back to Westlin. Oh and lest I forget, Stormy will be going with Lucious and Morgan. Are there any questions?" Each person seated responded with a no. "Good, let us all get some rest, we begin the defensive to-morrow!"

CHAPTER THREE

VENOM

S ebastian, Seline, and Uluck along with their new elec-
trified friend, Lux walked up the trail until there was a
sizeable distance between them and the scattered corpses of
the demon dogs. The group surveyed the area as best they
could in the failing light of day. Sebastian was first to break
the silence. "Well what do you guys think, camp here for the
night?"

Seline was not her usual commanding self since the
battle. "Looks as good as any other place." She opened one
of the packs on her horse and produced three white orbs,
each roughly three inches in diameter. Seline took the first
one and held it in front of her lips. With a light blow, the
white orb began glowing, illuminating the immediate area.
Gently she placed the white glowing ball on the ground.
Seline walked about ten steps away and again held one of
them up and blew on it. The second one reacted like the first
and began glowing. "Here take the last one and use it to find
some wood for a fire."

Uluck took the glowing ball and held it up in the air.
"Come on Sebastian, let's make this quick." The two men
ventured a short ways off between the trees to do as they
were told. The little creature that had saved them stayed

behind with Seline who was busy stripping the saddles and packs from their two remaining horses. She found a nice grazing spot conveniently close to their camp and let them eat their fill.

I'm exhausted, I've performed a lot of healing and never felt this drained. My leg is killing me, Seline thought as she rubbed the leg that was injured earlier. *Something is clearly wrong.* She sat down leaning on one of her bags. It took immense effort to keep her eyes open. Luckily, Uluck and Sebastian arrived with the firewood only a few minutes later.

Sebastian noticed immediately that Seline looked different. He knelt down next to her. "Hey are feeling alright? You look pale."

With a half hearted smile, "I'm fine, just tired from the battle that's all."

Sebastian wasn't buying it. Uluck, busy building the fire looked at him with concern on his face. The look Sebastian gave him back confirmed there was a problem. "Let's see what we have for dinner," said Sebastian as he rifled through the packs. "Here you go, Seline," handing her a small metal dish with some grapes, cheese, bread, and dried fish on it.

"Thanks, Sebastian." Taking the plate she began eating slowly. The Arabis by now was full so it quickly bounded over to sit next to Seline, gently nudging her arm to be scratched. "Alright, how's that little one?" She gave the creature what it wanted from head to tail. The purring started almost immediately.

Sebastian sat down with his meal after giving Uluck his plate. He watched Seline fall asleep mid chew, resting her plate on her lap allowing the grapes to roll off onto the ground. "Uluck, is this normal for her?"

The massive warrior shook his head. "No, I've never seen her like this, even after healing multiple wounded." Sebastian quietly walked over and took her plate. He then reached into one of her packs and found a blanket which he unfolded and gently covered her with. The Arabis nibbled away on the grapes as it watched Sebastian.

"Well Uluck, how about I take first watch if you want to get some sleep."

"Alright, wake me up to take second watch and let Seline sleep." Sebastian agreed that would be for the best. She needed sleep more than either of them right now.

Picking up one of the orbs, Sebastian proceeded to walk the imaginary perimeter around their camp. While walking, he thought back on the earlier battle hoping to find some clue as to why Seline seemed sick. We both suffered wounds from the creatures bite, his arm ached with a phantom pain when he remembered the bite that broke his arm. As far as I can recall, those beasts all looked the same so I should have the same symptoms as Seline. He knew the answer was right in front of him but he just couldn't see it. Sebastian, coming full circle back at the camp, sat down by the fire to warm up.

Uluck was already in a deep sleep, snoring with his mouth wide open. The newest addition to the party lay curled up in a ball on Seline's lap with its tail covering its face. Seline still slept but developed a twitch every few minutes and her face looked like she might be having a bad dream. For a moment, Sebastian thought about waking her but decided against it.

A few more minutes by the fire and then it will be time... The word instantly clicked like the last piece of a puzzle. Time, that's the only difference between our injuries. Seline treated my arm right away but her leg wasn't tended to until much later. I bet the monsters venom left untreated produces significantly more trauma to the person. The question now is how do we heal her. Those words rattled around in Sebastian's head for the remainder of his watch.

Thankfully it was a peaceful night and the changing of the guard took place without incident. Uluck added some more wood to the fire before setting off to patrol the perimeter. Sebastian wasted little time lying down next to Seline and falling asleep. She, nor the fur ball on her lap, gave any sign of waking.

The next few hours passed quickly as night began giving way to day. The twin moons sank on the horizon and the sun peaked ever so slowly into the sky. Uluck used the side of his boot to nudge Sebastian awake. In protest, he groaned under his blanket. "It can't be time to get up already?"

"Rise and shine everyone, I let you three sleep in late as it is." Uluck sipped from a steaming cup. "I made a fresh pot of spiced tea to get us going. We can eat on the way to Hemshire."

Sebastian sat up and looked towards Seline who was busy stretching as she yawned. The Arabis Lux was over by the horses that Uluck was putting the saddles on. What Sebastian saw was troubling. Seline was pale and looked sickly. When she threw off her blanket things became much worse. The puncture wounds that were healed yesterday were now open and oozing a foul smelling black liquid. Seline gasped at the sight. "What, I healed this all yesterday. How is this possible?"

"I'm not sure, but I think the venom from those creatures has poisoned you." Brushing off his pants, Sebastian walked over to offer whatever aid he could to Seline.

"I don't understand. You were injured every bit as much as me but your arm looks fine."

"I know, the only thing that was different was the amount of time the venom was in each of our wounds."

"This is possibly beyond my abilities then." Seline sat there silently in thought. A moment later with a look of determination, she began working her healing magic on the freshly opened punctures. The faint glow returned to her hands as she chanted the spell. Sebastian could only stand there and watch in amazement. Again the holes gradually closed stopping the flow of that horrible black fluid. When Seline finished, a bead of sweat rolled down her face and off her chin. She looked even more tired now and her breathing sounded fast and shallow.

Sebastian quickly poured a cup of the spiced tea and handed it to Seline. "Here, drink this it should help."

"Thanks." She took a few sips before vomiting everything back up. "Help me stand, please."

Sebastian grabbed her outstretched hands in his and heaved her onto her feet. He stood there for a moment steadying her, making sure she wouldn't fall. "Are you alright?" Even as he asked the question, he knew what the answer was.

"I'll be fine, thanks for helping me." Letting out a deep breath she carried on with the chore of breaking camp.

Uluck and Sebastian made sure to work quickly so their sick companion didn't have much to do. Soon enough, they were back on the road towards the town of Hemshire. Seline was kept riding in the middle and close just in case she needed help. Everyone but the little Arabis Lux felt on edge as if another ambush could happen at any time. Every time a creature of the forest made a sound, the trio stopped and readied their weapons, but no attacks were made. By mid day, the wooden gates into the town were visible. Each of them breathed a sigh of relief at the sight.

CHAPTER FOUR

SEPARATION OF THE SEVEN

L ucious and his companions slept little by the time the
first rays of sunlight shone through the tall windows.
"I guess we might as well get up and get ready, Morgan."
Lucious wanted nothing more than to stay in bed holding
her, but he knew his sister wasn't wasting any time to the
west.

Morgan rolled over facing him as she opened her
gorgeous blue eyes. Lucious could feel his pulse begin to
quicken. This young creature is the most beautiful thing he
had ever seen and his feelings towards her were growing by
the day. He only hoped that she felt the same.

"Is something wrong?" she asked in a hushed voice. Morgan panicked, quickly changing to her human form thinking
her Draconian form displeased him.

"No, no, no, you don't have to be anyone but yourself
around me. I think your natural look is beautiful, Morgan."

She shifted back to her Draconian form slowly. Her
face felt flush and she knew she must be blushing. Morgan's
feelings were growing for Lucious as well but neither of them

had any experience in matters of the heart. Not to mention, they were two completely different species.

Lucious gently placed a hand on the side of her face and brushed a stray lock of hair back. He never broke eye contact as he caressed her cheek. Up until a day ago, she had kissed him but not since then. Lucious didn't want it to be a one time thing, and he didn't want to over step her boundaries. With a knot in his stomach, Lucious found the courage to ask her. "Morgan, would it be alright if I kissed you?"

Morgan smiled and pulled him close. "You don't have to ask," she said following with a kiss of her own. *It was just as wonderful as the first time I kissed him.*

The two of them locked together hadn't noticed Ulandra standing there. "When you two are finished, the servers would like to come in and setup for breakfast."

Morgan and Lucious nearly leapt off the bed. "Yes by all means. Morgan and I were just getting up anyway." They were still using the great hall of King Elrick's castle as an oversized bedroom so Piercer could stay close to his master.

Ulandra gave the all clear and one by one the servants entered with plate after plate of delicious breakfast foods. The table they had used the night before was quickly filled. Lucious looked back towards Morgan to see she was already dressed and working on laying out clothes for him.

"Thanks," a smile was given for the kind gesture. Lucious didn't want a repeat of being partially naked with all of his friends present, so he quickly put on his clothes before everyone arrived this time. The gryphon who had been given the name, Piercer anxiously waited for some attention from Lucious. The majestic creature lowered its head as he approached. "There you go, how's that?" He stroked the soft feathers on the side of its neck. The occasional chatter like that of an eagle echoed in the great hall from the gryphon.

Morgan couldn't resist smiling as she watched the two bonding.

King Elrick and Queen Victoria were the first to arrive for breakfast. Unlike the night before however, they now wore more functional and practical clothing. Elrick gave a quick greeting to Morgan then headed straight for Piercer. The king was absolutely infatuated with the creature. "Good morning to you Lucious, I do hope you were able to get some sleep, because today is going to be very busy." Elrick's hands immediately went to petting the gryphon like a child that just couldn't keep his hands to himself.

"I did manage to get some sleep your highness, thank you for asking. How about yourself and the queen, were you two able to rest?" Lucious knew as he asked the question that nobody likely slept well.

"Ahh, there was some sleep but mostly just enjoying the last little bit of time together. Oh and Lucious, it's just Elrick remember?"

"Sorry about that your high... I mean Elrick. It will take some getting used to."

It wasn't long before the rest of the companions were chaperoned in by guards to have some food before embarking on their quest. Breakfast had a completely different pace than the night before. No tankards of wine and ale to drink this time. The meal was meant to be quick so they could all be on their way. No more than an hour passed and everything was cleaned out of the great hall including the table and bed. King Elrick signaled to have the newly made saddle for the gryphon brought inside. Two men carried in a true masterwork of fine leather and steel. The master tailors had nervously taken measurements the night before so the saddle could be finished for today. With help from Lucious they were able to get everything fitted with ease. "There you go Piercer, now you look like a truly fearsome mount!" The gryphon signaled with its ear piercing screech in response.

The massive doors at the end of the hall swung open. Elrick stood before everyone and instantly all eyes were on him. "Today we leave this castle and go our separate ways in hopes that soon we will all be reunited to defeat Arain Drake and her horde of monsters. There will be hardships and maybe even loss on this journey, but we willingly sacrifice everything to save this land and our world. Friends, let us go now to the courtyard where we will say our last goodbyes and begin this defensive."

Everyone filed out of the great hall and into the courtyard as instructed. Once they arrived, they could see caretakers loading the last of the supplies into the bags on the horses they would be taking. Each horse stood saddled, packs full and ready to go. While Ezra and Ulandra said their goodbyes, some supplies were loaded into the packs on the gryphon. Ezra stood before Lucious with pride. "I will see you soon son, stay safe. Morgan, please take good care of him."

She hugged Ezra. "I will and you take care of yourself and my sister."

"I will, you have my word." Ezra walked over and climbed up onto the saddle.

Ulandra was next, giving a one armed hug to Morgan and Lucious simultaneously. "You two take care of each other and I will see you soon." Onto the saddle behind Ezra she climbed.

Ezra leaned forward to Piercer's ears, "Fly" is the only word he said. Piercer spread his wings wide and with one powerful leap, raced skyward. Everyone in attendance stared on in awe. This would be one of many firsts to come as the three headed off into the clear blue sky. It wasn't long before they were completely out of sight.

Bibble, Bobble, and Selim were next to say their goodbyes. The massive Draconian's hand dwarfed Lucious' though his handshake was gentle. A hug for Morgan, and up onto his horse he went. "Good luck to you two, I hope we are reunited soon."

"Good luck to you three as well. We will meet up with you in the City of Tellium after my sister is defeated."

The Veasell's were fast, giving out only handshakes before climbing up into their saddles. Bibble and Bobble looked almost comical on the backs of such large mounts. With a wave goodbye, they exited the courtyard heading east. Mounted guards accompanied them so the city folk wouldn't be scared or try to stop them. Within the hour, they were out of the city leaving Westlin behind.

Morgan and Lucious walked over to Victoria and said their goodbyes. The queen hugged them both like they had known each other for years. They mounted their horses with Stormy leaping on last. Morgan's saddle had a new section designed just for the little Arabis. He settled in for the journey ahead.

Elrick saved his goodbyes for last, giving Victoria a long hug and a kiss. "I will see you soon my love," whispered the queen.

"As you wish, my love," replied Elrick with a bow. He climbed onto his horse with ease, and gave one final nod before the three of them were leaving westward with a large military force in tow. Banners of the king's gryphon crest were displayed and carried with pride.

Victoria and her generals waited and watched until the last of the cavalry had gone. "Let us get to work, generals."

They wasted little time as plans were enacted to prepare Westlin for WAR!

CHAPTER FIVE

NOT SO SMOOTH SAILING

"Drop the sails and secure those jibs!" hollered Captain Kander to his deck hands, as waves slammed into the port side of the cargo ship. "Where in the fucking seas did this storm come from?" The morning started out gorgeous and calm with a nice breeze blowing northward. That all changed in a matter of minutes when black clouds on the horizon headed their way. Winds quickly changed to the opposite direction halting the ships progress. Thunder boomed as streaks of lightning arched across the sky followed by thick sheets of cold rain. The deck load of somewhat docile ogres was turning into a dangerous place. With little to no protection from the storm, tempers began to flare between the groups. Sea sickness did little to help matters as the ship rocked and bounced in the large waves.

Talia ran over to the bridge to assist the captain. "What in the world is going on, Kander? I've never seen a storm of this magnitude before."

Kander just looked at her and shook his head. "I have no idea but it surely isn't normal!" When he looked back to the deck he could see some fighting starting to break out. "We need to do something quick, Talia before this gets anymore out of control. I want you to send as many of them as you can down to the oar galley. Get them putting all that energy into rowing."

Talia headed down from the bridge and onto the deck. Over to Adlin she headed. "I need you to pick eighty of your strongest and have them follow me down to the galley."

The massive chieftain seemed undisturbed by the weather as he collected the requested number of ogres. Only once did an irritated or sick one refuse. Adlin swung at the disobedient ogre connecting his enormous fist with the other's chin. A sickening crack rang out. The ogre slammed face down onto the deck unconscious. "Anyone else?" Adlin's point was clearly made, obey or there will be consequences.

Everyone that was selected followed Talia down to the galley without question. "You lot will be handling our propulsion today. Fill up the benches and use the long oars to row. Steady and even strokes is best. Any questions?" Talia scanned the room and watched as the oars were extended through the port holes. A few minutes later and the ogres were almost rowing in unison. "Their all yours, Adlin." Talia turned and headed back up to the main deck.

Kander now able to maneuver the ship pointed the bow into the waves. Up went the bow as the ship climbed the wave to its peak and down it crashed as it crested and pitched down the back side. The motion now long and rolling made the ogres even sicker. Every which way the giant beasts stumbled around the deck vomiting while trying to find somewhere that was rocking a little less, but the storm continued on relentlessly. Talia finally made her way through the maze of ogres and back to the bridge. "Captain, we need to find somewhere safe to wait out the storm. This ship won't serve us very well at the bottom of the ocean!"

Valin emerged from below deck a moment later to see what had awoken him. Wide eyed, the mage dodged an incoming volley of puke from one of the void ogres. "It's absolute chaos up here!" Without a second to waste, Valin headed straight for the captain.

"Good day Lord Valin, how may I help you?"

Valin did not look amused. "You can start by getting this ship out of this storm, NOW!"

"As you wish Lord Valin, but you may want to hold onto something." Kander spun the wheel hard to the right. The ship responded as the bow came around to face the coast line. At least a dozen ogres lost their footing causing them to roll across the deck. "Talia, we should be close to Eklin Bay. I think that's our best bet."

"Agreed captain, we should be seeing the entrance to the channel any moment."

The storm seemed to intensify in anger as the ship raced towards calmer waters. A bolt of lightning struck the forward mast sending a shower of flaming wood pieces raining down. The mast stood for a moment longer before collapsing across the deck with a loud crash. Two ogres were pinned under it, crushed to death.

"There it is, the entrance." With precision, spinning the rudder wheel this way and that, Kander navigated the vessel into the bay. "Talia, go make sure the anchors are ready to drop on my command."

"Right away, captain." Talia headed below deck and forward to the bow where the anchor winches were located. Along the way she enlisted two crewmembers to operate the release mechanisms.

Kander placed the ship in the most protected area of the bay. "Drop the anchors!" he shouted.

Talia gave the all clear to the two men and the locks were released. The massive chains raced off the drums as the enormous anchors plunged to the ocean floor.

"Stow the oars," came the next command. The rowing stopped and the oars were retracted into the galley. Now the wind took control spinning the stern around towards the shore. A moment later, the anchors dug into the ocean floor securing the vessel in place.

Talia returned to the bridge awaiting the next order.

"Lets get everyone below deck and out of this weather."

Talia nodded before heading off to round up everyone. Valin who had been standing idly by now spoke up. "Excellent work Kander, you truly deserve the title of captain." Before he could respond, Valin had already started heading back to the captain's quarters to continue his sleep.

Talia and Kander now had to share her room. They took turns on watch as they hid in Eklin Bay waiting for the storm to pass. Chores were dolled out to all of the passengers who slept in shifts below deck. Those that were rested headed back to the main deck where cleanup and repairs commenced. The mast that had been snapped off was lifted back into place by a combination of magic and muscle. Once it was attached, a group of ogres held it in place while the human crew members installed two large half circle clamps. Next the two sections were connected and pulled together by three large screws. Once the brace was installed it completely covered the damaged section of wood. A handful of ogres were tasked with collecting more food. With two larder boats and a large net, the group set about catching some fish. Kander watched from the bridge as they pulled up the net. "Wow it's actually working, the storm must be blowing schools of fish into the bay." They repeated this cycle of cleaning, repairing, and fishing for almost two days before the storm blew itself out. Finally the order was given to raise the anchors and hoist the sails. The ship and it's crew were at last back on their way to Castle Kragg.

CHAPTER SIX

THE DEEP ONES

A rain Drake emerged from the smoke of the burning tents around her. She looked like an apparition as she approached Timber. The werewolf just now finished regenerating from the vicious spell Corwin struck him with. The massive beast breathed heavily from the pain. Arain laid a hand on his muscled chest to comfort him. "Are you alright, my friend?" Timber nodded yes. We need to dig out all of your brethren before continuing on."

Timber took a deep breath and howled as loud as he could. Seconds later and the return howls could be heard from all directions. Legions of werewolves began closing in on their location. First one pair of eyes reflected in the dark, then another, then ten more, and so on until nothing but werewolves could be seen. Timber communicated what needed to be done and without hesitation they began excavating the collapsed portal and tunnel from both directions. Dirt, rocks, mud, and whatever else they came across was flung out of the way. The sight was impressive.

Arain watched her lycanthrope army work with a smile stretching from ear to ear on her face. One by one the buried werewolves were exhumed from the ground. Some were dead and in the process of regenerating while others managed to survive in small pockets of stable tunnel. At a certain depth they came across colonies of worms that were tossed aside with the rest of the refuse. Arain stood there noticing how fast the worms were able to bury themselves into undisturbed sections of ground. "I have a wonderful idea." Closing her eyes she began to picture a horrific new creature. Up until now, Arain had only created new life when under extreme duress. This time though she was going to use her powers when she decided to. Standing there silently she worked out the finer details of what she wanted to create in her mind. Just as an artist molds clay or chisels stone into a work of art she adjusted the image. Next she needed to tap into the feelings she had the last time her powers were awakened. One by one the crown of glyphs lit up around her head starting at the temples and moving towards the center of her forehead. Blood trickled slowly from her nose and ran down her face. As the last glyph lit completing the crown, Arain's body was completely surrounded by a swirling black mist. Minutes later she opened her eyes and the mist imploded in front of her. The lighted runes of her crown soon faded while a flood of warm blood flowed from her nose and off of her chin. "Did it work?" she asked herself.

It didn't take long to get an answer. In front of her the ground began moving as if something was digging it's way out. A twelve inch hole opened up and out came Arain's creation. An eight foot long, white bodied tube with multiple clawed tendrils on what she assumed was the head. It bent itself forward towards Arain and the entire top of it split into four equal sections that pulled back onto itself. Row upon row of hooked teeth lined the opening. A flower shaped appendage rose from the very center of the open cavity. Immediately Arain could hear a voice in her head. It didn't sound like male or female but something in between. "My queen, what is it that you wish of me?"

"Are there more than one of your kind here?"

"Yes, we are many."

"What is your name?"

A few moments of silence passed before it answered. "We are the Deep Ones."

Arain was so focused on this new creature she didn't notice the assassin creeping out from a nearby tent towards her. It was suicide for sure but the devoted attacker was not going to miss this chance. The werewolves were occupied with their rescue work, and her back was wide open. A long dagger was pulled from its sheath as the assassin closed the distance to Arain. Mid stab, the attacker froze in his tracks as if some invisible force took control of his body. The man struggled trying to fight it but his efforts were in vain. Turning around, Arain stood face to face with the paralyzed man. "What would you have me do with him, my queen," came the voice again in her head.

"Kill him," she ordered without hesitation.

That instant, the assassin began stabbing himself with his own weapon until he was nothing more than a bloody pile on the ground.

"How did you make him do that?"

"All of us deep ones have psionic powers which allow us to control weak minded creatures. I took control of his mind easily and made him do as I wished."

"Fascinating, absolutely fascinating. I have a job for you to do. There are a considerable number of enemy troops that have fled to the north and I would like you and the other deep ones to pay them a visit."

"By visit you mean to have them killed?"

"Haha, that's precisely what I meant! I can see these powers are going to be a lot of fun."

The worm like deep one closed back up and slid silently underground leaving only a circle of disturbed dirt where the hole once was.

Arain removed her right gauntlet and wiped the blood off her face. The fatigue now hit her as it always did after a creation was finished. This time was different though. "I don't feel as drained as the other times. I must be getting stronger."

By this time almost all of those trapped underground were freed. The massive pack now stood before Arain awaiting her next orders. In one night her forces grew ten fold.

"This conquest will be too easy if this is the best the opposition has to offer, how pathetic! Come Timber, let us head back to camp now for some food and rest." Timber had already changed back to his wolf form. Many of the others returned to their human selves. "All of you new bloods are welcomed into my army. Come with me and we will have you all clothed and fed. That is if any of you are still hungry." Arain chuckled to herself, most of the new bloods will be full on the remains of their brethren for days.

Into the night they returned, heading south where Seget and the rest of Arain's forces were staged. Her thoughts wandered during the walk, as she thought about the deep ones and their surprise attack on Hortus and his forces. Tomorrow she hoped to reach the general's new camp only to find it decimated and everyone slaughtered. Then nothing would stand between her and King Malik. I will need to devise something especially terrible for him when he is defeated.

Seget and the rest of her soldiers stood ready in case they were signaled for aid. It didn't surprise any of them that they were not needed. Hell, the enormous wave of werewolves approaching from the north didn't even faze them. This sort of thing was becoming the norm for the shrinking number of humans in her majesties army.

"Alright troops, you can stand down. Make ready for the queen and her new horde. We have a lot more bodies to feed and clothe before moving on."

The soldiers did as they were ordered, welcoming in the new recruits. Lines were formed leading to the armory and the mess hall.

Seget approached Arain, "I take it all went according to plan, your grace?"

"No not exactly to plan, those coward generals ran north just when we were starting to have some real fun. I guess Malik's generals are all female as they surely have no balls!"

"Very good, your grace. It looks like the recruiting went well." Seget eyed the long lines of half naked men and women lycanthropes as he spoke.

"Recruitment went amazingly well, three to four thousand new werewolves in just a few hours. Oh and the best part is, I finally created something with absolute control of myself."

Seget couldn't even fathom what she made this time. "Excellent your grace, should we be expecting them soon?"

"No, I sent them ahead to harass the remaining enemy forces. We should see them tomorrow."

"I cannot wait to see your newest creation, my queen. Until then, is there anything you need?"

"Just some dinner and a bath is about all." With her conversation concluded, Arain and Timber headed towards her tent. Seget nodded letting her know he would have her requests taken care of immediately.

Chapter Seven

WORM TROUBLE

Assassin Galena had been keeping a distant eye on Arain Drake's progress for King Malik over the last few days. Her orders were not to engage but observe and report back before Arain reached the castle. Galena had just witnessed the complete routing of General Hortus' forces. *It's time to head back to the king, things are much worse than anticipated.* Keeping down wind of those werewolves was a challenge, but she was the best at what she did.

Galena worked her way north to where Hortus and Corwin were now positioned. She needed to requisition a horse if she was to reach the castle quickly and it just so happened that there were now a few spares. The king's assassins usually worked as their own entity for the king and rarely served under one of the generals. They were given a special status that allowed them to take, use, and do whatever they needed to accomplish the king's orders. It would be perfectly fine for Galena to waltz into camp and just take the horse and that is exactly what she intended to do.

The master assassin stayed just out of range of the camp fire lights as she entered the compound undetected. Galena made her way to the northern edge of the camp where by some strange luck she happened upon General Hortus and

Corwin. They were sitting by a fire pit eating their dinner. It being her nature, she approached a bit closer to eavesdrop on their conversation. To her disappointment, the two generals were talking of nothing important. Galena almost turned around to leave when something caught her eye. It was very subtle at first, just a small patch of dirt moving behind the generals. Until a giant worm like creature burst out of the ground and began attacking the two men.

"Ahhh, what the blasted fuck is that thing?" screamed a startled Hortus. Corwin jumped up to see what it was when he suddenly felt a sharp pain in his head that forced him to put his hands over his ears in an attempt to stop it. The deep one had taken a chance that these two would have weak minds like so many of the others they had just controlled and murdered. This gave Hortus a chance to grab his weapon from the ground where he had been sitting. Realizing the mages mind was to strong to control, it stopped the psionic attack and went more conventional. Corwin still holding his head could feel the psionics stop. He looked in the direction of the attacker only to be struck in the forearm with a needle type projectile. The pain felt just as intense as the one in his head had been. The mage grabbed a hold of the needle and ripped it from his flesh. "Umm, Corwin look at your arm, something is inside you."

"Son of a bitch, this can't be happening." Corwin cast a fire spell on his own forearm trying to kill whatever parasite was under his skin. "Ignitus," is all he said and the skin on his arm began to burn. "Ahhhhh," he screamed in agony. "Extermose," barely left his lips putting the flame out and dropping him to a knee. To his horror, something still moved under his skin and was now heading up his arm. He hadn't killed it, only pissed it off.

Hortus thinking quickly, swung his blade severing Corwin's arm just above the elbow. The infected appendage hit the ground with a thud. Corwin didn't say another word as he passed out from the shock. The severed arm still moved until a smaller version of the worm creature wriggled out. Not wanting to give it another chance, he smothered it under his large boot. Now the monster whipped a needle towards Hortus who was ready and dodged it easily. Now it was his turn to attack. At a sprint, Hortus closed the gap between him and the demon worm. "Now you DIE!" Before the worm could slink back in its hole, the general split it in two right down the middle with his sword. Green fluid squirted in all directions as the creature expired.

Knowing Corwin needed immediate aid, he left the corpse and returned to his friend. Blood was pumping out from the stump with every beat of his heart. Hortus knew there wasn't a healer close by so he did the only thing he knew and grabbed the hottest stick from the fire. As it contacted the wet flesh, it sizzled cauterizing the wound in the process. Corwin remained unconscious through the whole procedure. Thankfully Hortus was an extremely large and strong man which allowed him to throw Corwin over his shoulder and head to the healers tent without anyone's aid. As he ran, a scream wailed to his left and soon another, and another, and another. *It must be more of those damn over grown worms, or worse the werewolves again.* Just the thought made the wounds on his face ache.

Galena took this as her queue to leave immediately. She grabbed a horse that was tied up nearby and bolted towards the castle.

In front of Hortus, another worm burst from the ground launching needles immediately in his direction. Hortus didn't slow his run as he dodged the incoming attack while swinging his sword cutting the worm in half. Finally he arrived at the makeshift infirmary just in time to see one of the patient's head explode sending bone and brain matter flying. In place of the man's head was one of those wretched baby worms. Hortus grabbed it before it could escape and crushed it in his gauntlet. Green juices squirted from between his fingers. "Disgusting little bastards," shaking the remains from his hand.

The blood spattered healer just stood in shock at what happened. "Snap out of it, man!" commanded the general.

"Sorry general, are you wounded?"

"No, it's General Corwin that needs your aid. Hortus promptly ripped the corpse off the bed and laid Corwin down so his feet were on the blood soaked end.

"I'll return soon, make sure you keep him alive. Oh and watch for the big worms, they shoot some sort of parasitic dart. I think we just witnessed the results of one of them."

The healer turned around to his other patients remembering one of them was struck with a similar projectile. He quickly ran over and threw a blanket over him. A few minutes later, the blanket puffed out as it contained the blast. Crash, the healer swung his mace into the bulging section of blanket killing the monster inside. He damn near broke the table in the process.

Hortus seeing his friend was in good hands dashed from the tent heading towards the nearest barracks. He burst through the entrance, "Get your asses moving now! We're under attack by...." A deep one burst out in the center of the tent at just that moment. "Watch out for the darts." The creature as if on queue loosed three in succession. Two were dodged but the third found its mark imbedding itself into one of the soldier's leg just below the knee.

"Ahhh," the soldier screamed falling to the ground in agony.

Hortus had enough, a downward angled swing of his sword and the worm was dead. His next move scared the shit out of his men. Hortus cleaved the injured man's leg off above the knee. Screams of agony followed by silence when the man passed out. "Get him to the healers and whatever you do don't get stung by those things."

Off went Hortus to alert as many soldiers as he could. Things were looking grim the further he went on. Suddenly the quiet made him stop. "Something isn't right here." There was no more screaming, but there was a familiar sound. *Marching?* Off just a little ways in front of him were his troops marching towards him. "Thank goodness you all made it here alive." Hortus lowered his sword and waited for them to catch up. Closer they came as he anxiously stood there. "Hurry the hell up, lads!" There was no response, just the continued slow march. Hortus was getting pissed off until he saw it. A glimpse here and there showed him that worms slithered behind his soldiers. "What the..." He didn't get to finish that sentence as bolts of lightning crackled past him and into the crowd sending worms and people alike flying. When Hortus looked back, he saw a haggard looking one-armed Corwin standing there.

"We need to leave now Hortus, those worms are psionically controlling those men now!"

Indeed those that weren't dead stood up and charged at the two of them, weapons drawn. Hortus was left with no option but slay his own troops. The first wave was slaughtered in seconds. Before the next wave, the two generals bolted north. As best they could, the two generals aided their subordinates that weren't infected or mind controlled. Tired and winded they looked at one another. "My friend, the battle is lost," remarked Corwin. "We should take as many soldiers as we can and retreat back to Castle Kragg. We'll have to deal with Malik's punishment later."

Retreating was the last thing Hortus wanted to do but he knew Corwin was right. "Alright, let's grab what horses we can find and leave this horrid place." One by one they collected stray horses that had escaped while fighting off the worms and their slaves. Everyone still left had a horse by now so they were sent towards the castle. Hortus was the last one still on foot at this point. Only Corwin remained to help his friend but his strength from the loss of blood was waning fast. "Go while you still can, I'll be right behind you."

Corwin was too weak to argue as Hortus smacked his horse on the ass causing it to take off with haste. He stood there for just a moment and watched Corwin race away. "Good luck to you mage." His minor respite was over. More of the mind controlled soldiers raced towards him. Even though exhaustion was setting in he still hacked through them with relative ease. Hortus rounded a supply tent running smack dab into one of the cavalry horses. The two scared the hell out of each other. Luckily for the general, this horse had been tied up quite well so it couldn't run off. Hortus had no time for knots so he severed the rope and mounted the steed. "Yahh!" he cracked the reins causing the war horse to take off leaving the smoldering compound to the worms.

CHAPTER EIGHT

LITTLE HELP

As the group drew nearer to the town of Hemshir, the signs of a recent battle could now be seen. They passed a dead woman and child that had been torn apart by the side of the road. Flies were already buzzing around the corpses feasting on the flesh. Uluck and Seline were used to the horrors of the battlefield, but Sebastian was not. The sight, smell, and sounds caused him to loose his lunch almost immediately. "Be ready messenger, we may have trouble up ahead," said Uluck.

Uluck's words did little to settle his already upset stomach. Cautiously the trio continued onward. "Stop right there," came the order from a ranger with his bow drawn atop the wall. "There will be no further looting of the king's property! Turn around now and I'll allow you to leave with your lives."

The group sheathed their weapons while continuing forward. Just as Seline began to introduce themselves as emissaries of the king, the ranger loosed his arrow. The projectile wizzed past Uluck's head so close that one of the arrows razor sharp edges cut his cheek sending a stream of red down his face. "Woah, woah, woah. We're on a special assignment personally issued by the king himself. Cease your attacks immediately! Can you not see we wear the king's standard?"

"How am I to know you didn't just lift that off of some dead soldiers?"

Sebastian could see Uluck was about fed up with this fellow. He raised his hand high with the sealed letter from the king. "I can prove it to you, if you would let me approach."

The ranger thought on it for a moment before signaling him forward. "Just you and no sudden movements or the next shot won't miss."

Sebastian dismounted his horse and carefully approached with the letter still in his hand. He made it to just before the entrance.

"That's far enough." With the arrow still trained on Sebastian, the ranger walked down from the wall. "Let me see it."

"I will, but you must promise me you will not break the seal."

"Very well, you have my word." The ranger lowered his bow and held out his hand.

Sebastian reluctantly handed over the letter. The man held it close to his face examining the royal seal. "Alright it looks official, you can come in." He handed the letter back. Sebastian put it right back in his inner pocket. "I'm Rickter, by the way."

"Nice to meet you, Rickter, I'm Sebastian. The woman there is Seline and the rather large fellow you cut is Uluck."

"Apologies for the rude reception, but ever since those black dogs attacked a few days ago, they killed half the guards and infected the rest. We now have an influx of looters who are mostly townsfolk looking to line their pockets on the way out."

"You mentioned that some of the guards were infected, how so?"

"It's those damned poisonous bites from the dogs that attacked. The wounds wont heal, they just keep oozing black fluid until the poor bastards die."

Uluck and Sebastian immediately looked at each other and then at Seline. "Don't worry boys, I think I finally cured it." Seline was bluffing of course. Her wound was not healing, but in fact getting worse. She just didn't want to worry them.

"Well miss, your one of the lucky ones then, that shook them off quickly and healed right away. There were only a few here that got lucky like that."

Seline stood in front of the ranger now. "Are you all that's left?"

Rickter shook his head "No, there are still a few decent folks who stayed. We still have a furrier, blacksmith, healer, and a woman fletcher. I'm the only one with any real fighting experience though."

"What about those black dogs, any idea where they came from?"

"No clue, they started picking us off a few days ago. They would usually attack at night when hunters were returning to town. At first we had no idea what was happening, it's not like hunters are on any kind of schedule. They leave and arrive to town all hours of the day and night. We all just figured whatever game they were hunting drew them far away. It wasn't until nobody returned that the guards suspected something foul was afoot. A patrol of ten went out to investigate but only one returned, and let's just say he was in pretty bad shape. Died that night as I recall. After that, they had softened our defenses up enough to attack. Twenty, maybe thirty of those creatures swarmed us and devastated the town in a matter of hours. We killed a handful of them, but by the time they left everyone was either dead, injured, or hiding real well. I'm very surprised you folks made it here in one piece."

Sebastian shook his head. "No, we ran into the rest of that pack yesterday and probably would be dead now if not for this little creature. He held up the Arabis to Rickter. Any clue as to what this thing is?"

Rickter looked the Arabis up and down. "I don't believe I have ever seen such a creature. You say this cute thing saved you three?"

"Indeed it did, this little ball of fur can put out an astonishing amount of electricity when it wants to." Sebastian set the Arabis down and watched it run over to the horses to play. Seline moved closer to the messenger and rested her hand on his shoulder for support. As he turned towards her to see if she was alright, she collapsed. His reflexes allowed him to catch her before she hit the ground. "Seline, what's wrong, are you alright?" The three of them helped lay her out on the ground with a blanket rolled up under her head. It didn't take long to figure out the cause when the black fluid from the Morlock's bite oozed through the bandage on her leg.

"She's been bitten, I remember seeing this sort of thing with the people here who were also infected. I'm sorry you two, but she has maybe two or three days before it kills her."

The only living town healer came out to see what the commotion was. "Oh my, this is not good, bring her to the infirmary immediately." Uluck picked up his sister and threw her over his shoulder. Sebastian was impressed how easy the warrior made it look. Uluck headed into town behind the healer while Rickter helped Sebastian with the horses. The Arabis bounded along beside them. Once inside, a hastily repaired gate was moved into place blocking the entrance.

Sebastian looked around and could clearly see the havoc those evil black dogs caused. Damaged homes and shops, blood splattered on a front door where someone must have lost their life. "This is terrible Rickter, how can anyone stay here now?"

"It's difficult, but this is the only home most of us have ever known. Walls and buildings can be mended, the king's soldiers will rotate in a new crew in a few weeks, and people will eventually come to take over for those that have fallen. I'm sure this isn't the first time Hemshir has faced similar challenges."

"I hope you're right Rickter, and I wish everyone here the best. Would it be possible for you to handle the horses while I go check in on my friend?"

"Absolutely, I'll tie them up over at the stable where they can get something to eat and drink. You go ahead and check in on her."

"Thank you." Sebastian handed the reins over and took off towards the building Uluck had entered. Up the steps and through the front door he ran. Inside was a decent sized medicinal facility with about fifteen beds. To his dismay, half of them had bodies on them with sheets pulled over. They must have been the ones that were bitten. Over in the far corner stood Uluck with Seline laid out on a white bed. The healer was chanting something and moving his hands up and down the injured limb. "Uluck, how is she?"

He said nothing, just shook his head side to side. The look on his face told Sebastian all he needed to know. It most likely would be a fatal injury. The healer finished his spell and the healing glow on his hands faded. "I'm sorry, but I haven't been able to find anything so far to neutralize the venom. All I can do is cast healing spells on it but even those will stop working soon. The only chance she has would be getting her to the healers in the City of Knowledge, and even then there are no guarantees they can stop it."

"Then that's what we'll do," exclaimed Uluck.

"You two are more than welcome to let her rest here while you go and resupply for the journey."

Sebastian held Seline's hand in his for a moment. "We'll be back soon, Seline." He let go and headed out the door with Uluck.

Rickter was just heading over after tending to the horses. "I take it you will be needing some supplies. Come, follow me."

They headed over to Peddlers Den. The front window was cracked and more of that black goo from those creatures was spread around the porch.

"Here we are, the best and now only outfitter in the city of Hemshir, Peddlers Den. The inside was clean and organized with shelf after shelf filled with supplies of all kinds. Provisions were the first thing to get picked up followed by some bandages for Seline's wounds and another saddle and bags for a third horse. They went up to the front desk to pay. Rickter was standing behind the counter like he owned the place.

"How much do we owe?" asked Uluck.

"Today the price is free. You all are in service of the king on a special mission. Everything you need will be written off as soldiers supplies." You didn't have to tell Uluck twice, back to the racks to pickup new blankets, some spirits, and some smoked venison.

"Thanks again, Rickter," Sebastian turned and ran out the door after Uluck. Over to the stables they went to requisition another horse for Seline to ride. The saddle, bags, and all the supplies were loaded and the horses were walked over to the infirmary. Sebastian waited outside with the horses while Uluck went in to get Seline.

Inside he could see his sister sitting up with her legs hanging off the bed. She was discussing possible salves or tinctures with the healer. "We are all set Seline, are you ready?"

"Yeah, I'm all patched up for now and the doctor here gave me a few things that might help give relief between healings. Thank you for your aid and I will be sure to come back to visit when I'm healed."

"Good luck," and a wave was all the man could give, he knew she would not be returning.

Rickter exchanged hand shakes and well wishes with the trio before opening the gate to let them leave. The ranger had given them some advice on the road ahead and the location of a shortcut or two to speed them on their way to the City of Knowledge. With some luck, they would reach the city in time for Seline. The pace from now on was as fast as they could safely travel. Every few hours they would stop so the horses could rest and Seline could cast her healing spells. This cycle continued on until nightfall came and sleep was needed. A quick meal, a small fire, and the use of the supplies the healer gave her let them make it through another night. There was still much ground to cover before they reached their destination, and every time the healing lasted a little less.

CHAPTER NINE

PUSHING THE PACE

King Elrick seemed like a different man when he led his army. Lucious and Morgan haven't known him long but his kind hearted demeanor was gone. It was all business now and nobody knew it better than Elrick. Every move they made and every break they took, the pace they rode was calculated for the best efficiency. It wasn't a difficult journey, just an extremely structured one.

Morgan as always rode side by side with Lucious. "Have you thought about what you will do when we meet Arain on the battlefield?"

Did I think about it, that's all I thought about. "I honestly don't know Morgan, she is growing stronger so much faster than I am. When I close my eyes and sleep she is always there in my dreams. Her legion of horrors seems to grow by the day. She has created at least three new species, all of which are geared for death and destruction. I know your people will be fierce on the battlefield and if we can find more gryphons that will surely help. Elrick's troops make up the bulk of our forces, but how will they react when fighting monsters? Fighting other humans is terrifying but it's something that skill plays a big factor in. These monsters have abilities unlike any human and we don't even know if they can be killed with normal weapons."

Morgan could see Lucious was spiraling and placed a reassuring hand on his shoulder. "We will figure it out together, Arain Drake hasn't won yet."

Morgan had a way of putting him at ease even if it was only for a short time. He needed that break from the fate of the world always resting on his shoulders. "Thanks Morgan, with you by my side I'm confident we can stop her."

Shady Vale came into view just up ahead. Elrick stopped to address his soldiers. "Let us take a break here before we continue on to the Vesper." Elrick could have stopped in the Vale but he didn't want his troops getting distracted or wandering off. No fires or warm meals, just some dried meat and fruit. The king was no different. If he expected his soldiers to eat like this, he did as well. The higher ranking officers ate with their respective platoons, and seemed to genuinely care about the men and women serving under them.

Lucious and Morgan went to sit with Elrick and the forward guard to eat their lunch. The guards quickly crammed down their rations when they saw Morgan. The looks they gave her were less than welcoming. They excused themselves politely and walked away. Morgan looked to the ground. "Should I change to my human form? I've noticed more and more humans looking at me strangely."

"Absolutely not! People need to see that their world has changed. They need to adapt or wallow in their mistrust and be left behind. Your beauty should not be hidden."

Morgan looked up at Lucious. "Thank you for saying that."

"You don't have to thank me, all I did was tell the truth." He put his arm around her as they continued over to where Elrick was sitting.

"Ahhh, Morgan, Lucious come and have a seat with me. Did you get enough to eat?"

"Yes, we should be fine until we reach the Vesper. Thank you." Morgan still felt a little uncomfortable and Elrick definitely noticed.

"What troubles you, my dear? You're not still nervous about talking to me are you?

"No, it's not that." Morgan didn't want to complain or get anyone into trouble.

Lucious finally spoke up. "It's some of the men, Elrick. They're scared of her and I'm concerned they may do something rash."

"I see your concern, my friends. I have already discussed acceptance with my officers but it looks like I will have to have another discussion with the troops when we stop for the night."

"On behalf of Morgan and myself, we thank you for your assistance in these delicate times."

"Not to worry Lucious, you two are more than welcome." Elrick stood up and signaled one of his lieutenants over. "Thadius, it's about time we get moving."

"Yes your majesty, right away." Thadius pulled out an ornate bone horn and blew into it. The noise it made was deep and intimidating. "Alright everyone, it's time to go. Pack up your gear and be ready to travel immediately." The command spread throughout the troops very quickly. King Elrick was brought his horse which he mounted with incredible agility. Lucious and Morgan were brought their horses next. Up went Stormy first to get settled in his spot and Morgan and Lucious followed. In no time, they were back on the move again passing by Shady Vale and heading west towards the Vesper.

The weather started changing as they traveled, gray puffy clouds began forming in front of them and the wind turned cooler. Lightning flashed in the distance followed by the rumble of thunder seconds later. Lucious saw what was coming and looked over to Morgan. "Looks like were going to be in for a wet ride soon." Lucious hoped the weather would be favorable the whole way but mother nature had other plans.

"I don't mind the rain Lucious, it's nature's way of taking a bath." He hadn't ever thought of it that way, but it made perfect sense now that she mentioned it.

"I suppose you're right, everything needs a bath now and then." As the foul weather drew closer, Elrick continued on as if it was still a beautiful day. The first few drops pattered off their clothes and saddles, but soon it was a steady rain. Morgan tried shielding Stormy but she only had her hands to use for protection. Lucious knew what she needed. He closed his eyes and concentrated for a moment. When he opened them he could see the emerald green cloak he created already on Morgan.

"What in the!" she said startled. One moment she had no cloak and the next she did. It felt warm and soft like no fabric she had ever touched before, and it was waterproof. Morgan covered Stormy with part of the cloak. "Thank you Lucious, it's so beautiful, I love it." She leaned over to wipe the drop of blood that slowly streaked from his nose. "You didn't have to do that Lucious, I was more than capable of getting soaked like everyone else."

"I know you're very capable, but I wanted you to be protected."

Morgan could see the caring look in his eyes. She couldn't help but to lean over and give him a kiss. "I will treasure it always."

It felt amazing being able to do that for her, and the re-ward wasn't half bad either. Lucious knew he needed to keep practicing so he could get stronger before he faced Arain. So many lives could be saved if he could neutralize her quickly. How he was going to do it was beyond him at this moment. *Practice, I need more practice,* was the only thing he knew for sure. Exhaling a deep breath, Lucious closed his eyes. *I should keep the item small so I don't wipe myself out, there's still a lot of riding to be done today.* As he gave himself over to the power, he no longer felt the rain or cold on his body.

Everything around him seemed to fade away as he en-visioned the object. Smooth polished metal, a razor sharp double edged blade, perfectly balanced. As he worked, he likened himself to that old smithy back in Addleberry. The one who he watched daily, hammering away on red hot metals at his anvil. Sparks flying with every strike, forming and molding the materials to his will. When finished, the end product was completely transformed into something beautiful and useable.

Morgan paid close attention while Lucious worked. His eyes were closed but they moved rapidly under his eyelids. The crown around his head glowed but not like before, she noticed. Usually the runes lit up fast, and were blindingly bright. However this time they were much dimmer. It looked to Morgan like the crown was slowly pulsing, with the light fading in and out in a repeating pattern. Whatever Lucious was doing, he looked at peace and that made her very happy. She continued on silently watching for quite some time before he opened his eyes. They exchanged a smile. "I take it you were creating something?"

Lucious held up the most beautiful dagger either of them had ever seen. The blade was dark blue about ten inches long. Its hilt curved forward on both sides and the pommel looked like wraps of the same material as the blade. The matte finish made it look almost soft. "You have to feel this Morgan, it weighs almost nothing." Lucious passed over the dagger.

Morgan took the flat of the blade and placed it on her right pointer finger where the blade met the hilt. "That's amazing, it feels so comfortable in my hand and it's perfectly balanced as well. Ouch! It's also unbelievably sharp." Morgan proceeded to place her cut finger in her mouth. "I barely touched it," she mumbled. "What is the blade made of that makes it able to cut on touch?"

"I call it coramite. I thought having a metal that once it was formed, would never loose its edge, never fatigue, and never break. I thought this could be handy."

"Indeed that metal will be highly sought after once more of it is discovered."

Lucious paused for a moment thinking. "Ya know, I'm not sure if creating inanimate objects produces the multiple effect like flesh and blood creatures do. It would be pretty neat if it did. Oh and I almost forgot to tell you the best part." Lucious picked out a random tree some fifty feet away and threw the dagger at it. The weapon made a puffing sound as it vanished, only to reappear imbedded in that tree all the way to the hilt. A second later it was back in Lucious' hand. When he turned to look over at Morgan, her eyes were wide open as was her mouth.

"That is by far the coolest thing I have ever witnessed! You are certainly beginning to master your powers."

"Thanks, I'm definitely better than the first time I used it. There's also a lot less blood and fatigue it seems when I can take my time. Hopefully I can get in a lot of practice before we reach the City of Knowledge."

"I'm sure you will have ample time, it's not very likely that anyone would be dumb enough to attack us." Little did Morgan know how wrong she would soon be.

CHAPTER TEN

ANOTHER BAD REPORT

Gallena rode all night and day to reach Castle Kragg. She was exhausted by the time she reached the outskirts of the city. Her horse was fairing just as badly. A thick froth coated the animals mouth from lack of water. "Come on girl, just a little further. All the water and hay you can eat is waiting for you at the castle. Just a little further," she coaxed. The two pushed on as best they could through the city.

Within the hour they reached the castle. Gallena gave no outward cues that she tired as she dismounted the animal. "Here, take my horse and get it water and food immediately!" She handed the reins to one of the grounds keepers before hurriedly heading into the castle. No one dared to stand in the assassin's way. Only when Gallena saw one of King Malik's stewards did she stop to converse. "Where is his majesty, I have urgent news?"

"Ahh, assassin Gallena, it's nice to see you in such good health. I believe he's supposed to be in the combat yard getting in his daily training."

Great, of all the places she didn't want to discuss this with him in. "Thanks for the info steward, Michale." Gallena was off towards the rear of the castle where the combat training yard had been set up.

The atmosphere in the city and castle was hectic with every available person preparing for war. Gallena knew it would be getting much worse after her report. As she closed in on King Malik's location, sounds of fighting could be heard. Thuds, and clangs rang out as weapons clashed. Just up ahead and down to the left was the exit. Gallena expected to see soldiers sparring, but in front of her stood two distinct sides fighting it out for control of the field. On one side was King Malik with roughly sixty soldiers. Opposing him were General Yuni, General Clink, and about sixty soldiers as well. Behind each squad stood a battle standard just waiting to be taken. *I suppose their running some sort of capture the flag drills.* Not wanting to interrupt, the assassin patiently waited. Currently Yuni was locked in heated combat with King Malik while the two squads of soldiers fought it out at center field. Clink however was quite a few steps back away from the fighting. He held one of his newer inventions in his hands. From where Gallena stood it looked like a tube about three feet long with a hand grip just off center. He shouldered the weapon like a crossbow and fired a four inch ball into the crowd of soldiers. A second later it exploded with an ear shattering bang followed by a blinding flash. Malik's troops were caught off guard by the attack. With loss of hearing and sight, they were easy prey for the opposing forces who knew what was going to happen. They had placed cotton in their ears to dampen the sound and closed their eyes when they heard the sphere hit the ground.

Yuni who had been holding her own against Malik now found herself reinforced by her troops. Like a wave, the soldiers surrounded Malik and over ran him. The king fought hard dropping attackers in every direction, but in the end he was defeated. Yuni held the king's battle standard high over head in victory. On queue, a group of squires entered the field to gather up the large quantities of equipment that was being shed by the combatants. The injured hobbled off the field or were carried. All the weapons were dull and blunted but the impact still broke noses, fingers, and legs. Cuts, scrapes, and bruises were carried by all who attended.

Malik noticed Gallena standing by the castle door waiting. Handing over his helm and gauntlets, Malik proceeded over to the assassin.

Gallena bowed, "Your majesty, I bring you news as instructed concerning Arain Drake and her forces."

"Very good Gallena, before you proceed I would like to gather Yuni, Clink, and Pogo and have them meet us back at the war room in one hour."

Another bow, "As you wish your majesty." Off she went to relay the orders to Yuni and Clink. Once that was done, she set off to track down the alchemist Pogo. *I would bet he's either in the mess hall eating or in his laboratory. Oh well, the mess hall is on the way so I'll just start there.* Gallena weaved her way through the castle's many halls and rooms until she entered the mess hall. As she carefully scanned the area, she did not find her target, only a handful of guards who just finished their watch for the day. The thought of going to Pogo's laboratory made her cringe. Quite a few people over the years have been killed or maimed by going into his lab unannounced, during an experiment.

Reluctantly she headed in Pogo's direction. She arrived ten minutes later and stood at the door to the lab. Warning signs were placarded across his door. *Keep Out, Authorized Personnel Only*, and her favorite, *You May Die Opening This Door*. Gallena grabbed the handle and slowly pulled the door open. "So far so good, no explosions or smoke yet." In she went trying to make as much noise as possible. "General Pogo, are you in here?" she shouted, but no reply was given. This room was a considerable size in order to house all the reagents, tubes, vials, samples, test subjects, and research books. Further into the lab she went, stopping ever so often to call for him again. "General Pogo, I have orders to deliver from the king!"

That finally got the alchemists attention. "I'll be right there, just give me a moment to put these rats away." Gallena stopped and waited. A few moments later and Pogo emerged from deeper in his lab. "Ahh Gallena, it is you. How are you doing?"

"I'm just fine, thank you. The king has asked me to inform his remaining generals to meet him in the war room by the end of the hour for an update on Arain Drake."

"Well, good, good, we need to learn as much as we can before she arrives. Thank you for relaying the message Gallena, I shall head that way shortly."

The assassin gave a nod and then proceeded back towards the mess hall for some dinner. She sat alone at a small table out of the way so she had full view of the room. *Hmph, once an assassin always an assassin. I can't even sit down for dinner without positioning myself in a way that sneaking up behind me would be impossible, and all the entrances and exits are readily accessible. I suppose that's to be expected though.* Pulling out the chair and sitting down was the highlight of the past few, somewhat crazy days. Gallena sat there silent for a few minutes just letting her stress and tension fall away.

It wasn't until the server arrived that she moved. "Good evening miss, what would you like for dinner?"

"Just give me today's special and some water, please." Off went the woman to put in the order. *I would love to have some mead or wine right now but drinking is strictly prohibited when addressing the king unless he is the one supplying the alcohol.* Years ago one of Malik's officers was drunk off his ass and insulted the king directly. It ended with the officer having a lance shoved up his anus and out through his mouth. That poor bastard was left there in front of the castle until the ravens picked his bones clean. *Ughh,* just the thought of it made her cringe. Luckily the server was returning with her food, so her mind didn't wander to such morbid occurrences.

The plate was laid down along with the cup of water. "Is there anything else I can get you?"

"No, that will be all, thanks." The woman headed over to wait on the other patrons in the mess hall. Gallena dug into the meat pie, ravenously finishing it within minutes. A few chugs and the water was gone as well. With a loud exhale, she pushed her chair back from the table and headed for the war room.

As she neared the room she could feel her pulse quicken. There wasn't much in this world that could do that, not even going in for the kill had the same effect. "Here we go!" Walking into the room she could see Malik and Yuni were already seated and waiting. Instinctively, she bowed her head when acknowledging the king. "Your grace, general."

Pogo and Clink could be heard coming down the hall. The meeting would be starting momentarily. No food or drink this time, it was all about the war today. Once the two remaining generals entered, the doors were closed behind them.

"Now that everyone is here you may begin, Gallena," ordered Malik.

All eyes were now on her as she recounted what she observed over the past few days on the southern front. "Hortus and Corwin's forces made it to within a day of Angor when they made camp. That night, Arain Drake staged a surprise attack with some sort of wolf man hybrid. Apparently their bite causes the affliction to spread thus creating more creatures. By the time they knew what was happening, about half of Hortus' troops were either turned or slain. Hortus himself suffered some grievous wounds during the battle. They managed to regroup to the north and setup a defensive perimeter. However, that held for only a few hours. Some sort of sentient parasitic worm creatures never before seen, attacked. General Corwin was seriously injured losing an arm in the confrontation. At that point, I deemed it best to escape while I still could. The camp was in absolute chaos by that point with these worms popping up all over the place. I do not have exact numbers, but a majority of the survivors from the first attack were slaughtered during the second attempt. Whoever wasn't killed should be arriving back here soon." Gallena finished her report and stood there in uncomfortable silence. Her audience sat in their chairs absolutely stunned by what they just learned.

Malik squeezed the armrests of his chair so tightly the wood creaked and cracked. Anger was all there was on the king's face. Yuni was first to speak up and break the silence. "Gallena, these wolf creatures from the first attack, did you notice any weaknesses or strengths that could aid us?"

"No general, I saw no weakness to exploit, only strengths. They are extremely fast and brutal in their attacks. Any injury they sustain is healed in minutes, and like I already said, they spread their disease by biting, thus creating more wolf creatures. I have witnessed them killed, but yet they still rise back to life moments later. No creature known can achieve such a feat."

"What we need is to capture one of these beasts for experimentation. Something has to kill them!" interjected the alchemist.

Clink was already figuring out what would be needed to successfully ensnare the creature. "I could have a working trap setup and ready to go by morning."

"Very well, Clink and Pogo. I want you two to focus on getting us one of these beasts. Build your trap and find us a weakness!"

Both generals acknowledged the king's order. "We will not fail, your majesty."

Yuni now moved onto the giant worms. "What can you tell us about them? Hopefully they are not immortal as well?"

"Quite the contrary, General Yuni, they seemed to stay dead once killed. As far as strengths, they can pop up almost anywhere from below. They also employ some sort of dart or needle that carries with it an adolescent worm. The victim becomes a host while the parasite feeds on your internals. The outcome I'm afraid, is death."

Malik leaned forward in his chair. "Enough about the bitch's pets, what have you discovered about her?"

Gallena nervously cleared her throat. "I regret to inform you your majesty, that Arain Drake has not engaged in any of the battles I have discussed. Her creations have done all of the fighting for her. I did notice one thing that has me concerned, her mentor, Valin seems to have vanished. He was missing at the fall of Angor and at the two routings of Hortus."

Malik stood up and grabbed his chair hurling it at great speed towards the doors just narrowly missing Gallena. On impact, the chair shattered into hundreds of little pieces that shot haphazardly around the room. "I want this woman dead. No matter what it takes Arain Drake will die by my hand!" The king's rage slowly came back under control. He knew he needed a clear head if he was going to defeat this opponent. "Gallena, your dismissed, go get some rest. I will have need of your services soon."

A wave of relief washed over her, the thrown chair was not meant for her. Gallena bowed. "As you command, my king," was her only response as she turned and left the war room.

King Malik grabbed another chair and sat back down across from his generals. It was going to be a long night as they planned the final defenses of Castle Kragg.

CHAPTER ELEVEN

AIR TRAVEL

Wind, cool air, and clear skies is all Ezra and Ulandra had to contend with on their first day of flight. Piercer did all of the work. All they had to do was not fall off, and judging by Ulandra's grip on the saddle, that seemed very unlikely. Ezra on the other hand was in pure bliss. Every time the gryphon dove downward quickly or banked a little too tightly, it excited the old mage even more. "How are you doing Ulandra, isn't this amazing?"

Amazing was not the word she would have used but showing weakness was not in her nature. "It is definitely a different sensation, I'll give you that. Where do you suppose we're at?"

Both agreed that staying away from the road and other populated areas would be best. The last thing they wanted to do was start a panic. Ezra took his best guess. "From what I can figure, we should be just north of Belrose. Not to bad for our first day of flying. We should probably land soon though and make camp. I'm sure Piercer here could use some rest." Ezra scratched the gryphon's massive neck.

Stopping for the night sounded wonderful to Ulandra. She couldn't wait to get some nice stable ground under her feet. "Yes, stopping to camp is a sound choice, whenever you're ready Ezra." Before she finished speaking the mage signaled Piercer to dive. The majestic creature folded its wings in to reduce drag and off they went. The speed with which they descended was terrifying, not to mention the fact that Ulandra felt like her stomach was trying to escape through her mouth.

"Weeeee," hollered Ezra as the three of them plummeted to the ground. He really enjoyed himself now, this day definitely ranked up there as one of the best he ever had. Just when it looked like they might actually crash, Piercer extended his enormous wings, and with one powerful flap brought them to an uncomfortably quick halt. Maybe thirty feet off the ground they gently floated on the wind currents. "Land over there," gestured Ezra. Like a floating feather, they gently drifted to the ground landing in a small clearing surrounded by trees. Ulandra hopped down from the gryphon and raced behind the closest one. Ezra could tell from the noises she was making that flying was not near as enjoyable for her. "Well how about we get this saddle off of you, Piercer?" Ezra undid the straps from around the gryphon's abdomen and slid the saddle off. Piercer shook his entire body fluffing his fur and feathers. He looked like an enormous dog shaking off water from his coat. "Thank you for all your hard work today, Piercer." Ezra scratched the gryphon one last time before focusing on dinner. "Ulandra, are you alright my dear?"

The poor Draconian just leaned against the same tree that she wretched by. Her scales looked paler than usual. "I'm fine Ezra, I just need a minute."

"Take as long as you need, I will take care of making us some dinner." The thought of food almost made Ulandra sick again but she managed to keep her composure. Going through the bag of rations he pulled out a small roast of salted venison and some vegetables for a stew. Within ten minutes, the mage had dinner cooking over a small fire. Ulandra was busy setting up the two, single person tents while Piercer flew off to scout the area for his own meal. The gryphon acted the same way a bird of prey would when hunting from above. Ezra and Ulandra watched as it circled for a short time before diving down and out of sight.

"Looks like he found his dinner. Speaking of dinner, how's the stew coming, Ezra?"

The mage leaned over the the fire stirring the contents of the pot. "I think it's just about done." He ladled out two full bowls and handed one to Ulandra. "Ya know, this reminds me of the last time I sat and had dinner with Lucious in our old farmhouse."

Ulandra could see Ezra was lost in the memory of better times. She waited a moment before bringing him back to reality. "Is that the same farmhouse Lucious said exploded into a million pieces?"

"Hahaha, yeah that would be the one. Nearly blew myself up with it, I was unconscious for days! But enough about me, how are you feeling now with some warm food in your stomach?"

The Draconian smiled, "I feel much better now, thank you. And thanks for making this delicious meal. I probably would have just went to bed if you hadn't cooked. Ezra, can I ask you something?"

"By all means, ask away." He sat back against the gryphon's saddle to get comfortable.

"I would like to know more about this vision you had all those years ago. Lucious has only really told us of how you found him and raised him, but why? Why did you and this Valin character get picked out of all the humans in the known world?"

Ezra just sat there for a minute thinking about the same question he has asked himself for eighteen years. "I'm sorry Ulandra, but that's one question I do not have an answer to. There is no reason I've come up with that makes any real sense. Who did all this is an even bigger unknown. Was it just some random cosmic anomaly that gifted those two with unimaginable powers? I'm afraid the questions far outweigh the answers."

"I appreciate you being honest with me. It seems we are all in the dark about many things. Did your vision reveal to you who would be victorious at the end of all of this?"

"I must say you have some very good questions. Sadly, the vision showed only snapshots throughout the revelation and it did not reveal anything past their confrontation. Whether that part of the future is still changing or that was all I was allowed to see, I do not know. The one thing I am sure of is, that we're in for a hell of a journey."

Ulandra nodded in agreement, "I do believe you are right about that, my friend." The two of them cleaned up and packed away the clean dinner dishes. "Ezra, would you like to take first or second watch tonight?"

"Ahh you go and get some rest, I think I'll stay up and have a pipe or two. Good night, Ulandra."

"Good night, Ezra," was the last thing she said before retiring to her tent.

Ezra pulled out his traveling pipe and a small leather pouch filled with tilly weed. *It sure is a beautiful night*, the sun had set and the first moon was high in the sky. The second moon was barely visible as it crept up past the horizon. The heat of the day was gone giving way to a cooler more comfortable breeze. *There we are, the pipe is packed, now time for the heat*. With a snap of his fingers, the weed began to smoke and burn in the pipe. A nice long puff and everything just got a little better. *I wonder where Piercer is? With the way that creature eats, he should have been back a while ago. Hopefully he isn't getting into trouble or we may be walking the rest of the way.* Ezra kept the fire stoked so the gryphon could see where they were even though he assumed its eyesight was probably good in the dark anyway.

It wasn't until just before the changing of the watch that Piercer seemingly dropped out of nowhere right next to Ezra. "Holy shit, you scared me half to death! Don't do that again feather head!" He had to walk around for a minute to let his pulse slow before proceeding to wake up Ulandra. Piercer just curled up by the fire and made ready for a nap of his own.

"Oh look, when did he get back?" asked Ulandra while exiting her tent and strapping on her weapons belt.

Ezra looked confused, "How did you know it was time for you to take watch?"

"I could here you muddling around out here so I figured it was my turn."

"Wha... I don't muddle young lady, and I'll have you know I was very quiet out here. You must have heard when the gryphon landed."

She knew it was him she heard but figured it wasn't worth bruising the mages ego. "You're right, it must have been the gryphon. Have a good sleep, Ezra."

He was still perturbed about the muddling comment when he retired to his tent. Ulandra made a quick walk of the perimeter before sitting down by the fire. She leaned back against Piercer's soft fur and waited for sunrise.

Chapter Twelve

SCATTERED LIKE LEAVES

Commander Seget rode at Arain's side as they reached the site where General Hortus and his troops retreated to last night. Nothing but death and destruction lay before them. "I take it this is the work of your deep ones, my queen?"

Arain was almost giddy viewing her creations work. "Yes commander, this is. I sent them last night to wreak havoc on the remaining enemy forces but this is better than I could have ever imagined." The carnage would have turned a lesser man's stomach but Seget expected this campaign to be extremely bloody. In front of them, hundreds of circular holes formed revealing both adult and adolescent worms. "You all have done exemplary work here, bolstering my forces yet again!"

A voice in their minds spoke. "We live only to serve you, my queen."

"Excellent work, were there many losses?"

"Our casualties were negligible, my queen. We made up for the loss ten fold in new broodlings."

"Very good, were there many enemy survivors, and were you able to kill Malik's generals?"

"There were few that survived the initial attack and most of them would be dead from parasitic infection by now. We did manage to badly injure General Corwin but General Hortus managed to help them both escape. We are still searching for any stragglers."

"Ahh to bad, I was hoping to play with General Hortus. I guess that will have to wait till another time." Arain looked disappointed for just a moment. "Seget, let us continue our advance on Castle Kragg. Deep ones, continue on with hunting our enemies."

Seget ordered his officers to mobilize the troops. "I want to be underway in five minutes or there will be consequences!" Seget's officers knew not to test him. Besides being a master swordsman, he was a master at doling out punishments. The last of his officers to offend spent the night cleaning out all the chamber pots of the Citadel by hand. None of them wanted to see what the punishment would be this time, so they dispatched with great haste to get all the troops assembled. Like clockwork, Arain's legion of humans and monsters were marching onward with time to spare.

Arain had given Malik's old Generals Ori and Vermillion a special contingent of werewolves to train in the assassin and archery disciplines. She dubbed them the silent howlers and they would become the first ever specialized werewolves to do covert operations for her highness. Timber however was unique as the only alpha. His lycanthrope genes were the purest of them all. He bowed only to his master and friend. There were still some humans and a hundred or so Krillox in Arain's army but the bulk consisted mainly of the Deep Ones and the werewolves. Her army was almost fully self sufficient, capable of producing more soldiers out of the enemies troops. It felt like victory was inevitable.

Timber patrolled the area staying just ahead of Arain. He would kill anything that posed even the slightest threat to her. Arain rode casually letting her horse keep the pace with Seget's mount while she pondered her next moves. *I wonder how Valin's doing with the ogres? It has been awhile since we've parted ways.* She assured herself that he was fine, of that she had no doubt. But how were a ship load of ogres doing? The thought of that made her smile. Controlled chaos I would imagine. A chuckle escaped her lips.

As Arain looked around there were all manner of mutilated bodies from the worms attack. Crows and other scavengers picked at the field of human meat. That sight continued on for some distance before petering out. "Awww, that must be the last one that tried to escape his doom." She looked down upon a young man no more than nineteen. His lower jaw was ripped off as were both his legs. His expression of horror was frozen on his face, eyes wide as the killing blow came.

Onward they continued leaving the remains behind to be erased by time. "Next time I pass here, there will be nothing left of this glorious battle, just memories."

"You sound sad about that, your grace. It is inevitable that all the battles we have and will fight are to fade away into memory and legend. When you have conquered all this world has to offer, your crusade will in concurrence be over. There will be no more war because there will only be one side, your side!"

Arain hadn't quite thought about it that way before. "A world with no war will be both grand and saddening in the same instant. Luckily we're just getting started and that day isn't even on the horizon yet, Seget."

"Indeed your grace, we're just warming up."

Arain Drake and her horde traveled until midday with not so much as a bird crossing their paths. The whole procession emanated ill intent. "Halt!" the queen commanded raising an arm in the air. Everyone stopped in their tracks and a great silence settled in. Not even the breeze dared to disobey her command and completely stopped.

Seget kept his voice low. "What is it, your grace?"

"There's a great deal of magic being used nearby. Be ready, something is happening." With those words, an ice cold wind came howling from the north. The sky overhead turned an eerie shade of gray as three tornados slammed to the ground hungrily devouring everything in their paths. Lightning bolts rained down incinerating anything they touched. It was as if nature itself was waging a war on Arain Drake and her forces.

"Scatter!" screamed Seget in vain. His voice drowned out by all of the noise. Humans, werewolves, and Krillox were sucked up and spit out all the same. Bodies were strewn over quite a large distance. The tornados threw barrage after barrage of dirt, rock, sticks, or whatever else they ran into making it extremely hard to see where the attackers were.

Arain Drake's anger grew to a boiling point, "Enough!" she yelled as a wave of energy burst out in all directions with her at its center. The crown of runes on her forehead blazed bright. As quickly as the storm was conjured it was destroyed. All manner of things fell from the sky now that the tornados were gone. The injured werewolves just healed but the damage done to her non-immortal soldiers was permanent. Eagerly, Arain scanned for the location of the attackers. "You have used a considerable amount of magic and I bet right about now you're completely drained."

Three riders on horseback bolted from the brush a ways up ahead. "Hahaha," she chuckled watching them flee with

Timber nipping at their tails. "You enjoy them my love, have yourself some fun!" By fun she obviously meant torture, maim, and massacre. "Nice one, Malik. I will be sure to return the favor very soon." Now was time to assess the damage. The healers that didn't die were hastily administering aid to those they could save. "Seget, are you alive?" Arain had lost sight of the commander during the attack and figured he must have been swept away like so many others.

In a labored voice, "I'm over here, your grace."

Arain turned around to see Seget slowly getting up from the ground. The commander's plate mail had been pierced during the storm. The hilt of a longsword protruded from his lower left torso. Blood ran off the blade sticking out the back side. Seget looked down at the sword. "Well would you look at that," is all he said before grabbing the hilt and in one fast pull, removed the sword from his flesh. Blood now freely flowed from both sides dripping off of his armor and pooling at his feet. "My queen, might I be so bold to ask you for aid?"

Arain stepped forward placing her hands on the wound. Closing her eyes she concentrated on healing the wound. Moments later she removed her hands leaving only the punctured armor behind. "There you are commander, good as new. Now let's get regrouped and see how badly that attack hurt us."

"Thank you, your highness. I will have an assessment of the damage to your forces very soon." Seget bowed and headed off barking orders this way and that, getting troops to pickup supplies and soldiers that were littered around the area. Carts were repaired and spooked horses were rounded up. The day was pretty much ruined now so Arain decided to set up camp early. It would be better to take some time and get everything that was damaged repaired before pushing onward.

"We shall not be surprised again by such tricks. Ori, Vermillion, take your howlers and set up a perimeter ahead of us. Kill anyone or anything that gets in your way, understood?"

The group bowed, "As you command, our queen." They gathered their supplies and headed out to setup the perimeter. By the time the sun began to set, Seget had the losses figured out down to the last bag of carrots.

Standing at the threshold to the queen's tent, he announced himself, "Commander Seget requesting an audience with the queen?"

"You may enter, commander."

Inside Seget stepped. "Your majesty, I come to bring you the final tally of the damages. Thirty nine humans, twenty three Krillox, thirteen horses, and one werewolf dead. Approximately a third of our supplies and rations and two carts have also been lost."

"That son of a bitch! Wait, did you say they managed to kill one of my werewolves?" Arain stood up from the table she was eating at to move closer to the commander.

"That is correct you highness, one of the turned ones from a day ago. After thorough questioning, the only probable conclusion is that they are dead. All the others no matter how far they were thrown have returned some time ago."

"Hmmm, that is most unexpected. Maybe there is a way to kill a werewolf. Very good commander, I wish to be underway at sun up."

Seget nodded, "As you command, your grace." He exited her tent and headed to inform his officers of the request.

About twenty minutes passed as Arain finished her dinner. She was just about to question Timber's absence when the massive gray wolf walked in. "There you are, did you have fun with those nasty mages?" It was easy to tell by the swollen abdomen and the bloody muzzle that he did indeed take care of the combatants. Arain scratched behind his ears. "Good boy, Timber." Very gently she dipped her cloth napkin in a glass of water she had been drinking. Then she meticulously cleaned the blood from his fur. He loved the attention, sitting there patiently as his master took care of him. "I can see you won't be needing dinner tonight, boy." Timber's tail wagged on the ground. "There you go all done, what do you say we get some sleep now." She never had to ask him twice. Timber took one leap and landed on the bed. Besides tearing out peoples jugulars, snuggling with Arain was his favorite thing to do.

CHAPTER THIRTEEN

THE GENERALS RETURN

"Open the gates!" yelled the sentry from atop the wall. Outside were what remained of General Hortus and Corwin's forces. A paltry twenty nine souls including them, out of ten thousand strong that left just days earlier. From the looks of them, a few more would be discounted from that number very soon. Every single man and woman showed signs of serious injury.

The metallic clink of the gate mechanism and the portcullis slowly opened. The wait seemed like an eternity to those outside the protection of the walls. Finally, the entrance was open to welcome in the weary soldiers. The worst injured were ushered off to the infirmary immediately. Hortus made sure Corwin arrived there with no problems. The mages stump looked nasty, bubbled skin from the fire and puss oozed from the mutilated limb. The healers Corwin was left with at their camp didn't last long enough to properly heal him. Worms attacked killing them and almost finished the work they started on Corwin. Little did they know an injured Corwin was still as lethal. A volley of magic missiles shredded his attackers giving him ample time to escape with Hortus.

The infirmary had been given considerably more room in the castle courtyard in preparation for the uptake of new patients from the war. Hortus laid Corwin down on one of the many new beds. A healer, Eliss and her assistant rushed over to begin administering aid. "Ohh," gasped Eliss' assistant at the sight of the wounds. Eliss herself had seen worse, much worse. "What was the cause of this injury? Did he get hit by some sort of flame attack?"

"No, his wound was done by my hand." Eliss and her assistant weren't to sure how to take the admission. "It's not like that, he was infected with some sort of parasite that would have eventually worked its way to his brain and killed him. Loosing his arm was the only thing that was going to prevent that. The explanation seemed even more disturbing now that he said it out loud.

"What in the world happened to your face, general?"

Hortus grimaced when he ran his fingers over the wounds. "That one is an even wilder story than the last one! Let's just say it was caused by a huge wolf and leave it at that."

"As you wish, General Hortus. Now let's get this arm taken care of, General Corwin." Eliss gave her assistant a list of items she was to bring back with her. "Alright general, I will need to sedate you, cleaning off all that infected burned flesh is going to be excruciatingly painful."

"Do what you must, I leave my care in your able hands Eliss." She placed her hand on his forehead and said something quietly under her breath. Corwin fell into a deep coma like state.

Her assistant returned with the requested supplies on a surgical cart. "Thank you, now hold up the injured limb so I can get started." The assistant did as she was told, getting in a comfortable position holding the half arm up and steady. Eliss began cutting off the dead flesh.

"That's my queue, please take good care of him Eliss," then General Hortus turned and walked out of the infirmary. It was time to go inform King Malik of his failure to kill Arain Drake. Hortus wore his failure for all to see. He fully expected serious consequences to be waiting for him. He was a shadow of his former self after being so utterly defeated. The only other time he lost like this was when Malik dueled him for control of the southern regions. He felt everyone was looking at him differently, like a weaker man. Hortus banged and bruised with gashes on his face and dried blood on his armor walked through the crowds of people that were preparing for the coming conflict. *People used to look up to me as if I was something more than a man, but now I feel invisible to them.*

Finally he reached the steps that led up to the castle entrance. Each one he walked his vision changed from blurry to clear. His skin felt like it was on fire and he began to sweat profusely. "What the fuck is going on?" Reaching the last step felt like a monumental accomplishment. Hortus was shaky at best and almost fell before two of the sentries grabbed his arms to steady him.

"General Hortus, are you alright?"

"I need to see King Malik, you gents mind giving me a hand?" The two did their best to assist the general in reaching the king.

Talo Grey was finally released from the care of the king's personal healer, Vazeer, today. "I humbly thank you again Vazeer, without your skills and quick thinking I would surely have perished from General Ori's poisonous kiss. Is there anything you need or anything I can do for you before King Malik assigns me another duty?"

"Talo go on now, I did what I was trained to do and this time it worked. You walking out of here healthy is the only reward I need." Vazeer smiled as he gave Talo a wave goodbye from across the room. Without another thought on the matter, Vazeer went back to work mixing large batches of healing potions so they could be administered more quickly. Everyone knew that getting to a skilled healer or cleric was your best bet, but in a pinch healing potions could keep you from dying until you could get help. As healers and clerics were not as plentiful as say your typical swordsman, the potions become an absolute necessity in a war time scenario.

The first order of business was to find King Malik. He had sent a squire to deliver a message. *Come and see me when you have a chance today, I have a job for you.* The last thing he wanted was to keep the king waiting. Talo was off down the hall and up a flight of stairs, arriving outside the king's throne room. Just ahead of him was an injured man being assisted by two guards. When he finally had a better look, he could see the injured man was none other than General Hortus. Into the throne room the four of them went.

Malik was standing inside pouring over maps that were laid out on a large rectangular table. The king looked up at the four entering. "Talo, you may take a seat over at the table while I talk with Hortus."

"Certainly, your majesty." Talo walked past the small group and sat down at the table as instructed.

"General Hortus, is that you? I must say you look like shit at the current moment. What do you have to report?"

Hortus composed himself so the sentries released him. "Your majesty, I come before you to report that my mission was a complete and total failure. Arain Drake still lives and her forces have grown exponentially. If anything, our attack aided her considerably. A small group of mages stayed behind to lay a trap for her and to give us enough time to return here to warn you."

Malik clasped his hands behind his back while he slowly walked around Hortus. "Continue on with your report, general."

"She does in fact command monsters. I have proof to show it, on my face from when I fought one. Corwin and myself watched this creature come almost completely apart only to return to full health within minutes. Their bite spreads their disease, making more of them. Then there were the...

"Worms, finished Malik.

"How did you know about the worms?"

"I have had a spy watching Arain Drake for some time now and that spy just gave me a very similar report not long ago. She also mentioned how you were taken by surprise not once but twice in the same night. Either this bitch is that remarkable or you were just to cocky and lazy to put her down!"

Each word stung like a dagger piercing his flesh. Hortus exhausted and sick with pain dropped to his knees.

"Oh come now Hortus, you wish to grovel at my feet?"

The general sat slouched on his knees silent and unmoving. One of the sentries knelt down to check on him. "Your grace, I think he's dead."

That poor sentry never saw it coming as Hortus latched onto his neck, ripping out a large chunk of flesh and artery. A shower of blood sprayed uncontrollably from the wound. As he changed, Hortus' bones snapped and cracked, his face elongated and rows of razor sharp teeth came in. His chest grew larger than his armor could hold breaking the bindings that kept it together. It sounded like somebody dropped a large pot or pan when the plate male fell off and struck the ground. The second sentry was frozen with fear at what stood before him. Hortus grabbed the man's head with one of his massive claws picking him up at least two feet off the ground. Screaming and flailing about the man tried to free himself. In one fluid motion, Hortus now fully transformed, used his other claw to rake downward on the man's body. In that one swipe, the victim's chest plate, flesh, and innards fell to the floor in a bright red pile.

Talo was so shocked he fell over his chair trying to get up. Malik wasn't so easily frightened, drawing his sword he launched at the beast landing what would have been a killing blow to the heart. Hortus just stood there barely fazed. Before he could counter though, Malik withdrew his sword and side stepped to safety. Hortus stood there breathing deeply, his inhuman size now dwarfed the king. It was his turn now as he charged Malik with his claws open wide. The king was fast dodging and blocking with great efficiency. Two guards from outside the door rushed in to defend their king. "No!! Get Clink and his cage now!!" he commanded.

Hortus' attention was now focused on the two intruders. Before he lunged, Malik arced his sword downwards slicing the beasts back wide open. The two fleeing guards were quickly forgotten. Malik backed up slowly with his sword held out in front of him. Hortus matched his pace towards him. The blood had already stopped flowing from the three foot gash on his back.

"Holy shit, this can't be happening," muttered a distressed Talo Grey from behind the table. His body shook from the adrenaline being pumped into his bloodstream. Looking over at the man that was bitten, he could see the slumped body twitching and quivering on the floor. He couldn't help but stare at whatever was about to happen. Suddenly the body stopped moving all together before dissolving into a disgusting pile of whatever the hell that was. "I have to help the king, I have to help the king," trying to summon enough courage to stand and fight. Malik was holding his own but with every attack, Hortus came closer and closer to landing a massive blow.

Talo pulled his magic sword the king had gifted him. As the blade left the scabbard, Talo whispered its name, Vixor. Somehow just holding this weapon made him less afraid of the monster he was about to face. His shaking stopped and his mind was clear. In slow motion, he watched Malik finally get caught by one of the creatures attacks, sending the king sprawling across the floor on his back. His sword clanged as it careened away from his hand. Hortus wasted no time pouncing on the dazed king pinning him to the ground. With a horrifically wide mouth, Hortus went for the kill. Before he could finish though, Talo charged Hortus, driving Vixor through one side and out the other. The general reared back on his knees letting out the most blood curdling screams. Not sure what was happening, Malik siezed his opportunity and retrieved his sword. The werewolf twitched and flailed about for a moment before its body started to smoke and sizzle.

With the worst timing possible, Clink and Yuni burst through the doors dragging a large barred cage on wheels. "Where'd it go?" questioned Clink somewhat confused.

Malik pointed to the shriveled, smoking body lying on the floor with Vixor sticking out of it. They all looked at one another completely speechless.

CHAPTER FOURTEEN

CAMPING WITH ENEMIES

The base of the Vesper mountains were just a short distance ahead. King Elrick scanned the surroundings looking for the best location for them to camp for the night. He stopped and waved one of his officers over. Elrick pointed to the spot he wanted. The officer left relaying the king's command to the rest of the officers, who in turn commanded their designated platoons. Lucious likened their synchronization and teamwork to that of the ant colonies he used to watch as a child. Everyone contributing for the greater good of all. It gave Lucious hope for the human races survival and the future of this new world.

King Elrick climbed down from his horse, handing the reins to the caretaker. This group of men and women took care of all the animals that the military used. They did not fight, primarily staying well away from the front lines. When a battle was taking place they watched over the various supply and cargo hauling carts. It was a common courtesy to not injure or attack the opposing sides caretakers.

Without hesitation, Elrick pitched in with the camp setup. He worked side by side with his soldiers and expected that his officers would do the same.

Morgan and Lucious dismounted their horses and set a newly awoken Stormy on the ground. The fur ball stretched and yawned before he was ready to play. "Stormy, you stay close. No wandering off, do you understand?" Lucious waited until Stormy looked at him to be sure the little Arabis knew how serious he was.

The three of them pitched in helping unload one of the many carts with supplies for the night. A line was formed to make the work quicker and more efficient. It didn't take long before the camp began taking shape. Lucious smiled at Morgan, "You know today is turning out to be a pretty good day."

Morgan agreed, "It really feels like people are getting used to us. It was a bit rocky earlier on but since then there hasn't been any more issues."

Lucious was still fairly guarded on the acceptance from all the troops. He knew too well the lengths some people would go for their ideals. "That is good Morgan, but don't forget to be on guard for those who would try and deceive you."

Just then, two of the king's royal guards arrived. Both men did the obligatory bow. "Do forgive the interruption King Lucious, but King Elrick requests your presence immediately."

"What for, has something happened?"

"I am not privy to that information your grace, we were just told to escort you to his majesty post haste."

"Alright, Morgan, Stormy lets go."

"Sorry your grace, but the king insisted it was only you he wished to speak with. Your companions are free to do as they please while your away."

Lucious didn't like this one bit, especially the part about leaving Morgan and Stormy alone. "I am sorry, but you will need to return to King Elrick and inform him that I will not leave my companions."

The guard was about to object when Morgan pulled Lucious aside. "It will be alright Lucious, go and meet with Elrick. Besides, I have Stormy to protect me if anyone decides to do something stupid."

Every fiber of his being told Lucious not to leave them, but denying a king's request for an audience was not a very smart choice. "Alright, I will go see what the king needs then I will come right back, ok?"

"Yes Lucious, go and we will see you when you return." Morgan kissed his cheek then shooed him on his way. Lucious headed off with the two guards. He stopped to look back only once to make sure she was safe. One last smile was exchanged between them and then a wave.

Morgan bent down to Stormy. "Well what do you think we should do now?" Stormy just stared back with that cute little face. She couldn't help herself as she reached out and scratched his little head. Upon standing back up, a female archer approached.

"Excuse me miss, would you be Morgan Drake?"

Morgan blushed when she heard Lucious' last name after hers. "Yes I'm Morgan, what is it that you need?"

"Oh sorry, I don't need anything I was just told to let you know your tent was ready just over there." The woman pointed in the direction it was located at.

"Thank you for letting us know. It is greatly appreciated."

The archer bowed and excused herself. "I guess we should go check out the tent and make sure it's ready for when Lucious gets back." The two of them headed off in the direction the archer had pointed. Their tent was pretty easy to spot, the dark blue one with a white top. "Here we are Stormy, home sweet home." That was the last thing she remembered before everything went dark.

Three of the royal guards that shunned Morgan and Lucious earlier were waiting in the tent for her to arrive. One man clubbed Morgan in the side of the head with a mace knocking her out cold. Stormy met a similar fate taking a club swing to the side. The little Arabis screamed in pain as the blow broke multiple bones as well as sending the creature flying across the room. The three soldiers hastily stuffed Morgan's limp body into a large burlap sack used for keeping potatoes in. The top was tied and the bag with its contents were flung over the shoulder of the biggest man of the three. "Alright, stick to the plan. Once we leave, head south until we're far enough away from camp so that we can dispose of this abomination!" The leader of the group, a tall slender younger man with blonde hair and a scar on his left cheek, headed out of the tent first. The sack carrier exited second and the third guy followed at the rear. Nobody gave a second thought to the three royal guards carrying a large sack. They were supposed to be the top tier of Elrick's army and nobody questioned them except for the generals and the king himself. It was to easy how they worked their way through the congested camp and southward to where they would commit their horrible deed.

Lucious was escorted to the king's tent for the supposed meeting, but when he entered, Elrick was not inside. "This isn't right." Turning to leave he was greeting with a dagger through the neck and out his spine. The royal guard in front of him took pleasure in twisting the blade as he ripped it out.

Panic gripped Lucious as he fell to the ground. *No, what are they doing? I can't scream or move my body. No, what will they do to Morgan?* He was as helpless as when the Morlocks attacked. His windpipe split and his spine severed, all he could do was lay there suffocating as the two guards looked on laughing at his demise. Soon the noise faded and it felt like he was falling into the dark void. *Blackness, that's all I can see is blackness. I no longer feel like I'm falling, actually I no longer feel anything. The fear, the pain, the hate, it's all gone. Morgan, I have to get back and save her,* but he did not know how. Just as before, a small light appeared far in the distance. *That has to be the way out,* so he began running in the blackness towards the light.

When Lucious finally reached the source of the light, he could see it was an open door. Cautiously he stepped through out of the blackness and into the light. Nothing could have prepared him for what he saw.

Lucious snapped awake, *I'm in some kind of bag or sack.* He couldn't see what was happening but the sound of shovels digging into dirt was immediately discernable. This is bad, they mean to bury us here. Frantically his mind raced trying to come up with a plan that didn't involve him or Morgan dying. That all went out the window when Morgan screamed.

She was defending herself fiercely. "Lucious, help me please!"

Time stopped at that moment and everything became clear to Lucious. *No longer will I allow the innocent to be preyed upon by the wicked!* The bag he was in and the cart he was on melted away falling to the ground. Morgan stood there bound at the wrists with blood running down the side of her face. A total of five men encircled her with nothing but ill intent in their eyes. Nothing moved except for Lucious. It was as if everyone was frozen in place. Lucious walked up from behind two of the men and placed a hand on each one. Upon contact, the skin, flesh, and blood melted from their bodies leaving only the clean white skeletons behind. Lucious continued on touching the next two offenders, and again everything melted from the bones and pooled on the ground. He now turned to face the leader of the group blocking his path to Morgan. Lucious took in a deep breath and exhaled loudly. Lucious had released time again. The murderer before him stepped back in shock, wide eyed.

"I, I, killed you."

Lucious snapped his fingers and the four skeleton guardsmen boxed in the man. Morgan was still trying to get her bearings on the situation and figured it best to stay silent. "You're right, you did kill me and it was an excruciatingly horrible way to die. Why though? Do you truly hate us this much to murder us the first chance you had?"

"You and your lizard woman are abominations and have no place in this world!"

The man's words weighed heavy on Lucious. "You're frightened by us, I can see it in your eyes. It is your own fears that have now forfeit your life."

Lucious was about to give his skeletons the order to finish the man but Morgan intervened. She placed a hand on his shoulder, "Lucious, this man deserves to die for what he has done and what he was about to do. But maybe we should let King Elrick deal with this traitor?"

He nodded in agreement. "You're right Morgan, he should be brought to justice in front of everyone. Take him away." On command, the four skeleton guards disarmed the captive and carried him in the direction of the encampment. Lucious remove the remaining shackles from Morgan before giving her a vise like hug. "I don't want to be separated from you ever again."

Morgan hugged him equally as tight resting her chin on his shoulder. She cried tears of joy, "I will never let you leave me again." Her loving moment was cut short as she realized Stormy was missing. "Lucious we have to find Stormy, he must be so scared." Frantically they checked for any sign of the Arabis where they were at. "Stormy, where are you?" she yelled hoping to see the fur ball bound in from the brush.

Lucious picked up one of the guards weapons, a mace with a chunk of fur stuck to it. "Oh no." His stomach dropped. "Where did you see him last?"

"I think he was with me when I walked into our tent, after that it's all blank. He must still be there!" Lucious had been learning a teleport spell and now seemed like the time to test it out.

"Amne, Patress," he spoke along with a hand gesture and the two vanished. Seconds later they appeared back in camp, totally scaring the shit out of a group of soldiers sitting around a fire pit. "Morgan, which way?"

"Follow me," she took off running. Lucious was no slouch but he had a hard time keeping the pace that Morgan set. Moments later the two burst through their tent entrance. "Stormy, where are you boy?"

Crawling out from underneath the bed the little Arabis whimpered dragging his broken leg. Morgan's heart broke seeing this gentle creature battered and broken. She raced over gently cradling him in her hands as she picked him up. "Lucious, can you help him?"

He had never healed anything before but the way Morgan looked at him with those pleading eyes he knew he had to try. Kneeling down next to Morgan, he placed his hand on the injured animal. "Here goes nothing," closing his eyes Lucious focused his energy on healing the creature. Slowly the crown of runes lit up. They always started at the outer runes working their way to the most front and center rune. Lucious opened his eyes to see Stormy fast asleep in Morgan's arms. A streak of blood ran down Lucious' nose and hung on his upper lip. Instinctively Morgan wiped it away. "Do you think he's alright now?"

"Yes Lucious, I'd say so. I'm sure he would thank you with lots of licks if he wasn't passed out." Morgan chuckled under her breath not wanting to wake Stormy.

There was some commotion outside which quickly reminded Lucious that the four skeleton warriors were still marching the prisoner this way. "We need to go now before there's more senseless loss of life. Follow me." Lucious grabbed Morgan's free hand and the two headed towards the noise as quickly as they could. The camp seemed like a maze as they weaved their way through the sea of tents. Just up ahead a crowd was beginning to form. He looked back at her, "Please stay close to me." Letting go of her hand Lucious picked his way through the crowd of soldiers making a path for Morgan to follow. Finally he reached the center of the gathering where he saw the prisoner being escorted by four skeletons with swords. The crowd was becoming agitated seeing one of their own surrounded by monsters. Lucious raised his hands trying to get the attention of the masses. "Everyone calm down and listen."

"Why don't you and your monsters go back where you came from!" shouted one onlooker. Others shouted similar insults directed at all the non humans.

The louder Lucious talked and the harder he tried to explain these circumstances the more dangerous the mob became. A handful of soldiers had their weapons drawn while others picked up small rocks and began throwing them at him and his companions. Lucious wished the king would show up to end this squabble but he wasn't that lucky. A rock hit Morgan and Lucious snapped. "If you want to be violent then I'll show you violence!" Balling up his fists over his head the runes ignited. In a split second, Lucious slammed his balled fists into the ground. Boom!! The force of the impact sent soldiers flying. Large fissures formed outward from the companions in all directions. Not one of the motley group still stood. All of them were dazed. Some were injured, but none were killed. Lucious stood there next to Morgan with blood coming from his nose and mouth. "I think I pushed it a little to hard today."

Morgan wrapped her arm around him offering support. Stormy was wide awake now and a bit pissed off that the humans hurt them and were trying to do so again. "Easy Stormy, we're alright. Nobody is going to hurt us again." She kissed the fur ball and set him on the ground.

"What is the meaning of this!" shouted King Elrick who just arrived with a battalion of troops. Elrick stopped and looked around wide eyed at the destruction. "What happened here?"

Lucious stepped forward as the king's troops drew weapons to defend him. "So this is how our races coexist? The peace couldn't survive one day." Sadness welled up in him and his eyes became teary. "It's my fault though to think humans would willingly accept change without a fight, and if this is any indication of how things will be, then surely my sister has already won... You ask what is going on King Elrick, well let me tell you." Pointing towards the skeletons and prisoner. Your royal guard, or at least five of them conspired to get rid of us and our kind in a most brutal fashion. This beautiful Draconian woman and this magnificent creature were brutally attacked under pretense of comradery. The man you see guarded here lured me to your tent Elrick where he proceeded to insert his dagger through my throat and out my spine. Then him and his companions watched, waited, and laughed while I suffocated to death. Unbeknownst to them however is that I tend to not stay dead for long which is very fortunate for my friends here who were about to be murdered and buried out to the west in the brush. Please by all means, go have a look. You'll find two graves dug and ready to be filled by their new owners as well as four puddles of human remains from those four royal guards right there. We were bringing the last of the murderers to you for judgement when this mob became hostile. I assure you Elrick that I pleaded with them to stop and listen to reason. What you see here is their failure to listen!"

Elrick stood there ashamed for himself and his soldiers. Lucious was right, if they couldn't make it one day without turning on him and his companions what chance did we have against Arain Drake? "My deepest apologies to you three. I should have addressed the issue as soon as you brought it to my attention. I was naïve to think we could all put our differences aside so easily. I, King Elrick, make it known to all who serve me that the behavior displayed here today will not be tolerated! We humans are the eldest race on this world and must lead by example not by betrayal. Lucious, may I have the prisoner now?"

"Sure," with a motion of his hand the skeletons parted releasing the traitor.

Right away the man began pleading that Lucious and Morgan were the ones that attacked him and his accomplices. Elrick looked him in the eye and raised a hand to silence him. One of the king's officers had just returned from visiting the site Lucious had described. "Your highness, he is telling the truth. Two graves, shovels, and a bloody burlap sack just west of here."

The accused knew his fate was sealed. He pulled his dagger and tried to subdue Morgan as a hostage. That was his next mistake. Morgan in a head on fight was not the easy prey he presumed. With lightning speed she unsheathed her sword and drove it through his throat and out the spine. "A fitting punishment for a murderer." She removed her sword and watched the soldier collapse to the ground gurgling on his own blood. His eyes wide with terror as he slowly suffocated to death.

CHAPTER FIFTEEN

TRAVELING WITH TWINS

G eneral Robert and Selim were getting along just fine on the journey eastward. Bibble and Bobble on the other hand were more akin to children who couldn't sit still on a long trip. One was always picking on the other, which usually ended in a fist fight on the back of a horse or on the ground.

"Alright, that's quite enough!" Selim grabbed Bobble by the scruff of the neck and hoisted the Veassel up onto his horse, setting him down in front of him so he could correct any further issues.

Bobble sat there pouting with his arms crossed. "This is horse crap Selim, and you know it. Bibble should be up here, not me!"

Bibble chuckled at his brother for having to be babysat.

"Shut up Bibble it's not funny, I'm a strong independent Veassel who should be free to roam."

Selim put his hand on Bobble's head and gave him a little scratch. "It's ok little fella, you're safe with me. The Veassel quickly shooed his hand away, as he fixed his hair. Then went back to the pouting.

General Robert did as best as he could trying not to laugh at the situation. A wide smile couldn't be helped though. "I'd say our first day is going swimmingly, wouldn't you agree Selim?" The Draconian shot the general a side eyed response, "Or not," came the rebuttal.

It would take them about two days to reach the coastal city of New Haven, where they would need to requisition a ship to take them further east to the Veassels land of origin. The only foreseeable problem was going to be Bibble and Bobble's funny business. Robert was assigned as their escort to bridge the gap between humans and non-humans. Hooded cloaks were worn as well to cut down on the attention. The area which they would travel through was fully under the kingdom's control. Patrols up and down the road from Westlin to New Haven were conducted daily, thanks to the regiment of the king's soldiers always stationed there.

A few hours had passed before Bobble was released from his prison, and able to ride his own horse again. He was a bit less troublesome but still managed to get his jabs in on Bibble. It only took a disapproving glance from Selim to correct the two now.

Selim missed his mate and yearned to be reunited with her as soon as possible. This short trip seemed extremely long already. He was thankful that the first day was already coming to an end. "This looks like as good a place as any to sleep." Selim's three companions agreed. There was plenty to eat for the horses, some trees for shelter, and a small stream zig zagging by it.

Dinner was lackluster at best, not one of them knew a thing about cooking so it was dried meats and bread for all. Bibble and Bobble didn't mind, they ate their rations and headed straight for the water. Veassels loved anything to do with water. They both threw off their clothing and weapons leaving nothing but their furry behinds to view as they raced for the stream. Robert looked over at Selim, "Odd little fellows those two."

"You have no idea Robert, just make sure to keep your valuables hidden or anything else you may hold dear. Those guys can swipe anything without you being the wiser."

Robert did a hasty inventory of his belongings. He stopped when he felt his neck. "Those thieving bastards stole my necklace!"

"Hahahahaha," Selim laughed hysterically almost coming to tears. "I told you they were amazing thieves."

"But how, when did they even have the chance?" Robert recalled their interactions throughout the day. "I don't even remember them being close enough to snatch it."

"Well unless it fell off, those two have it. I certainly couldn't do it." He picked up one of his massive clawed hands.

"I suppose I might have noticed if you had tried." The two of them chuckled at the thought. "Do you trust those two enough to take a watch tonight?"

Selim looked back at Bibble and Bobble who were now playing a game of grab ass running in and out of the stream naked. "Nope! I will take the first watch if that's alright with you?"

"Fine with me." Robert stood up and went about preparing his one person tent. It was dark by the time the twins wandered over to camp. A nice campfire was burning encircled by three tents. Bibble and Bobble plopped down by the fire. Their fur was already dry, in fact it never got wet. The Veassels fur was continually replenished with natural oils that secrete from their skin, keeping it smooth, soft, and waterproof at all times.

"I think today was pretty fun, don't you Bobble?"

"It wasn't bad, just the part where that Draconian manhandled me."

"Heheheh, that was so funny, Bobble." Whack! "Ouch, you don't have to hit me."

"You deserved it Bibble, and if you keep it up I've got another one right here." Bobble held up his furry little fist menacingly.

"Isn't it time you two went to sleep?" Selim had just returned from a perimeter walk and went back to sitting by the fire.

The twins were pretty tired, letting out the occasional yawn. "You're right Selim, it is about that time, goodnight."

"Good night, Bobble, see you in the morning."

"Good night, Selim."

"Good night, Bibble." Finally there was peace and quiet. Only the occasional crackle from the fire dared break the silence. The Draconian's thoughts went back to Ulandra. *I wonder how she liked flying for the first time? It looked like it would be a lot of fun.* The night was as uneventful as the day. Eventually Robert took his turn on guard so Selim could sleep. Time passed quickly, the sun chased away the night and the four of them were back on the road bright and early.

It must have been about midday when the group ran into the patrol from New Haven. Fifteen strong, mostly foot soldiers with a mage and a couple archers. "You three wait here while I ride ahead to educate them." It was a sound decision to pre-warn them of what they were about to see. The last thing they needed was to surprise them and possibly invoke a fight.

Robert and the patrol greeted each other some twenty yards away. It was evident from their body language that they were acquaintances. Selim, Bibble, and Bobble wait-ed impatiently. Well maybe just Bibble and Bobble, Selim waited so still you might think he was a statue. "Settle down you two, or does one of you want to ride with me again?" The twins immediately stopped the horse play. Another day riding with the large Draconian was not something either of them wished to do.

Robert and the patrol finally headed towards them. "Behave yourselves boys, this is going to be an eye opener for them." Selim pulled his horse just off the road so the patrol could pass. Bibble and Bobble followed the Draconian's lead. Sure enough, everyone of the patrol had that half scared half amazed look on their faces as they passed on by.

"Alright my companions, the first fifteen people to the east seem to be handling the news of the new species quite well." How much of that was due to Robert being a general in his majesty's military is unclear, but at least they didn't attack, and that is good on any day. Robert took the lead to intercept other possible human encounters. "Shall we get moving? We can make New Haven before dark if we have no further intrusions."

Selim, Bibble, and Bobble fell in line behind Robert. Looking back Selim could see the patrol continuing west was gradually fading out of sight. As predicted, they arrived at the front gates of New Haven just as the light of day was waning. Just as before, Robert went ahead first to catch the guards and soldiers up to speed. Again, those looking on were wide eyed and open mouthed at the sight before them. Wasting no time, Robert headed straight for the docks and the harbor masters office. He looked back at his three companions, "No sense in waiting till morning, let us procure the ship tonight so we can be ready to go at first light."

All were in agreement with the plan. Robert hopped down from his horse and proceeded into the office. Selim followed soon after. Robert was already inside talking with a thin elderly fellow. He had curly white hair on top of his head along with a pair of thick round spectacles. Selim stepped next to Robert and flipped back the hood of his cloak. "Holy shit, what is that?" yelled the old man.

Reaching out a big clawed hand he introduced himself. "My name is Selim, nice to meet you."

The old man looked like he was in shock as he just stood there and stared. His eyes went to the general then back to Selim. Slowly and cautiously the man stepped forward to shake hands with Selim. "N, n, nice to meet you, I'm Chester Burbot." Selim smiled with as little tooth as possible.

"Alright now that the introductions are over, back to the task at hand. King Elrick sent us here to take his largest ship east. We will need food and supplies for around four hundred mouths, and we need to leave at first light."

Chester's eyes never broke contact with Selim even while he confirmed the general's orders. "I think we can accommodate that request, our night shift will be starting in about thirty minutes."

"Wonderful, myself and my companions would like to board the ship now and settle in so we don't have to traumatize anyone else today. Oh and would you send for a caretaker for our horses and possibly some dinner for four?"

"Four, there's more outside?"

Right on time Bibble and Bobble came in agitated that they had been waiting so long. Bibble approached the counter where Robert and Selim stood, "What's the hold up? We've been waiting forever out there!" He looked up at the old man. "Well do we have a ship or not?"

Chester was dumbfounded that a four foot tall otter was giving him attitude. "Yeah you have a ship but I think I'm going to call it an early night." Chester grabbed his things and rushed for the door.

"Chester, you haven't told us which ship we're taking yet?" interjected Robert.

"It's the Sea Spirit, second vessel on your left, can't miss it."

Bobble's ears perked up, "Did he say there was a Veassel?"

"No ding dong, he said vessel as in a ship or a boat," retorted Bibble.

"Ohhh, haha my mistake, I'm just so excited to see home. Well what I think is home."

The four of them headed out of the office and down to the docks. Chester was right, there she waited for her next sea voyage.

CHAPTER SIXTEEN

HARD TIMES

"Ahhhh!" came the screams in the middle of the night. "It's alright Seline, you're safe with me and Sebastian. Here drink this, some of that special tea the healer back in Hemshir gave you."

Seline was sweating profusely and looked shockingly pale. She took the tea and drank it slowly. It wasn't the worst thing she had ever tasted but it also wasn't the best. Sebastian, and Uluck could easily see the black tendrils running up her leg. It had been three nights since leaving the town of Hemshir, and every night she woke delirious, screaming. They had been splitting the watch between them and both were getting worn out. "Uluck, how much further do you think until we reach the City of Knowledge?"

"A day, maybe two at the most."

"Uluck, I'm not sure she's going to last that long. The poison is spreading faster with every day that passes."

"I know, I know but what can we do, Sebastian?"

"The only thing we can do, ride faster, it's her only chance." The trio rode long and hard over the next few days, while Seline's condition worsened. By the time they could see the majestic white pillars of the city she was barely clinging to life. "Uluck."

"I know, I know, just a bit further were almost there. Hang on Seline, were gonna get you some help real soon."

At a flat out sprint, they drove their horses to their limits. The animals did not falter delivering them to their destination. Guards stationed at the front gates yelled for them to stop. "We are emissaries of King Elrick sent to deliver this letter to the high council. We are also in desperate need of help for our friend who was injured on the journey, she needs immediate medical attention!"

The lead guard was a older, black haired woman, she could clearly see that these three were dressed in royal attire. "Come, follow me. I'll take you to the hospital right now." Uluck and Sebastian quickly followed the guard while leading Seline on her horse behind them. Uluck had to lash her to the horse for fear she was too weak to stay on. Her head hung so her chin rested on her chest. She barely moved or made a sound. The marvels and wonders of this city were wasted on the companions as they rushed to keep up with the woman guard. "Bring her in here." The guard dismounted her horse and rushed inside an enormous white and black building with the words *Hospital of Healers* written across the front just above the main entrance.

Sebastian and Uluck were quick to follow, jumping down from their horses and untying Seline. The massive warrior carried his sister in his arms as if she was as light as a bag of grain. Sebastian tied the horses to a long hitching post out front where water buckets and hay bags were waiting. Into the hospital they ran. There they were greeted by at least five healers along with the black haired woman. A floating bed of white waited for its patient. Uluck set her down as gently as he could. The bed continued to float in place until the group of healers moved to the triage area, then it followed silently behind them. "Uluck, you go with Seline and I'm going to deliver this letter. I will return as soon as my job is finished." Uluck and Sebastian shook hands before going their separate ways. "Excuse me miss, but would you know where I can find the high council?"

"The name is Helena, and yes I know where to find the council, follow me." Sebastian did his best to keep up with Helena as they weaved through the enormous city until they reached an incredibly tall tower made of white and gray marble. Magical sconces ringed the tower all the way to the top. Helena pointed upward, "There on the top floor is where you will find the high council. They should just be starting their nightly meeting."

"Thank you, Helena for all of your aid. I will take my leave now." Sebastian entered into the lowest level of the tower. A half moon counter stood at one end of the room with a young man dressed in a green shirt and pants.

"How can I help you today, sir?"

"I have an urgent letter for the high council from King Elrick of Westlin."

"Sounds important, right this way," ushered the man. He took Sebastian to another area with large black circles on the floor. "Stand here and please make sure to keep your hands and arms inside the circle at all times." Before Sebastian could say a word, the disc he was standing on rushed straight up. He could feel his stomach drop as the disc accelerated upward. Floor after floor of people whizzed by around him until suddenly it stopped.

A woman in green now greeted him. "Hello sir, and welcome to the top floor, level one hundred and sixty three. This is the floor of the high council chamber. Do you have an appointment with the council?"

"I have no appointment but I do have a sealed letter from King Elrick to the high council." Reaching in his tunic pocket,

Sebastian produced the letter showing it to the attendant. The woman confirmed the seal of the king was unbroken on the front. With great haste she rushed over to a white and gold trimmed door. Knock, knock, she wrapped on a gold knocker. A few moments later the door quietly slid open. A scrawny old man stood in the entrance. His hair was completely white except for the bald spot in the middle of his head. The robes he wore were gray in color and in his left hand he clutched a six foot long staff. Briefly they conversed before waving Sebastian over.

"Bishop, this here is the messenger from Westlin, his name is Sebastian."

The old man reached out to shake his hand. "Nice to meet you, please come in."

"Nice to meet you as well Bishop, and thank you miss for your help." The woman in green simply smiled and took her leave. Sebastian followed Bishop into the council chambers. It was an understatement to say this room was amazing. Columns of marble reached to the ceiling around the perimeter. Long rectangular windows were between each pair of columns, stretching some twenty feet tall. Intricate stained glass mosaics were located right above each window depicting a different council member on each one. Snake shaped sconces wrapped each column, with a magical flame emanating from the wide open mouths. On the ceiling, it looked like a massive painted mural depicting the last great war between Elrick and Malik. In the very center of the room was a long rectangular wooden table where the council members now gathered. Bishop opened the sealed letter and began reading while Sebastian stood there waiting. He urgently wanted to get back to Seline.

A minute later Bishop lowered the letter, folding it closed. His happy demeanor was gone replaced by a more serious disposition. "Thank you for bringing this letter so quickly, we have been hearing rumors out of the west and were just about to discuss this very issue. By all means you are welcome to stay if you wish."

"Many thanks to you Bishop but I must decline. One of my companions suffered serious injury on the journey and I desperately wish to rejoin her in the hospital."

"Then by all means Sebastian, take your leave and good luck to your friend."

"Thank you." Off he headed out of the chamber and back down towards the entrance. The crowds were thick down on the bustling city streets making it difficult for the newcomer to navigate. He managed to get turned around more than once, luckily though a few of the merchants helped him out. "There it is." He was close enough now to see the sign, *Hospital of Healers*. In through the front glass doors and up to a long gray counter where there sat a man and woman receptionist.

The woman looked up first, "Hello, how can I help you?"

"Yes I'm looking for my friends, a large soldier carrying in a sick woman and a small dog like thing. They came here a little over an hour ago."

"Ahh yes. She's in the intensive care wing, all the way at the end of the hall to your left.

"Thanks," and off down the hallway he went to find his friends. Sebastian passed at least twenty unused rooms before he reached the end of the hall. A large glowing sign with the words *Intensive Care* written across it were above the entrance. Before him spanned a large off white room that was partitioned into thirty private rooms. The farthest back wall looked like it housed all the different reagents and elixirs a healer would use. The rooms had no occupants except for the far corner one to his left. The lights were on and Uluck's voice could be heard. "That must be them." With long strides Sebastian reached the open doorway. To his surprise and joy Seline was sitting up talking. He could feel the anxiety and tension leave his body like an exercised demon had been purged. Their gaze met and the two of them exchanged a smile. Her injured leg was coated with some sort of concoction while the black liquid slowly drained into a catch pan below. The two healers in the room walked past Sebastian as they left. "Hi Seline, how are you feeling?"

"I feel much better now that their draining all of that liquid out of my system."

"That's wonderful news, so they are pretty confident they can cure you completely?"

"I hope so, but the healers have never seen anything like this before. They were surprised how difficult the venom was to purge and it still looks like the bite wound has more of it under the skin."

Sebastian could tell she had her reservations on the prognosis. "Well you look pretty damn healthy to me!" Sebastian had decided it would be his mission now to keep her spirits up until she was a hundred percent healed. What other choice did they have if the smartest and most powerful people in the City of Knowledge couldn't cure her.

Uluck had been sitting there silent the entire time with the Arabis on his lap. "Did you get the letter delivered?"

"Yes, they are meeting on its contents as we speak. They offered me a chance to stay but I needed to get back to see how Seline was doing."

She tried to hide her blushing, but failed miserably. Uluck noticed as well and chuckled. "You two visit while I go and get us a place to stay." Uluck stood from his chair and kissed his sister on the forehead. "I'll be back soon." He walked past Sebastian as he left and gave him a wink.

What did he do that for? I hope he isn't going to stick his tongue in my ear again. Sebastian kept an eye on Uluck until he was out of sight to prevent any disgusting tricks. He walked in the room and over to the chair besides the bed. It was still warm as he sat down. "So did they say if you had to stay the night or not?"

"No they haven't even mentioned it, but if everything looks good maybe they'll let me go. I'm not very fond of hospitals especially if I'm the one being treated." Seline held out her hand gesturing Sebastian for his. "I just want to let you know how grateful I am for your efforts to get me here alive. Without you and Uluck I would surely be dead by now, so thank you and know that I am forever in your debt."

Sebastian had never seen Seline so vulnerable, she usually was kicking ass and taking names but coming this close to death had an effect on her. "You're certainly welcome, I know you would have done the same for me. So what will you two do now that the escort mission is complete?"

Seline sat in bed quiet for a moment. "You're right, the king's orders have been fulfilled so I guess we will be heading back to Westlin for our next assignment. Shouldn't you be heading back as well?"

"Indeed, back to my simple, safe route. Who knows maybe I'll ask to be moved to somewhere new just to keep things interesting."

"If that's what you choose good for you, but I would surely miss seeing you around Westlin." The two of them sat there silent, holding each others hand after that statement.

It felt like butterflies were bouncing around in his stomach when she professed she would miss him. *I had no idea she saw me as anything other than a job.* Summoning up the courage, Sebastian leaned in towards Seline. To his surprise she did the same. Both met in the middle sharing a first kiss. It was amazing, as waves of excitement coursed through his body. Seline looked like she was enjoying herself as well. Everything was great until one of the healers came barging in to check on his patient. "Sorry for the intrusion, I just needed to check the dressing on her leg." The old man by the name of Fennil inspected the wound and replaced the dressing. "I think it best if you stayed here for the night. The venom has stopped draining, however it looks like there is still some more by the punctures. We may try some other techniques if the issue doesn't resolve by tomorrow. I'll have the nurse bring you something to eat and drink shortly." Fennil left as quickly as he arrived leaving the two of them alone again.

CHAPTER SEVENTEEN

A BITTER TASTE

Castle Kragg with its sprawling city and mountainous backdrop came into view. "There it is General Seget, the first of my castles, haha." Arain's mood was borderline giddy, thinking about the upcoming battle and its ensuing carnage. "I can't wait to see what pathetic defenses good King Malik has put in place for us. I just hope they put up a good fight and don't roll over submitting as quickly as his other cities did."

"I would think our opposition will be much more formidable with Malik and his remaining generals on the battlefield. In the end however, they will fall just the same as the rest your majesty. Would you like me to give the order to set up base camp here my lady?"

"Not yet, let us head northwest for the remainder of the day so we may rendezvous with Valin. Barring any trouble, he should have my ogre contingent here very soon." Seget nodded his acknowledgement before giving his officers the queen's command. Like a river following a bend in its path, her forces diverted northwest. Any and all humans they crossed were slain without mercy. Most of the farmers and herders past the outskirts of the city had been evacuated to the castle but some were stubborn, refusing to leave their homes. Those few signed their own death warrants, paid for with their lives and the lives of their families. All of the livestock was eaten or added to the queen's food stores for later consumption. Arain and her armies faced no resistance as they marched on to the designated location.

Just before dusk set upon them, they finished setting up camp. Castle Kragg loomed off in the distance, just waiting to be attacked. Seget and the other high ranking officers were having a council with Arain over dinner. Glub Widegrin as always, made the other human officers cringe as he snapped up his meal with that long sticky tongue. The Krillox general didn't even need to get up to grab more food, a snap of the tongue and the entire tray of roast lamb was in his gaping maw. Ori chuckled as she watched the accuracy the giant frog man possessed. The assassin threw a chunk of meat high into the air, "Get it Glub!" With ease, the pink weapon shot forth some twenty feet easily snatching the morsel.

Seget always sat next to the queen whenever these types of dinners were had. "Your majesty, our scouts have yet to locate Lord Valin and the ogre army. Do you plan on waiting for his arrival before beginning your assault?"

Arain now finished, sat back in her chair. "That was the plan Seget, but now with my immortal army of werewolves I don't see the need. We may as well just dispose of Malik and capture the castle, that way when he shows up we can all move on to the City of Knowledge."

"I beg your pardon your majesty, but do you think King Malik will be defeated so easily?"

Arain looked at Seget with a slight rage in her eyes. "I will take the castle and city by daybreak general!" Having her judgement second guessed infuriated her. If anyone besides Valin or Seget did it there would be dire consequences. Arain rose from her seat and stared down the table at those assembled. "Dinner is over! General, assemble the lycanthropes, archers, and battle mages immediately."

"Yes, your majesty." Seget turned to those still seated. "You heard the queen's orders, now move! I want lycan squads of three hundred supported by mages and archers, ready for battle by the top of the hour!" Those in attendance almost tripped over one another as they all raced for the doorway. "Your majesty, we will be awaiting you on the battlefield." Seget bowed and exited the dining tent.

The speed at which the orders were fulfilled even had Arain standing there in awe. Row upon row of werewolves awaited the order to unleash their fury on the capital city's occupants. The streets would surely run red this night and her horde will grow ten times over by daybreak. "Oh what a splendid night for war don't you think, Timber?"

The massive werewolf stood next to his master obediently waiting for her command. The lights of the city and castle reflected off the creatures eyes making them look as if they were glowing. Arain walked up beside Seget who stood looking out over the battlefield ahead. "Your majesty, still no movement or visible defenses of any kind. It's safe to say that there will be traps to contend with."

"Send in five squads and have the mages and archers hold their fire until contact is made with the enemy forces."

"Squads one thru five attack, mages and archers set up a support line but hold until my command!" Fifteen hundred nightmares raced towards the city. A mass of glinting eyes and snarls approached at unbelievable speeds. Nothing would stop them until their appetites were satiated and their affliction was spread.

Arain, Timber, and her generals stood motionless waiting for the massacre to ensue. Little did they realize the massacred would be them. As the werewolves reached the city's perimeter, Malik released his trap. Two columns sprang from the ground in front of the attackers and quickly zipped past them. It happened so fast the silver razor wire was almost invisible as it sliced through the lycanthropes with little resistance. In one fell swing, the fifteen hundred crumbled into a hundred thousand bloody pieces. Screams, groans, and howls shrieked out as their immortal lives were taken so easily.

Timber snarled in anger as he watched his children be destroyed. "How can this be? Nothing can kill my wolves. I don't understand." As they stood there in shock, an incredibly large contingent of soldiers formed outside the city walls. Humans and steam machines made up the opposition.

Giant metal and wood contraptions with spikes and ballista's rolled onto the battlefield. Steam and smoke billowed from exhaust pipes protruding from the roofs. General Yuni and General Clink were at the forefront of Malik's forces shouting commands and building confidence in their ability to defeat the monstrous hordes. Their battle cries rang out across the field as they advanced towards Arain Drake and her armies. Catapults loosed large black barrels which were lit on one end. They looked like giant fire flies sailing through the air.

Seget by far had the most battle experience which let him instinctively react to the counter attack. "Mages destroy those incoming barrels, now!" Fireballs lit up the night sky as they raced to intercept the incoming artillery. BOOM!! BOOM!! BOOM!! one after another they exploded the barrels on contact, leaving only a glittering dust that twinkled as it fell to the ground. Almost all of them were stopped except for two that made it above Arain's forces before exploding on their own. More of that glittering material floated down to the ground.

Arain held out her hand to catch some of the debris. Shiny little metallic flecks coated her gauntlet. "Oh no!" Looking to her lycan warriors they began to burn and cough as the silver dust coated their fur. Even the mighty Timber was choking. "Werewolves, retreat!" Arain watched as more of her lycanthropes succumbed to the buildup of silver in their systems. Piles of the dead lay strewn about around her. The bulk of her forces however managed to retreat before being fatally poisoned. All that were left to fight were the remaining humans and Krillox warriors.

"Your majesty, the enemy forces outnumber us a hundred to one. We should retreat and regroup."

"Come now Seget, we owe them some recompense for our losses, do we not?" Arian's smile looked like that of a mad woman. "Archers and mages fire at will, Krillox spare no one!" Arain peered out at the wave of attackers with delight. "Meteoric strike!" Her crown of runes blazed bright. The sky above her turned red as a volley of flaming meteorites rained down onto the battlefield. Hundreds of Malik's soldiers were incinerated on impact. Rocks, metal, dirt, and flames shot out in all directions. Blood ran down Arian's face from her nose. She stood there with arms and hands outstretched. "Acidic cubes!" Again her crown blazed bright as a mass of bright green jelly like cubes formed from nothing. They were large standing at about ten foot square and emitted a hissing sound like when oil hits a hot cooking pan. Off the cubes went, rolling haphazardly into the oncoming forces. Screams of pain and suffering cried out as the green jellies engulfed everything in their paths. Bodies floated in the substance as they melted to nothing. With each life taken, the cubes began to grow. A fair amount of blood was now flowing from Arain's nose and corners of her mouth.

Seget grabbed her arm. "My queen you must stop, I fear the further use of your powers may kill you." Arain turned to look him in the face and he could see she was already conjuring something else. Her crown blazed bright yet again.

"Step aside Seget, and witness as I destroy them all!" Little did Arain realize but her glowing crown made for the perfect target. Thwack! and a cloud of red was all Seget could see from the blood in his eyes.

Hurriedly, he ungloved a hand and wiped at the fluid. With blurred vision he could now see what had happened. Arain Drake laid there on the ground some twenty feet away with a ballista through her chest nearly splitting her in two. "Dammit!, retreat, retreat, fall back!" he yelled as loud as he could. A quick glance back and he could see the gelatinous cubes were still blindly absorbing everything they could touch. Seget ran to his queen's limp body and ripped out the huge ballista bolt, throwing it off to the side. With ease, he scooped her up and flung the leaking body over his shoulder. Back to their makeshift base he ran until a Deep one sprang out in front of him. Startled, he stopped and just stared at the grotesque worm in his path. "Move out of my way."

A voice spoke as clear as could be. "We will protect your retreat, now go."

Seget looked left then right trying to see where that voice came from. "Did you just talk?"

"I have psionically communicated our intentions to you, now go and get the goddess to safety."

With no time to waste, Seget shook his head as if he was shaking something loose back into place. Off he ran west as quickly as he could. Every few steps another Deep one sprang up to defend against any would be assailants. There would be none. Malik's generals were suffering a large amount of casualties from the ever growing acidic slimes and deemed it tactically sound to retreat back to the castle while they figured out the best way to dispatch them. The slimes were lethal but they had one disadvantage, they were terribly slow, relying on attackers to get close enough to be sucked in. Eventually the battlefield was quiet once more. Only the smoldering meteorites and the hiss of the slimes absorbing dead bodies could be heard.

Back at the camp, the werewolves had reverted back to their human forms. Bucket after bucket of fresh water was dumped on them to rinse off the painful silver dust. Krillox and human soldiers alike began trickling back into the camp. Seget out of breath and sweating profusely lumbered in from the dark. A handful of soldiers rushed over to aid their queen. "Take her to her tent and have the healers assist her immediately." It took every bit of his remaining strength to keep from collapsing to his knees.

Ori seemed to appear out of nowhere next to him. "What are your orders, sir?"

"The worms are out there protecting our borders for now so make sure the injured are tended to and setup a rotating watch," Seget said in between labored breaths looking towards the ground. "I don't think they will be attacking again tonight but we need to be ready if they do."

"Yes sir." By the time Seget raised his head, she had vanished like a ghost.

"I guess I should get cleaned up." The amount of Arain's blood that ran down the left side of his armor made it look like he had a crimson curtain draped over one side. It was drying now and becoming quite sticky. Inside his tent his assistant aided in the removal of the soiled plate, then quickly went to work scrubbing and cleaning the armor. Seget wasn't sure if he should be concerned or not about the condition of the queen. This wasn't the first time Arain was killed only to be resurrected later. He figured it in his best interest to at least check on the body. Arain's tent was close to his so the walk was short. When he entered, there were two healers tending to her while Timber laid at her feet. Looking past one of them, he could see the gaping wound already looking much better.

"Amazing, isn't she commander? She healed this much on her own, as it seems our magic has little effect on her. We cleaned her up and made sure she would be comfortable when she woke."

"Thank you gentlemen, continue on with your care and have me notified the moment she wakes."

"Yes commander, as you wish." Seget glanced over as he was about to leave and saw the damaged armor they had stripped from her. It was unbelievable that anything could survive a wound that big.

Seget made it a point to inform one of the blacksmiths that her majesties armor would need to be repaired post haste. He settled down in his tent and had something to eat. "All I can do now is plan and wait. Either she'll wake up or Valin will arrive before we can continue on with this campaign."

CHAPTER EIGHTEEN

FAITH

Sleep for Lucious and Morgan was poor at best. The previous days trials weighed heavy on the couple, and more than once nightmares forced them to wake.

His four skeletal soldiers stood silently outside guarding the tent and its occupants. King Elrick went so far as to set up his own sentries a little further out from the skeletons. He wanted to be damn sure that nobody had anymore ideas of harming them.

.   Lucious' last nightmare came just before dawn. With a scream he awoke, breathing heavily like he had been holding his breath for a very long time. "You're alright, shhh you're alright," came Morgan's soothing voice as she held him. His body quivered against hers as he sobbed. "You're safe Lucious, no one will hurt you."

"That dream felt as real as when it happened. I could feel myself lying on the ground unable to move, desperately trying to breathe. But all I could inhale was blood. I have never felt so helpless as I did when they killed me."

Morgan didn't know how to respond to something like that. For her and every other living creature, dead was dead. There is no reliving like he is forced to. "It must have been awful to suffer like that Lucious, and I'm so very sorry for not being there to protect you."

Lucious looked her in the eyes. "Don't you dare blame yourself for what happened! I should be the one apologizing to you. I blindly placed too much faith in the human race and because I was so naïve you were injured and could have been killed. Never again Morgan will I blindly trust anyone!" He leaned in and kissed her gently on the lips before getting out of bed.

Sounds of people breaking down the camp could be heard outside. Lucious dressed and headed out to secure their breakfast. Outside the tent stood two of the four skeletons. Both their heads turned towards their master. "Stay here and guard Morgan." Their eyeless gaze turned forward again. Looking around he spotted one of the mess halls which were designated by a blue roof.

As Lucious worked his way over to the tent he noticed all eyes looking his way. The king's soldiers gave him a wide berth as well. It seemed like everyone was scared of being turned into a skeleton, or worse. Lucious didn't intend for them to fear him but he wasn't going to apologize for it either. *Let them fear me then, if they cannot be civil to non-humans.* The line of people waiting for food dispersed allowing him to walk right up to the front. A pair of young cooks nervously waited on him. Lucious was given the best of everything they had, delivered on a wooden tray.

"I, is, is, there anything else we can get for you, sir?" one of the cooks asked in a very shaky voice.

"That will be fine you two, and thank you for such splendid service." Lucious grabbed his tray of food and headed back to his room. Morgan was already up and dressed.

"That smells wonderful, thank you so much for grabbing us breakfast." Morgan grabbed the tray from Lucious and took it to their small, two person table in the corner. She took the plates off the tray and sat down to eat. Typical Stormy, he had to sit on her lap.

"Don't worry little guy, I didn't forget you. I had the cook put some cabbage and carrots on a plate for you." The Arabis looked up at Lucious while he spoke, twitching his little nose.

Morgan promptly inserted a nice orange carrot into Stormy's eagerly waiting mouth. The Arabis made short work of his breakfast before jumping back down on the floor to play. Lucious joined his Draconian friend and the two had a nice little meal.

In less than an hour, the camp was packed and ready to travel. They started their long ascent up the Vesper Mountain road. It was cold this morning and the temperature only dropped more the higher they went. Frost clung to the rocks and a light dusting of snow coated the trail. "What is this white stuff that crunches under my horse's hoofs?"

Lucious chuckled. "Sorry I didn't realize you've probably never seen snow. When it gets cold enough, rain freezes and snow is the result."

"That's amazing, is it dangerous?"

"No, not usually unless you get stuck outdoors in a snow storm or you don't dress warm enough. Most of the time it's perfectly safe."

"Hmm, does it snow everywhere?"

"Almost everywhere, we get a fair amount in Addleberry. Further south not so much though, it's just too warm."

Stormy was surely enjoying himself with the change in weather as he bounded all around playing by himself. He tried to lure Morgan's horse into a game of chase, until she gave him a stern look to knock it off.

The road was only wide enough to ride five abreast which caused the king's army to stretch from where they previously setup camp all the way to the peak. Lucious looked back. "Wow would you look at that, soldiers and wagons as far as you can see. It's sure going to be a long day for those at the rear."

"Yes indeed, hopefully they rested while everyone else went ahead." It amazed Lucious that Morgan was still genuinely concerned for the humans well being just a day after they tried to murder her.

The company crested the peak by midday and were just starting their decent. The town of Tellium could barely be seen way off at the bottom of the mountain. King Elrick walked his horse up besides the couple. Sheepishly he struck up a conversation. "How are you two doing today?"

Morgan responded seeing as she was the only one who still had any injuries. "We're doing good your grace, a bit sore but good. How about yourself?"

"Physically I'm doing great but I have to say what happened yesterday is weighing on me greatly. I would have never imagined any of my subjects, especially my royal guard committing such atrocities. It saddens me greatly."

Lucious felt bad for Elrick, he knew this probably would not be a one time offense. "Try not to carry all of the burden, Elrick. It's impossible to know what lies in people's hearts, you would have a better chance guessing how many grains of sand are on a beach or snowflakes on this mountain."

Elrick was silent for a moment reflecting on what they were saying. "I thank you both for being so honest and kind. It comforts me to see two young leaders who are so level headed. This gives me hope for our two races and for our world." Elrick rode with the couple for the better part of an hour, while they discussed more personal things. The king's upbringing, Lucious' abilities, and even Morgan's favorite color green were talked about. "Well we're almost to Tellium city, I best be off to greet the towns people and inform the guards of the recent developments. I will see you both later in camp." Elrick took his leave, heading to the front of the procession.

Morgan and Lucious continued down the mountain with their skeleton escorts. She stared at the one closest to her trying to figure out which person it used to be. "Lucious, do you think that these four remember anything about their human lives?"

Up until this moment Lucious hadn't thought much about it. "That's a great question. I don't think anything remains from those four men except for their bones."

"That's good, I would hate to think of them as slaves deprived of their free will. Not that free will would help them much in their current condition."

The day carried on with little fanfare. King Elrick had camp setup just West of Tellium and provisions were restocked. The town was instructed to prepare for a possible invasion, and that General Erin with a regiment of thirty thousand soldiers would be arriving. Elrick also informed the townsfolk that a new race called Veassels would be joining them as well. If it wasn't for the sight of Morgan, the citizens would have surely thought the king had lost his mind. Most still couldn't believe the Draconian in front of them was real. Tellium's blacksmiths were ordered to begin producing weapons and armor immediately. While the miners were told to focus only on materials required by the blacksmiths. This city could not be taken by the enemy as it would cripple the kingdom's ability to arm and defend itself.

Over at camp, Lucious and Morgan were spending some time alone in their barracks. Morgan sat at their small dining table with a mirror propped in front of her. She used a cloth and some ointment to clean the wounds she had gotten from her captors. Mostly just scrapes and cuts, nothing too serious. Lucious tried not to stare at the half naked Draconian while he cleaned mud from their boots. Morgan knew he was watching and it excited her. She also knew how shy her human interest was so she decided to play with him. "Lucious, could you please come help me? I can't reach the wounds on my back." Morgan sat backwards on the chair straddling it. In one smooth motion she undid her top letting it fall to her hips and tail.

Lucious swallowed hard seeing the beauty waiting for him. This was all new to both of them but Morgan wasn't half as shy as he was. "Sure, I think I can help you." He dropped the polished boot onto the floor and walked over to Morgan. Pulling up the other chair, Lucious sat behind her with the ointment and cloth. Very carefully he dabbed the cloth into the small jar and then onto the first of a handful of abrasions. "Let me know if I'm doing it to hard, alright?"

"Mmmhhmm," was her only response.

Slowly and gently he worked at the spots making sure not to miss one. She smelled so good and her skin was amazingly soft and warm. He couldn't help but let his thoughts wander as he cared for her. His body showed signs of reacting to this as well. Oh no, his face felt warm and his breeches were uncomfortably tight now. The panic began setting in. *What if she sees me like this I'll be so embarrassed.* "All done, is there anything else you need help with?"

Morgan grabbed her shirt from the table and slid it back on. Gently she leaned back against Lucious. "Can you just hold me for a while?"

With the greatest care he wrapped his arms around her waist. "How's this?"

She rested her hands over his before letting out a sigh. "This is perfect."

CHAPTER NINETEEN
ALMOST HOME

E zra and Ulandra started the time consuming task of saddling the griffin. Piercer being as patient as ever stood there while the two of them situated everything. Ulandra secured the straps across his massive chest and his abdomen. Being underneath Piercer gave Ulandra a first hand view of what one would see before the gryphon ripped you apart with its intimidating looking talons.

Stepping out from his underbelly, Ulandra brushed off her pants before giving one last reassuring tug on the saddle. "Piercer, is that comfortable?" Extending his wings he did a test flap. Retracting them he let out one of his signature ear piercing screeches. "I take that as a yes." The Draconian wasn't quick enough to cover her ears so now she would have to deal with the ringing punishment.

Ezra stood there smiling, looking silly with his pointer fingers buried as far as they would go in his ears. "I believe at some point we'll need to figure out a way to protect ourselves from that. Especially if we wish to be able to hear later in this life. That should be it," as he packed the last saddle bag. "Why don't you sit in front today? Maybe handling the reins will help with your air sickness."

Ulandra thought about the offer for a moment. "Sure why not, it can't be much worse than the back." The two of them climbed into their respective spots. Her nerves were already on edge making her stomach knot. It felt like somebody just punched her in the gut. Clenching the reins tightly in both hands, she commanded the gryphon, "FLY."

Piercer flexed his wings out wide before leaping straight up. The massive wings cut into the air forcing a cloud of dirt to form as the air slammed into the ground below like a wave on a rocky shore. Piercer continued his powerful flaps until they ascended to a considerable height. Now he could mostly just glide on the air currents, conserving his energy. All other birds steered clear of the enormous predator for good reason. The next biggest creature in the air was a blue eagle which paled in comparison to the mighty griffin.

"Wooohoo!" yelled Ezra from behind. "I could fly like this every day of my life and never get bored."

"I'm glad you're enjoying yourself Ezra, but today will be spent flying straight ahead. No twists, spins, loops, or dives will be included." She looked back over her shoulder to see Ezra frowning with his arms crossed in front of him. "Come now mage, no need to pout. You can take Piercer out by yourself when we land to make camp later."

Ezra nodded, "That's fair I suppose. For the time being I'll just enjoy the journey and update my journal." He reached into his thick robes and produced the red book and pen. Settling back in the saddle he set about to chronical the past days events.

Ulandra settled in for a long flight herself, gradually loosening her iron grip on the reins. Looking out at the clear blue sky ahead, the knot in her stomach started to loosen. Thoughts of Selim crept into her mind now. *Oh my dear Selim, how I wish we were together. Your toothy smile and all engulfing hugs are sorely missed.* Sadness wished to visit her but Ulandra denied it adamantly. *We will be together soon my love, keep yourself safe. Enough of this longing, I'm about to visit my homeland.* That thought made her smile. Soon she would be the first outsider to witness this new land and its people. Soon she would be home.

It's so nice and quiet up here as if all the troubles in life were subject to only the people on the ground. *Nothing can touch us up here*, thought Ezra. The constant hum of air passing his ears slowly lulled the mage to sleep.

Ulandra sat there silent, with only the occasional wing flap to break up the calm. A sucking, grumbly sound could be heard every so often now. Looking back, she could see the source. Ezra, head back and mouth wide open, was snoring. "You've got to be kidding me." All she could do was shake her head and turn back around.

They traveled for a very long time, not stopping for a single break that day. It wasn't until the rocky coastline and the dark blue sea came into view that they decided to stop. Piercer landed gently on a cliff overlooking the churning surf below. A cool salty breeze flowed inland bringing with it a slight fishy smell. Ulandra and Ezra dismounted the gryphon and started removing the saddle and bags.

"Tomorrow Ezra, tomorrow we will reach a new civilization." The Draconian smiled uncontrollably with joy.

"You're right, this is going to change the known world. But first I must venture to the port town of New Haven and deliver the king's letter for us to be given the use of his ships. The division of soldiers he sent to aid us are still a few days behind, so you'll fly over and tell your people the situation we are facing. Get them ready for the journey ahead."

"That sounds like a good plan, Ezra. I'll have them ready and waiting to board when you arrive with the ships."

"Good, now that that's settled why don't we have some dinner and relax for a bit."

"Great, I'll do the cooking tonight while you setup the tents, Ezra." Ulandra unpacked everything she would use. "Alright, now all I need is some wood for the fire." She quickly realized a problem. No trees grew this close to the ocean, just some vinery, bushes, and moss. "Well that's not going to do. Hey Ezra, do you mind helping me with the fire?"

The mage finished setting one of the tent posts before walking over to aid Ulandra. "Oh dear, you're quite right, not much to burn is there? Let me see." Ezra put a hand to his chin, stroking his beard as he tried to recall a fire spell that would work. Sure he knew plenty of spells to start fires but not any to make a self sustaining campfire. "I have an idea." Scanning the ground he found what he was looking for, a handful of orange sized rocks. Carefully he placed them in a tight circle near Ulandra. "Alright now this is a first, so if I catch fire please put me out." She gave him a nod that he hoped meant she agreed. Kneeling down, Ezra placed his left hand over the opening made by the rocks and recited a couple incantation words. "Ligamen, funiculus," and with a snap of his fingers the fire sprang forth under his hand. Slowly he removed it to reveal a perfect orange flame.

"That's fantastic Ezra, how does it work?"

"Well I tethered my magical aura to the stones so when I placed the fire spell inside, it continues to burn. The flame is basically using my magic as fuel." Standing up, he brushed off his knees.

"Won't that tire you, having a constant drain on your aura?"

"Ahh, it's not using much as long as I don't make it large or walk to far away. If I don't stay close, the tether could break causing the fire to go out. Now if that's all you needed I'll be off to finish setting up the tents."

"That should be all, thanks for the help. Oh, and I'm glad you didn't catch fire," she said with a joking tone. Ulandra went about the chore of cooking dinner while Piercer sat close by preening himself. "Not heading off for a meal tonight?" The gryphon paid her queries little attention. *Hmm, he must not need to eat every day, one large meal apparently lasts awhile.*

The companions ate their meal and headed off to bed. Piercer curled up at the entrance of both tents in front of the small fire. All three were sleeping in no time.

That night was especially dark as the clouds above blocked out the twin moons. Their fire was much easier to spot because of it. Out in the dark, downwind from the campers someone was watching them. Slowly and silently they approached, circling around to Ezra's tent. A quick glint of steel from a dagger sliced through the fabric of the back wall. There was the human mage slumbering peacefully with his head pointed towards the newly made entrance. It looked down upon Ezra with hatred in it's eyes. The dagger came down quickly in an arching motion towards the sleeping mans chest. Boom!! an explosion went of sending the attacker flying at least ten feet backwards. The tent didn't fair much better as its sides were blown clean out. Piercer let out a startled wail as he jumped up defensively, facing the remains of Ezra's tent. Ulandra, scared half to death sprang from inside with weapons drawn. Ezra hurried over to the incapacitated assassin with a light orb floating over his head. "Ezra, are you alright? What just happened?"

Ezra stood over the body. "Yes I'm perfectly fine, thanks to my barrier spell but you may want to come look at this."

Rushing over she could now see what the mage was staring at. A Draconian male lay there in the weeds. His dagger hand burned from the explosion caused by Ezra's spell. "Why is there a Draconian here, and why was he trying to kill you?" Ulandra sheathed her weapons and knelt down to search the body.

"I'm not sure to both those questions. It's possible not all the Draconian's created by Lucious ended up on their island."

"Looks like all he had was that dagger on him, and I'm guessing from his hand that it's probably destroyed."

Piercer wandered over to inspect the body at the same time the young man regained consciousness. "Ahhhhh!!!," he screamed staring up at the gryphon.

Ulandra quickly placed a hand over his mouth. "Quiet!"

Wide eyed and shaking, the Draconian looked over at her. Ulandra removed her hand while giving him a look that told him he better listen to her.

Ulandra stood with her hands on her hips. "Why in the world did you attack us, and I better like your answer."

The young man sat up cradling his injured hand. "I thought you were this human's prisoner so I tried to free you."

Ezra and Ulandra looked at each other puzzled. "Why would you think she was my prisoner? Are there more of you here?"

"I won't answer a traitorous human!" he said with a clear look of hate and disgust.

Ulandra wasted no time stepping forward and smacking the man upside the head with her open hand. "You will show us a little more respect. Do you understand?" Still wincing from the blow, the young man nodded. "Good, now answer my friend's questions."

"A few days ago a small group of us were sent out by boat to investigate this new landmass that just appeared out of nowhere. Myself, Victor, Ellie, and Crook came over and landed on a beach not far from the nearby city. We watched these humans for awhile until we decided they were relatively safe to approach. How wrong we were. We tried to tell them we meant no harm but they labeled us as devils and bound us in shackles. I managed to slip mine, escaping to go get help. I went back to where we left the boat but the city guards had already confiscated it. Alone and with no way to sail home for reinforcements, I decided to stay near these cliffs so I could watch out for a possible Draconian rescue boat. That's when I saw you two fly in on that bird and assumed you were his prisoner."

"You're lucky he's a powerful mage or you would have committed murder on an assumption! Not all humans act as rashly as the townsfolk did, you might want to remember that next time."

Like a scolded child, the man looked to the ground in shame. "Please forgive me, I have made a terrible mistake."

Ezra leaned in offering his hand to help him up. "It's alright, no harm done." As he said that last word, he looked down at the blackened blistered hand. "Well mostly no harm done. By the way, my name is Ezra and this beautiful Draconian to my right is Ulandra." Piercer reminded them he was still there with an ear piercing screech. "Sorry, how could I forget this magnificent creature. It's called a gryphon and his name is Piercer."

With his ears still ringing, the Draconian introduced himself. "It's nice to meet all of you, my name is Trisk. By chance, do either of you know any healing spells?" He held up his damaged limb.

Ulandra shook her head. "Sorry my skill set is more for causing injuries, not healing them."

Ezra raised his brow. "I can give it a try but I haven't used healing magic in quite some time." The mage placed his hands on the injured arm just below the elbow, and began focusing on the spell. "Inum, colibre, suth," he recited. A greenish hue now emanated from his hands causing the blackened scales to mend. In only a few minutes time, Ezra finished and removed his grasp from Trisk's arm. With a critical eye he examined his work. "Not bad, it looks much better than before. How does it feel, Trisk?"

The Draconian held up his hand while flexing his fingers. "It's still a bit sore, but other than that I feel much better. Thank you for aiding me."

"Glad I could help. Now let us talk more about your falsely imprisoned companions."

CHAPTER TWENTY

OGRE LANDING

"Lord Valin, the port town of Seaside will be in view within the hour," relayed Captain Kander. He stood on the bridge, manning the wheel while a calm breeze gently filled the sails. Out on the deck in front of him were the sunbaked ogres, along with a fair amount of excrement and food waste. Kander thanked mother nature herself for keeping him upwind from the putrid smell. Valin and Adlin Bonecrusher walked over to speak with the captain.

"Kander, if you were to guess, how many troops should we expect in Seaside?"

"Well Seaside is a good sized city, and on any given day there's four maybe five hundred of Malik's soldiers present. Now with word of his towns being sacked, I would say there will be quite a few more there to welcome us."

Valin's face lit up with joy upon hearing this news. "You and Talia are truly fortunate that you get to bear witness to the might of the first ever ogre invasion. This is going to be a sight to behold. Kander, I want you to stop the ship just short of the city so we can go ashore. I'm not sure how well these beasts can swim so having them wage war from land is our best option."

"As you command, Lord Valin. We can begin off loading just up ahead. What are your orders for us after your departure, may I ask?"

"I will get back to you on that later. Right now I have some last minute business to attend to below deck. Adlin, get everyone ready to go ashore. When Kander here gives you the signal, I want you to fill the boats and have everyone stationed on the beach head where you will wait for my arrival. Understood?"

The towering giant bowed his head, "Your command will be done, Lord Valin." Excusing himself, Adlin headed over to get the others prepared. Valin took his leave as well, heading below deck.

"I have a nagging feeling that mage has something evil planned, I just don't know what yet," Kander said quietly. *For the time being I'll play along and follow order*s. Spinning the wheel to the right, he redirected the ship towards the beach. "All hands on deck!" hollered the captain. "Stow the sails and prepare to drop anchor on my command!" The crew scurried around the deck completing the tasks requested of them. Without the wind to push it, the ship slowed as it drew closer to the shore. "Drop the anchors!" With a click, the locks were released sending the massive anchors racing to reach the ocean floor. Kander gave the signal to Adlin. "Launch the boats!" In unison, the small vessels were loaded and lowered to the ocean below. For hours, a constant procession travelled back and forth between the shore and the ship carrying with them the harbingers of death.

Valin and Talia appeared from below deck. It seemed odd to the captain that the two mages seemed to be getting awfully chummy over the past few days. Noticing Kander, the two walked over to speak with him. Talia smiled, "Good day captain, looks like things are going well."

"Indeed they are Talia, soon the ship will be empty, giving us time to do a much needed cleaning. It'll take us at least a week to get her back to pre-ogre shape again."

Valin chuckled, "Do you think a week is enough time?"

There was an awkward silence for a moment until Adlin Bonecrusher showed up. "Lord Valin, the last of your army has disembarked for the beach. We are the only ones left."

Valin slapped his hands together, rubbing them vigorously. "Now it is time for some chaos!" The way he said it made the hairs on the back of Kander's neck stand on end, and before he knew it everything went black. "There, a simple sleep spell to subdue the captain and now the helm is all yours, my dear Talia."

"Why thank you, Lord Valin now we can use the ship as a decoy without any objections from him." Little did poor Kander know that Talia harbored a deep hatred for King Malik. After all, it is he who assigned her to travel the same stretch of ocean for the rest of her days. She hated this ship and the monotony it brought. Valin offered to end her life sentence of sailing, in return she would become his protégé. Talia graciously accepted.

Valin simply smiled at Talia before heading to the boat with Adlin. "I will see you soon my dear," is the last thing he said to her before the giant ogre started rowing towards land. In a matter of minutes, the two of them were on the shore with the ogre army.

Talia wasted no time getting the massive ship moving towards the city of Seaside. "Hoist the anchors and raise the sails!" The crew moved with added haste knowing that Talia did not tolerate slacking. Her ship moved easily through the water with all of the weight now removed.

On shore Valin laid out their plan of attack. "We will skirt the shoreline until we reach the front gates. After that, I want total carnage unleashed on this city. Focus on military units first and then have fun with the townsfolk." The crowd of ogres now came to life with the promise of bloodshed. It took them no more than twenty minutes to reach the gates. Valin with the biggest most evil grin looked over to Adlin, "Their all yours to command."

Adlin now stood in front of his brethren. "Mages, destroy the gates and the adjoining walls. Make a big enough entrance so we don't create a choke point. Berserkers will be the first line in to soften up any large human regiments. Next the warriors followed by the mages and the void." Off in the distance came the sounds of cannons being fired. "That would be our decoy, so now we attack!" Valin watched in amazement as this horde of monsters executed their orders perfectly. A wall of giant fireballs came hurling from the ogre mages. With an ear splitting crack, they impacted the gates and perimeter wall leaving only small chunks of rubble behind. The berserkers now charged in a chemical induced rage. Their spiked gauntlets swung about with brutal precision killing anything and everything in their way. The vessel captained by Talia worked like a charm diverting the bulk of the heavy weapons and troops to the piers.

Valin and Talia had spent the last couple of days coming up with a plan wherein the ship would draw most of the firepower from the cities defenders. Charming the ships crew and cloaking them in illusions that resembled ogres helped to sell the façade, and from the sounds of it, it worked perfectly. Malik's troops used cannons to pound the massive ship while mages lobbed fire and lightning. Talia had long since departed in the last larder boat and was waiting off shore for confirmation it was safe to come in. Valin walked through the gaping hole in the wall without a care in the world. "There are truly no words to describe the total destruction before me." Fires burned all around while homes and shops crumbled. Screams came from every direction as the human inhabitants met their demise. Some were smashed to a pulp while the majority of them were eaten.

By the time the guards realized the ruse, it was too late. The ogres pressed on forward like a wave of death consuming everything. Malik's soldiers were trapped now between the ocean and the ogres. They fought valiantly but in the end, they were no match for the sheer strength of their attackers. A few chose a watery grave over being eaten as their heavy armors dragged them to the oceans bottom.

Talia rowed her small boat into the blood stained bay of Seaside. Valin waited patiently for her on shore. "Welcome Talia, to the newest town in her majesty's kingdom." The black robed mage extended a hand to aid Talia off of the boat.

"Thank you very much, Lord Valin, I can see now why you had been so excited to unleash them."

"Her majesty, Arain Drake will surely be pleased with her new soldiers. Come now, we need to hurry and put an end to these hostilities before there is nothing left to call a city." Side by side the two mages headed to the front lines as the ship they sailed in on burned and sank behind them.

Adlin stayed close by to protect Valin in case of an ambush. He nodded in respect when the mages approached. "Give the signal for an all stop Adlin, and have any survivors brought back to me. The city is ours, no need to destroy it completely." The hulking ogre took a few steps away from Valin and Talia before blowing on his war horn. Its tone was low and eerie as it filled the air around them. There is no mistaking such a sound for any other. Adlin repeated the call every few minutes until all the ogres returned to their location. Valin scanned the crowd assessing what injuries they suffered. "All in all it looks like only minor damage was received while maximum damage was given. You all have done an exemplary job winning this town for her majesty, Arain Drake. Now where are the surviving citizens of Seaside?"

The horde of ogres parted letting the humans file in. Maybe two hundred were spared out of almost ten thousand souls. Most of them were understandably distraught, crying, and whining for mercy. Valin looked to Talia, "Go ahead and convey what we have discussed."

"With pleasure." The beautiful mage stepped forward in front of her former brethren. "Citizens of Seaside, this city is now property of her majesty, Arain Drake. Your lives have been spared as long as you swear absolute loyalty to her majesty." Talia paused for a minute, waiting for a response. It didn't take long before the humans all knelt down and swore their devotion.

One woman however did not kneel as she stood sobbing. "I have nothing left, you bastards have taken everything, my home, my family, my future!"

"Oh poor dear, let me rejoin you with your family." In one fluid motion, an ogre stepped behind her placing one hand around her head and the other hand on her shoulders so her neck was between the pointer and middle finger. With ease he pulled up on her head, ripping it along with her entire spine from her body. The sound it made caused more than one person to vomit. The woman's limp body was hurled out into the bay, while her head and spine were crunched on as a snack. "Is there anyone else who wishes to be reunited with their recently deceased loved ones?" Not a sound came from the kneeling subjects. "Good, for the privilege of being allowed to dwell here, each and everyone of you is charged with rebuilding Seaside into an even better version of itself. Her majesty, Arain Drake will one day return when all the known lands are conquered, and for all of your sakes she better be pleased. I will leave the election of your city officials up to you fine people to decide." Talia turned from the crowd and walked back to Valin. She could tell from the look on his face that he approved of the way she handled the situation.

"Alright now that all of the formalities are out of the way, who's hungry for dinner?" Everyone in attendance looked over at Valin, who just smiled back in return.

CHAPTER TWENTY-ONE

REPELLING THE QUEEN

King Malik stood up high on his ramparts looking out onto the battlefield. The defenses worked perfectly as he watched the masses of werewolves get slaughtered below. Malik couldn't help but smile at the sight. General Pogo walked up beside him. "Looks like you were correct in concluding that the silver of Talo's blade was the catalyst that could kill them."

Malik continued watching the chaos unfold below. "The only thing I did was remove the knowns from the unknowns, Pogo. You see, the sword, Vixor that I gifted Talo is enchanted with speed and dexterity spells and those only effect the wielder. The sword blade is high grade carbon steel with a pure silver inlay. We know from fighting the late General Hortus that steel only wounds them momentarily, so the silver is the only thing left that it could be."

By now, Arain Drake had her forces in a full retreat leaving only piles of flesh and fur littering the field.

"Shall we pursue them, your majesty?"

The battlefield was now vacant causing Malik to loose interest. He turned to face Pogo. "No general, we will not pursue. We don't have enough silver weapons at this time to properly equip a large strike force. Her numbers have been depleted, let us not replenish them. Send out a group to scour the field and reclaim whatever silver arrows we can. Also, have the silver collection throughout the city continue."

Pogo gave a courteous nod, "As you command, your majesty." The alchemist took his leave heading to relay the new orders, leaving Malik with his royal guard behind. Meanwhile tens of thousands of soldiers were dispersed throughout the sprawling city. Door by door they went collecting anything that was made from the semi precious metal. Mirror frames, silverware, cups, jewelry, and even teeth were piled high in wagons destined for the smithy. Making silver swords and arrow heads were the top priorities for the blacksmiths. Fletchers were given the task of removing the steel broad heads and replacing them with silver ones. Pogo on the other hand had his disciples converting some of the silver into a fine dust that was placed into small bags before being loaded into explosive ordinance. After he passed on the commands to the other generals, the alchemist returned to his workshop to oversee production. Tables full of finished ordinance lined the massive lab. "Yes these will do the job nicely," as he gently examined one of the projectiles before placing it back in line with the others.

One of Pogo's lieutenants approached before slightly bowing. "General, as you can see the production is going well. We have nearly thirteen hundred air burst shells completed and ready for use."

"Excellent work lieutenant, are there any areas of concern with the process at this point?"

"As expected general, the lack of silver is our biggest problem, everything else is running smoothly."

"Very good, continue on until we run out of materials, and have these finished rounds distributed to the artillery batteries for use at once."

"Yes, general!" The lieutenant called over a handful of lower ranked soldiers to carry out Pogo's orders. Carefully they loaded up and delivered each cartful of ordinance until the tables were empty. Satisfied, the general headed to his library to continue his research on the remains left by Hortus. His shriveled charred cadaver now laid out on a metal table. Pogo stood silently looking down at his deceased friend, remembering better days long past. "Ahh Hortus, I bet you never imagined your life would end with you in my library like this. Hopefully you can find peace now wherever you may be." Walking over to a cabinet on the far wall, the alchemist gathered his surgical tools and a journal to record his findings. Once he had everything he needed, Pogo started the dissection of Hortus. He meticulously documented the entire procedure. The organs were removed and weighed before being placed into liquid filled jars for preservation. Occasionally he would stop just long enough to fetch certain regents from the other room to test their reaction when placed in contact with the flesh of the werewolf. To his surprise only one thing besides silver had any effect, a fungus called monkshood that would cause blistering when placed on the skin. "Hmm, I will have to try this on a live subject to see the full extent of damage it can inflict." Monkshood grew on the cliffs that protected castle Kragg's northern approach. *That would truly be good fortune to have another weapon so close and plentiful.* Pogo continued on with his research for as long as he could, before succumbing to the need for rest.

Meanwhile on the battlefield, Malik's soldiers led by General Yuni were busy disposing of the gelatinous cubes that Arain Drake had left them. First the mages used cold attacks, but that only managed to make more slimes when they shattered. Fire based spells were used next with much more favorable results. The green slimes sizzled as their liquids evaporated from the high temperatures until nothing was left but the skeletons of the poor few that were consumed. Once the monsters were dealt with, burning corpses and collecting the precious silver arrow heads would be the next priority. Care was taken to not venture too far away from the protection of the archers perched atop the castle walls. Every so often something would move at the tree line where Arain Drake had retreated earlier. Yuni looked on with disgust as a Krillox scout observed them from afar. "Come a bit closer, you fucking toad!!" she hollered trying to bait the enemy to attack, but the scout just stood there watching. Feverishly the troops worked while keeping one eye on the monster. An attack would be quick and none of them wished to be turned into a lycanthrope. They threw body after body onto a blazing bonfire. The corpses seemed to burn extremely well as if they were made of kindling.

Two soldiers picked up another body and headed off to the fire without even noticing the worm that now stuck some two feet out of the ground. Silently it launched two projectiles hitting the targets with ease. Before either of them could alert the others, the deep one launched a psionic attack. Their minds being weak were overcome easily. The parasitic needles had plenty of time to deliver the juvenile creatures into the hosts. Wanting to remain hidden, the worm retracted back into its hole leaving only the head exposed above ground. Like puppets, the worm controlled the two soldiers making it look like nothing was amiss. Before leaving, the creature placed a murderous hatred for their commander into the two men's brains. Instantly they dropped the werewolf corpse and headed for the general. They were helpless against the rage building inside them. The soldier named Earl remarked, "There that bastard is!" In front of them no more than thirty feet away, sat General Yuni atop her sable colored horse. She barked orders for her subordinates to hurry up, totally unaware of the danger approaching at her right flank. Once in range, Earl unsheathed his sword burying it deep into the horses back just behind the saddle. A scream of pain filled the air as the horses rear legs collapsed sending Yuni tumbling backwards into the mud. Earl silenced the horses screams with one forceful slash across the neck. The mighty steeds front legs buckled sending it to the ground with a thud. Yuni scrambled to right herself and identify the attackers. She was a moment too late as the other soldier buried his sword through her left side just below the breast plate. Her mace was unleashed with amazing speed, smashing into the man's legs. Leg bones shattered like glass from the force of the blow sending him sprawling to the ground in agony. The general, despite her injury stood to face Earl. Through clenched teeth she removed the sword sticking through her, throwing the blood coated blade to the ground. A constant flow of red ran down her armor from the wound. The resolve and tolerance of pain she possessed was unbelievable. A weaker person would be bleeding out, whimpering as they died in a pool of their own blood. Earl lunged swinging his blade in a downward arc at Yuni. She parried with her war mace deflecting the blow. On the follow through, the butt of her weapon split the side of his face open from cheek to chin. She didn't wait for a second attack as she quickly swung her mace connecting with the back of his head. A loud crack sent blood, bone, and a bit of brain flying. Earl crumpled in a lifeless mass to the ground. By now more soldiers rushed over to assist Yuni. "Stop where you are!" she shouted, causing everyone to freeze. "Continue gathering the silver so we can get back behind the walls as soon as possible, and group into teams of four from now on. I'm not sure what happened to those two so be cautious, the enemy may have laid a trap." Reluctantly her subjects did as they were commanded.

Yuni looked down at her slain horse shaking her head. "What a waste." Her eyes went to her wound that still bled freely. "I suppose I should get this fixed." Carefully Yuni walked to the portal through the city wall where she was met by one of her clerics. A young woman by the name of Alissa immediately began assessing the injury.

"General, let me take care of this for you." Yuni only gave a nod to proceed. Alissa stood facing the general's side. Gently she placed her left hand over the exit wound and her right hand over the entrance. Alissa closed her eyes to concentrate as she began the spell. Within seconds, a faint green aura could be seen around her hands. The flow of crimson gradually slowed before stopping completely. A few minutes later Alissa opened her eyes and removed her hands. "That should do it, general."

"Thank you, as expected excellent work." Alissa smiled and nodded before returning to her post. Yuni did the same. A new horse already waited for the general. All black with a white diamond shaped spot on its muzzle. She ran her fingers across the animal as she inspected it, ending at the head. "I think Blindside is a fitting name for you. It will remind me of that potentially fatal error I made just a short time ago." With agility and grace Yuni mounted the steed and headed outside the wall to finish watching over her troops. They finished collecting the silver and burning the corpses just before dark. The two traitors were thrown in the fire to burn as well. Yuni had no idea that one of Arain's deep ones had forced them into action.

The last thing to do was reset the silver mesh trap and cover it over with dirt. Chances of an attack coming from this direction again was slim but the general was not about to take any chances. All the soldiers exited the battlefield with Yuni following up the rear. An eerie calm and silence settled over the area. Only the occasional crackle from the bonfires dared make a noise. In place of the Krillox scout, there now stood the werewolf, Ori. Her night vision easily allowed her to watch the city walls and its guards. There would be no surprise attacks coming from either side this night.

CHAPTER TWENTY-TWO

CHAOS

Patience, patience, patience, that's the mantra poor Selim kept repeating to himself. Bibble and Bobble being contained on a ship drove their annoyance level substantially higher. "Nothing on the ship is safe from those two," proclaimed the Draconian as he watched Bobble climbing up the center mast. Bibble wasn't in view which only meant he was below deck getting into trouble.

Robert let out a chuckle, "You better learn to relax, Selim. Just imagine hundreds or even thousands of these Veassels all packed on this one ship." A sudden look of despair shown on Selim's face. He even looked a bit sea sick. The general placed a hand on the Draconian's shoulder. "Cheer up and look on the bright side, at least the landmass is close so we shouldn't be more than a day getting there and back. Hell, I think you could stay drunk the entire voyage."

Selim's brow raised, "That's not a bad idea, but maybe not a useless drunk. Maybe more like enough ale to numb some of the irritation away." He stood silent for a moment, lost in thought. "Well I'll be in the galley if anyone needs me." A renewed vigor took hold of him as he quickly headed below deck in search of alcohol.

Robert and the captain just stood together watching Selim leave. "He is an amazing creature, don't you think captain?"

"Amazing? If you say so, but scary, lizard man that's gonna give me nightmares is what I think of him."

The makeshift crew nervously went about their duties running the ship while the captain and first mate took turns at the wheel. As expected the sailors were a bit freaked out. Just a few short hours ago they believed that only humans existed and now they sailed to a new landmass populated by another race. It was a lot to take in for sure.

"Tighten the aft sail!" shouted the captain. Once in a while the skipper would bark out an order, but for the most part the only noise came from the sea parting on the bow. This ship wasn't the biggest of Elrick's fleet but it was the largest one docked in town at the time.

Robert made his way from the bridge to the ships bow. The cool, clean sea air blowing in his face caused his hair to tussle about. *I sure miss the freedom of being on the ocean. Life as one of the king's generals is great but it leaves little time for trips to the coast. Oh well, I should enjoy this moment while it lasts.* Robert placed his hands on the railing while taking in a deep breath, *ahh perfect.* He could already see their destination off to the west. Two, maybe three hours at most. The general stood on the bow a while longer before heading down to the ship's galley for some food.

Slam!!! The door heading below deck flung open just as Robert went to reach for the handle. Bobble came barreling onto the deck as if the devil himself were chasing him. "I didn't steal anything. It was just lying there inside the locked chest," professed the Veassel.

Totally caught off guard, Robert looked back at the door to see a burly, weathered man charging up the stairs with a dagger in hand. "There you are rat boy, I'll show you what we do to thieves!" Bobble cowered behind the general.

Putting his hands up to stop the man. "Woah, woah, woah, hold on a minute. I'm sure there's been some misunderstanding."

"Misunderstanding? I caught that rat thing rummaging around in my foot locker stealing my valuables!"

Robert turned around to question Bobble. "Is what this man says true? Have you stolen something?"

The Veassel lowered his ears. "I was bored until I found a mysterious locked chest that just begged me to open it. What was I supposed to do, it needed my help?" Robert gave him a look that suggested he didn't believe him. "Alright, I opened the chest and rummaged through it a bit, but all I took was this little leather sack."

Upon producing the sack of trinkets, the sailor lunged to grab Bobble. Robert's reflexes took over as he slammed the man onto the deck. A little kick and the man's dagger skipped across the smooth wooden decking. "I told you to hold good, sir. An order from his majesty's generals is the same as an order from the king. You will obey or face serious consequences. Is that understood?" The sailor still on the ground nodded his compliance. "Bobble, would you be so kind and give him back his belongings?"

The Veassel looked up at Robert as if to object, but decided against it. He reluctantly went over to the sailor and handed him the leather pouch. "Sorry for borrowing your valuables."

Grabbing the bag, the deckhand stood back up. "My apologies for getting out of line general, it won't happen again."

"These are new and wonderous times my friend, we need to all exercise some lenience in the years to come. On your way now, I'm sure you have much to do. He quickly excused himself and retrieved his dagger. "Well what do you say Bobble, how about you stay close to me for now. I wouldn't want anymore locked chests getting you into trouble." Like a pouting child, Bobble walked past Robert who held the door open for him. Down to the galley the two went. Below deck looked to be much busier than above. Their were sailors doing maintenance and cleaning throughout the lower decks. They entered the galley to see Selim sitting at one of the tables alone with a giant tankard of ale in one hand and a turkey leg in the other. The Draconian's razor sharp teeth tore all the flesh from the drumstick in one bite. Bobble and Robert looked at one another as if to make sure what they just saw really happened.

"I sure would hate to be bitten by him," professed the Veassel. "Two bites max is all it would take and bye, bye, Bobble."

"Oh come now, if he really tried I bet he could do it in one!" Robert walked over to take a seat with Selim. Bobble just looked on in horror as that vision played itself out in his head.

Selim took a single gulp and the tankard of ale was gone. Wiping his face with his forearm he looked towards Bobble. "What's up with him he looks like a statue standing there all frozen and stiff?"

Robert smiled at the sight. "He'll be fine, I just told him that you could consume him with one bite. Apparently Bobble has a paralyzing fear of being eaten. Hmph, who new."

Selim burst out laughing. "Come on over and have something to eat. I promise I'm already full." The Veassel's ears dropped pointing out to the sides. He knew they were making fun of him and he didn't like it one bit, but he really wanted some food. With his head down, Bobble walked over and sat down at the table.

A squat older woman with a greasy apron approached the three. "Will you two be dining with us this evening?"

Robert spoke up, "Yes, me and my furry friend here are famished. Two ales and two turkey dinners if there's any left."

"Yeah, we should have plenty as long as your lizard buddy is finished."

Selim gave the cook a toothy grin. "I think I'm done for now, thanks for asking." The woman grunted before turning away and heading to the kitchen. "I think she like's me."

The three companions chuckled. In all the commotion, the group completely overlooked the fact that they were one Veassel short. Bibble enjoyed himself standing in the crows nest of the tallest mast. It gave him a better vantage point to see all the stuff he had been missing down below. A few barrels were tucked away over in the far corner near the stern, and an interesting looking group of crates hidden to the port side midship. Not to mention the assortment of various ropes strung about between the masts and the deck. "Lemme see which one looks like the best ride." As if it was an important decision, he examined them all carefully. "Ahhh, this one." Bibble settled on the one that stretched towards the stern deck. Without giving it a second thought, he threw his empty pack over the rope and jumped out of the nest. Zzzzzz, was the only sound as the leather pack slid across the coarse rope. His hair blew backwards from the high rate of forward travel until just before the bottom when he let go and rolled to a safe stop.

"Woohoo, that was so much fun!" He held up his pack which now had a permanent rope burn mark across it. "Huh, now that looks cool," as he put it back on. Bibble rubbed his hands together fiendishly. "Let's see, those barrels were this way," and off he went to investigate. It didn't take long for him to sniff out his target. Three barrels with the king's griffon emblem burned into there lids along with the words, Property of King Elrick do not open. The Veassel craned his neck back. *Hmph, why leave something out for everyone to see, yet tell them they can't touch it?* The thought just blew his mind. *Surely the king would be alright if I opened one of them,* he reasoned with himself. Bibble being so transfixed on his debauchery hadn't noticed the two men coming up from behind until it was too late. Whack! a small club to the back of the head and Bibble fell unconscious. Almost thirty minutes passed before he slowly opened his eyes. *Why are my hands and feet tied, and what the heck's in my mouth?* Looking around gave him his answer. *I'm definitely below deck, someplace not cleaned very often.* Some coils of rope lay stacked nearby along with half full crates of maintenance supplies for the ship. *This isn't good, from my throbbing skull I get the impression there are some humans on this ship that wish us non-humans harm.* As he finished that thought, two of the shadier looking crew showed up.

"Look, our little rat boy's awake." Bibble tried to speak, but the gag in his mouth turned every word into a mumble. The second sailor didn't speak he just carried what looked like a small tool box in his left hand. Little did Bibble know, but the talkative man happened to be the same one Bobble had a run in with earlier. At a quick glance, Veassels look almost identical to one another. The sailor with the tool box set it down on the floor and began quietly removing some of its contents. "Oh don't worry rat boy, my friend Cless is just getting us some toys to play with.

Robert and Bobble sat back in their chairs full and fat. Selim finished his fifth or maybe his sixth tankard of ale and felt pretty good at this point. But something nagged at him from the back of his mind. Something important. Like a slap across the face it hit him. "Have either of you two seen Bibble?"

A silence fell over the table. Bobble was first to spring from his chair. "Bibble wanders but he's never gone for long, and definitely not this long." A certain note of concern could be heard in his voice.

Robert quickly headed from the table while issuing orders. "I'll go to the bridge and get us some help from the captain, you two start searching deck by deck, he has to be here somewhere. Selim and Bobble acknowledged as they headed out of the galley with great haste.

The levels below deck were long and sprawling with lots of rooms and cubbies to check. Selim called out, "Bibble where are you?" He interrogated every one of the crew they passed. Nobody had any information on the whereabouts of their friend. Again the Draconian called out, "Bibble give us a signal if you're on this deck!" No reply of any sort followed.

Robert raced above deck scanning for their companion. "Dammit, where are you?" He ran to the ship's bridge to ask the captain, "Have you seen one of our veassel companions, he seems to be missing?"

The captain pointed towards the stern of the boat. "The last time I saw one of them, he was sliding down that rope there. I can't be certain which one it had been though, general."

"Alright captain, I need every available man and woman on this vessel to search for him, is that understood?"

Robert raced off to the ship's stern while the captain barked orders to his sailors. "The general is missing one of his companions, all hands find that critter or you'll be scrubbing the deck with your tongues!" You've never seen people move so fast.

Robert followed the long rope to its end but no sign of the Veassel. He carried on toward the stern. Everything looked normal until he glanced over at a small cluster of barrels. His stomach dropped and despair crept in. There on the deck lay a clump of bloody fur as well as half a dozen semi fresh blood drips heading away from the scene.

CHAPTER TWENTY-THREE

SHATTERED HOME

A little sable haired girl frolicked and played as the first snow of the season began to silently drift down to the ground. Her two brothers joined in with mouths open and tongues out trying to catch snowflakes. Their father worked nearby patching a whole in the barn wall. The sound of the hammering could be heard for quite some distance. Their mother worked in the house preparing some lunch.

This surely seemed to be a serene moment, that is until the cracking and falling of trees could be heard coming from the forest. The three children stopped and looked in the direction of the sound. Closer and louder came the sound as each minute passed. It drew their father's attention now causing him to pause the hammering and go investigate. "What's making that awful racket?" He could see his three children standing together with their attention fixated in the direction of the noise. Whatever it was made the hairs on the back of his neck stand up straight. Not wasting another moment, the farmer grabbed his children and ran for the house. "Hurry now, into the storm cellar." One by one the children walked down a rickety staircase and into the cellar. The little girl was oldest so she was put in charge of the lantern. "Keep them safe and no matter what, keep them quiet."

She shook her head that she understood, tears welling up in her eyes. "I will, papa."

"I'll be back as soon as I get your mother, alright?" Three tear streaked faces nodded back at him. Up the stairs he went closing the doors behind him. The noise outside grew to a deafening pitch before stopping altogether. Through the open front door, he could see his wife standing there looking up at something much larger than her. Her eyes wide, as the fear of what she saw paralyzed her. He only made it to the front door when a massive hand snatched his beloved. Grabbing his sword, the farmer rushed out to aid his wife, but instead witnessed her horrific demise. The last thing she did was scream before being ripped in two like a piece of bread. Intestine hung from the torso like links of sausage at the butchers. Blood rained down splashing on the frozen ground. The ogre consumed her, savoring each bite.

Now more ogres arrived behind the first. The smell of the fresh kill lingered in the air making the others ravenous for food. Instantly, their focus went to the little farmer standing in the open with his sword. They started to advance and he knew what had to be done. *I have to lead them away from the children.* As fast as he could, he ran into the forest away from his home and the precious occupants below. "Come on you ugly bastards, come and get me!" Two ogres obliged, giving chase. *Those things may be big and strong, but I know these woods better than anyone.* Weaving in and out of the trees he ran, drawing his attackers behind. Their size hindered any kind of agility as they crashed through the forest.

"Get back here human, I wanna taste your flesh" pleaded one of his pursuers. Recklessly they plowed through shrubs and trees or whatever else happened to be in their way.

Neither recognized the subtle changes in their surroundings. A human snack is all that mattered. This mistake would cost them their lives. Bursting through the trees and onto a steep drop off they went. Tumbling like rag dolls, the ogres were picking up speed. A massive hammer went flying, it's owner no longer able to hold onto it. Splash, as both ogres landed in a lake of molten tar at the bottom.

"I'd like to welcome you both to black lake, where you will spend eternity." The ogres fought a futile battle against the scalding tar. Layers of flesh were stripped away every time they tried to free themselves.

One of the ogres sank out of sight as the other cursed the farmer. "Damn you human, one of my brethren will enjoy your flesh!" The tar silenced him, completely submerging the second ogre.

Wasting little time, he headed back for his children. The devastation just two of those things caused to the forest surprised him. It also made the run back much easier due to the path being cleared. He slowed his pace the closer he came to the farm house. "There's another one of those things around here somewhere." Cautiously creeping up to a cluster of trees, he could see his front yard. *It looks clear, but somethings not right here.*

"Come on out, we know you're there," came a older man's voice from somewhere to his right.

Sword in hand he walked into the clearing to face a man and woman clothed in mage garb. In front of them stood the three children. "Who are you, and what do you want with my family?"

The male mage spoke again. "My name is Valin, and this is Talia. I do apologize for the destruction, it's just your bad luck that we came across you today. We are on our way to an important rendezvous so if you don't mind, I'll trade you my two ogres for your three children. Seems like a more than fair trade."

Pointing his sword at Valin, "Your abominations are dead, and you will be joining them if you harm a hair on my children's heads!"

Valin shook his head in disappointment. "Hmph, that is most unfortunate." In a single motion, the mage shot his hands forward while uttering, "Extricate!" The two young boys flew up ten feet in the air, and in an instant were twisted by some unseen force. The children didn't even have a chance to scream. They were twisted so tightly, so fast that everything but bone shot out through whichever path offered the least resistance. Below their mangled bodies lay everything that was expelled. The little girl stood motionless in shock as the blood from her siblings hit her like a wave.

The farmer ran straight for Valin with his sword poised to strike. Smash!!! From out of nowhere, Adlin Bonecrusher intercepted him with his mighty warhammer. The audible cracks and crunches indicated severe damage had been done. The farmer landed at least fifteen feet away with his broken sword falling next to him. To everyone's amazement, he survived writhing in pain in the dirt. Adlin went to finish the man. "Ahah leave him be, I want him to suffer with the slaughter of his family while he succumbs to his wounds. Excruciating pain for his body and spirit." The mage's words had a note of enjoyment to them. "Oh and I hope you don't mind, we're going to take your last child for servitude."

Cough, choke, through blood filled breaths he pleaded. "Please I beg you, do not take her."

"I believe we're doing you a service, we wouldn't want her left all alone when you're so close to expiring." Snapping his fingers, the two small husks of the boys fell to the ground.

"Adlin, I want you to stay back and make sure nobody eats him. I want that man to suffer as long as possible."

"Yes Lord Valin, I will see it is done." Nothing else needed to be said as the procession of death and destruction continued on towards Castle Kragg. Talia took it upon herself to wipe the blood from the girl's face and hold her by the hand as they walked. Talia made it a point to walk the little girl right past her mangled father so the two could exchange one last horrified glance.

More than an hour went by before the last ogre walked past them. Adlin gave the broken man one last look before traveling on with the others. The fortitude of the man impressed him. Normally he would end the man's suffering but the repercussions from Valin would be too great, and the man would die soon anyways. Without a further thought on the matter, Adlin left the farmhouse of broken lives behind.

He was left alone, on the freezing ground. Tears flowed down his face while he sobbed in despair. His two contorted little boys laid next to him. "I'm so sorry I couldn't protect any of you..." Every word stabbed at his heart like a dagger. "My end must be close, I don't feel the pain anymore, and the cold doesn't seem as bad." He watched the snowflakes fall for a few seconds more until his eyes closed for the final time.

A layer of snow gently covered him and his sons like a fluffy white blanket. It almost seemed peaceful, with only the sound of snow crunching under someone's boot to be heard.

A woman's voice spoke. "Not yet, you have a larger role to play, my Judas."

CHAPTER TWENTY-FOUR

FIGHTING FOR SURVIVAL

T he curtain slid to the side as the nurse walked in. "Good morning you two, and how is our patient?"

Sebastian stretched, standing from the chair he used for a bed last night. "Good morning," he replied. Seline still a bit groggy, sat herself up in bed while letting out a big yawn.

"Let's have a look at that leg so I can change the dressing before the master healer arrives." Seline pulled the blanket off her bandaged leg. Gently the nurse unwrapped layers of protective bandage before removing the salve infused last pad. The quick inhale combined with the shocked look on her face told them everything was not alright.

Panic struck Seline, "What is it, what's wrong?" The nurse made sure to keep the leg covered. "Master Fennil, I need your assistance in room thirteen please!" She tried her best to keep her voice even and calm but failed miserably.

Fennil rushed in unprepared for what he would see. "Yes nurse Hadley, what's got you so, oohh....." he said as she lifted the bandage mid sentence.

Sebastian and Seline were completely freaked out at this point. Leaning forward in the bed she yanked the bandage away. The cleric's leg wasn't at all better. In fact it looked way worse. Black veins streaked upwards from her foot to just below her groin. The bite punctures oozed out the healing salve that had been used to help, and the smell. The smell is what you would imagine an animal carcass baking in the summer sun for a week would smell like, but worse. Seline immediately broke down into tears. She knew what would need to be done, amputation. Her eyes met Fennil's, she gave a nod to proceed. There just isn't enough time to try other methods and have any hope of containing the poison to just the limb. Sebastian sat halfway on the bed and held her tightly to his chest. "It'll be alright, there must be something they can do?"

"There is, but the price is high. My leg must be removed."

Seline could feel Sebastian's breathing stop at the revelation. "I'm so sorry, if you would have taken care of your wounds first this wouldn't be happening to you. If I had been more observant and a better swordsman you wouldn't have needed to aid me." His heart felt heavy taking the responsibility for this.

Seline pushed him back to look into his eyes. "Don't you dare blame yourself messenger! As a royal cleric in his majesty's service, it is my duty to aid others before myself. How were we supposed to know those creatures bite could do this? It's Arain Drake's fault for creating those evil things, not yours." He knew it to be a lost cause arguing with her so he decided to bury the guilt he felt until he had time to deal with it alone. All he could do was hold her and be there during this life changing moment.

"I must go prepare for the operation, nurse Hadley will come get you when we're ready." Fennil exited the room with the nurse in tow. Hadley went on to notifying the surgical staff of the procedure so they could get ready.

Uluck rushed into the room carrying the little fur ball. He stood beside the bed opposite of Sebastian. "What's going on? They said something about an operation and that I should come here as soon as possible."

"Yeah....my leg got worse. It's just a cancer now that must be removed if I am to have any chance of surviving." Bouts of great sadness washed over her. The two most important men in her life did what little they could to keep her comfortable until they took her away for surgery.

"Don't worry sis, I'll keep Sebastian safe until you get back."

Sebastian bent down to give her one last kiss and hug. "We'll be right here when you're done." The two exchanged smiles.

Nurse Hadley returned to collect her patient. "They're ready for you Seline, it's time to go." Hadley placed a hand on the corner of the bed and it began to move. Out of the room they went and down a hall through two light blue double doors.

Uluck and Sebastian watched her disappear. "Uluck, she'll be discharged from the king's military after this, won't she?"

The big man let out a grumble. "I fear so, a one legged soldier is a liability on the battlefield. Even one as fierce as my sister. She will need us both after this. Do you think you're up to the task messenger?"

Sebastian looked up at him. "Seline saved my life, I will stay by her side and support her to the best of my abilities. You can count on that, Uluck." He could see from the look in his eyes that he meant what he pledged.

Seline entered a large, brightly lit, white room. Three stainless steel tables will all manner of apparatus on them were positioned around the central operating table. What must be medical books lined the far wall. The opposite wall held vials and jars with all different reagents, potions, and salves inside. Two assistants gently heaved her onto the main table. Two new nurses entered to take over for nurse Hadley and aid in the procedure. Last to enter had been Fennil's colleague, and master, Ceil. She would take over the procedure if something caused Fennil to not be able to finish.

A cold hand touched Seline's forehead causing her to immediately go unconscious. The nurses covered her entire body with sterile blankets, leaving only the dead leg uncovered. Fennil immediately went to work. He placed a mark along the circumference of her thigh just above the highest reaching black vein. He started calling out commands to the nurses. "I need forty inches of mithrite cord with a helix loop, as well as four pink searing leaves." Within seconds the requested items were handed to him. The pink searing leaves secreted an extremely sticky and flammable sap. Very carefully he wrapped the leaves around the circular shaped cord. Next he wrapped the mithrite cord around her thigh just above the marks he had placed earlier. Lastly, Fennil placed his hands on her thigh directly above and below the leaf wrapped cord. Closing his eyes he concentrated on the spell. "Hixs, Rengas, Hixs, Rengas, Hixs, Rengas," were the only two words he continued to repeat. The mithrite cord started to tighten without being touched. Just before it cut through the skin, the searing leaves ignited making the cord instantly white hot. Into her flesh it synched, cauterizing as it went. The less than pleasant smoke funneled upwards and out through a conical portal in the ceiling. Fennil continued chanting in deep concentration as the cord continued to synch and cut. Soon it reached the femur and the smell went from nauseating to down right putrid. The thick bone slowed the mithrite cord for only a few seconds before yielding. A moment later and the procedure was complete. More research needed to be done so they wrapped the infected leg and sent if off to be studied. Fennil took a couple cleansing breathes before wiping the sweat from his brow. "She should recover nicely now. Let's coat the area with some healing salve before bandaging."

"Yes master Fennil," acknowledged the male nurse.

"Excellent execution as always, master Fennil," congratulated Ceil before taking her leave to tend to her other patients.

Looking down at Seline now disfigured, he shook his head. "Damn shame this happened to such a caring soul." It became more personal for Fennil when treating a fellow healer. All healers belonged to a family, is the way he and so many others saw it. Sure she would still be able to help and heal people, but in more of a hospital setting now. Ahhh to much uncertainty this early on, some amputees continue on with life like nothing happened while others are just a shell of their former selves and unable to adjust. Time will tell.

Fennil went back out into the hallway towards the two men anxiously waiting for good news. "The surgery went well, she should be rid of the poison that infected her now. My assistants are finishing up with the dressings and then she will be brought back to room thirteen."

Sebastian and Uluck breathed a sigh of relief. Each man took turns shaking the hand of and thanking the healer for all he had done. "I will be back in later today when Seline wakes to see how she's doing. Until then if you three need anything don't hesitate to call on one of the nurses." A quick smile and a wave, then Fennil took his leave to tend to other patients.

"Uluck if you don't mind, I'd like to leave for a bit to go pick up some flowers for Seline."

"I don't mind at all. Do me a favor though and pick some up for me as well, I don't want to be empty handed when she wakes."

"Sure thing, Seline could use as much cheering up as we can give her." Sebastian headed out of the hospital not entirely sure where he would find flowers. Streets full of people lay out before him. Merchants, teachers, students, tourists, and many others with their own reasons walked every which way. "I can't be gone long, better just ask the hospital receptionist." Behind the front desk sat the same woman from the day before. "Excuse me miss, where can I go to purchase some flowers for my friend?"

The receptionist smiled, "Sure thing, you'll want to go out the front door and turn left. Keep going until you see the blue and white sign that says Marvin Gardens. Follow the signs and you should be in the botanical district in just about ten minutes or so. Is there anything else I can help you find?"

"No that's it, thank you so much for your help." *Alright, so left here until I see the sign.* Into the swirling masses the messenger waded. *I can't believe how many people are here. Is there some sort of special occasion or is it always like this,* he wondered? A few minutes later the big blue and white sign in the shape of an arrow came into view. Marvin gardens this way. Slowly and without cutting off too many people, Sebastian worked his way in the direction of the arrow. *Whew that was crazy.* He wasn't one for big crowds and that had been the biggest crowd he had ever seen. This street seemed more his speed. Still plenty of people but plenty of room to move as well. The fragrant aroma in the air assured him this way is where flowers could be found. Just as the lady at the front desk said, in just a few minutes he arrived at the entrance to the largest gardens he had ever laid eyes on. Sprawling out in front of him, the garden stretched on as far as he could see. Trees, flowers, shrubs, mushrooms, and everything else that could be grown. The sun shown down the entire area as rain fell in specific locations.

"Hello sir, and welcome to Marvin Gardens, the place where every living plant in the known world is grown. How can I help you today?"

Sebastian just stared out into the garden with wide eyes and an open mouth. "It's beautiful."

"Yes sir, it's the most beautiful garden in the world. What can I get you?"

"Umm, I have a dear friend in the hospital and wanted to get her something nice to cheer her up."

"Awww that's so nice." Quickly the woman produced a binder containing three dimensional images of what she had available.

"Wow, that's pretty amazing how the pages show a rotating depiction of the different bouquets." It didn't take long to pick what he wanted, and only minutes later the arrangements arrived.

"That will be six silver mister."

Nine silver was the wage for the messenger per month, but with zero hesitation Sebastian handed over the coins. "Thank you so much for your help."

"Anytime mister, we're open all the time so come visit us again soon."

Sebastian had already started heading back to the hospital before the saleswoman finished. Getting back before Seline woke being the top priority now. Retracing his steps landed him back at the hospital entrance. As fast as he could walk he headed to room thirteen. Two massive bouquets of flowers blocked his vision, making navigating difficult but he managed to make it back without falling. Uluck could see the wall of flowers in the hall so he ran over to assist. "Very, very, nice my friend, but did you need to buy all the flowers in town?"

His brow raised, "Uluck if you had seen the garden where these came from you would realize how ludicrous that statement really is." Sebastian set his flowers on the stand next to the bed where Seline slept while Uluck put his on the table at the foot of the bed. The arrangements so bright and fragrant contained a mix of no less than ten different flower species. "Has she woken up yet?" Sebastian asked while returning to the seat by the bed.

"No, not yet. Fennil stopped by for a moment and told me she may be asleep for quite a while due to the strain on her body from the venom."

"That's understandable I suppose. All we can do now is wait until she's ready." Sebastian looked over to the side of the bed where her leg should be and the blanket laid flat. It felt like someone just hauled off and punched him in the stomach. The realness that the woman in front of him had now been changed forever really sunk in. Their little Arabis however didn't seem to have a care in the world as it laid curled up on the bed next to Seline. "If you have something to do I can watch the two of them."

Uluck shook his head, "No I really want to be here when she wakes." The two of them sat and patiently waited for her.

CHAPTER TWENTY-FIVE

FEAR OF THE FUTURE

I t seemed a bit cooler today as Elrick's forces assembled on the border of the Hemshir forest. As common practice scouts were sent in first, ahead of the main army to look for traps or ambushes. Six to seven men wide is all the room the road through the forest offered. A bit more restricted than Elrick liked, but it was by far the quickest way to the City of Knowledge.

Morgan and Lucious stayed in their own little section with just Stormy and the four skeletons to deal with. "Morgan, I just wanted to let you know how much I enjoyed our time together last night." His tongue tried to trip him up every chance it could. "You're an amazing woman."

She quickly blushed at the compliment. "I enjoyed last night very much as well. You fascinate me."

Now it was Lucious' turn to blush. "This forest sure is beautiful but eerily quiet. I thought this place is supposed to be ripe with all kinds of creatures." Suddenly the column of soldiers stopped.

Elrick called out to have Lucious and Morgan brought up at once. Soldiers moved aside so they could pass. As they reached Elrick, they could see his concern. Parts of Morlock bodies littered the ground. A handful of them were even burned to the forest floor as evidenced by the charring around the corpses. Stormy immediately perked up and jumped down sniffing the air then the ground. Morgan looked over at Lucious. "Something sure has his attention. Don't wander to far Storm," called out Morgan like a protective mother.

Lucious knelt down to examine the charred bodies, the smell instantly reminded him of the hunters his Arabis had killed. "I think this bunch here ran into one of Stormy's kind, wouldn't you agree."

Morgan nodded, "I agree but these other ones were killed by human weapons, sword and mace by the looks of it. Look over here, dried blood and not that black ooze that's inside the Morlock's. I think from the prints that a small group of humans were attacked here. Weather the Arabis came with them or just happened to show up is unclear."

King Elrick walked over looking concerned. "You have a very keen eye my dear, there had in fact been three humans. One cleric, one swordsman and a messenger to be exact. No doubt this is the group I sent out ahead of us with a letter to the elders. It looks like they all survived the encounter as the only corpses are these horrid creatures. We should head on to the town of Hemshir, maybe there we can gather some more information on the health of my three vassal's." Stormy popped his head up from the grass before running back to Morgan. He knew without a doubt that there had been one of his kind here and he couldn't wait to meet her.

They arrived at the ruins of the once great town, with only a handful of its occupants still alive to greet them. Rickter, being the towns protector as of late, handled the conveyance of what transpired to make the town look as it did. Rage boiled in Elrick's stomach, "Those damn demon dogs were smart enough to sack this place on their own!" Shaking his head in disbelief, "How is that even possible?"

"Those things, Morlocks you called them are extremely intelligent, your majesty. They watched and waited until everything lined up in their favor before making themselves known. We did however learn a bit about them which may help us in the future. Their bite is poisonous and must be purged and healed within the first few minutes or it will set in like it did your cleric, Seline. We did all we could here but I'm afraid she most likely did not survive the last leg of the trip."

The news saddened Elrick. "Even one life wasted is too much. unfortunately many more will be slain in the coming weeks. War demands its tributes... We'll camp here for tonight, I want roaming patrols doubled and barrier spells reinforced, there's no telling what else may be lurking in these woods." The officers acknowledged the orders before dispersing them through the ranks. A ring of campfires were setup at the camps perimeter to aid the sentries and keep them warm. Mages cast three different barrier spells layered like the peels of an onion around the site.

It seemed to Lucious and Morgan that King Elrick had yet again accelerated his plans. Only half of the usual tents were erected to save on time. The extra patrols meant more soldiers would be awake so why waste the effort. Elrick enacted the procedure he liked to call hot swapping. When someone wakes for duty their bed is given to another that is finishing their shift. Lucious looked at Morgan and raised his brow. "I have to say it's not ideal but it is an extremely efficient way to do it."

"I agree it's efficient Lucious, but these poor people have no privacy, no personal space to call their own. I know we're headed for war and I'm not naïve but at the end of the day you need that piece of something to remind you what you're fighting for. A picture, a letter, maybe a memento, just something that has nothing to do with war and death." She noticed that Lucious had been staring and smiling at her the entire time. "What's that look for?"

"You're just so amazing, everyday you show me new levels of compassion that I'm not sure humans even posses." Stepping forward and grabbing her by the waist, Lucious embraced this magnificent creature. Morgan did not resist. A few passionate moments passed before Elrick stood outside the door requesting to enter. "By all means your majesty, come in." Their small dining table only had two chairs so Morgan decided to sit on the edge of the bed while Lucious pulled one out for the king. "Welcome King Elrick, can we offer you a seat and maybe some wine?"

Elrick walked over and sat down. "Thank you, and good evening to the both of you. No thank you on the wine though." Lucious sat down across from the king. "After our findings today I wanted to ask you a few questions about your abilities, if I may be so bold?"

Lucious sat back in his chair, folding his hands on the table. "By all means ask, though I'm afraid I may not have many answers."

"Your sister, Arain made those Morlocks which she sent to kill you and your father correct?" Lucious gave a nod. "If all of them were killed when you summoned the Draconian's, then where did these one's come from or did she just make more?"

"I'm pretty sure that once something is created its entire species becomes part of this world so it cannot be created again. At least that is what I have found when trying to duplicate Stormy. I also feel that when a more feral species is created like the Morlocks, they also spawn throughout the land with no rhyme or reason. Just like in nature, a type of deer could live in this forest and at the same time be found across the continent. As far as how many are created I have no clue. For all I know that could have been the last of them back there but I'm not going to bet on it."

Elrick put a hand to his chin thinking about what he just heard. "Is there anyway you could transport us all to the City of Knowledge or even make a portal to take us there? I get the feeling we won't have much time to prepare for your sister if she's already on Malik's doorstep."

"I don't currently posses the means to cast such a spell nor do many in existence. To tear a hole in space is no small feat. I could try teleporting a few of us but without ever being there I have nothing to focus on. We could easily end up in some very bad places, sorry."

The king scoffed, "Nothing to be sorry about, the last thing I want is to be transported into a wall or the foundation of one of the hundreds of buildings there. That wouldn't do us any good now would it? Alright one last question, you have seen your sister on various occasions in your dreams I recall. Is it possible to give us an idea of where she's at or what she's planning with her assault on the Kragg?"

Lucious had to think for a minute. "Every time something like that's happened I've either been asleep, unconscious, or dead. I can sure give it a try though and let you know if it's something I can control."

Elrick stood up from his chair. "That's all I can ask, is for you to try. Information on her will surely be valuable in our cause. Well I've pestered you two enough so I will take my leave. Morgan, Lucious I thank you for your time and insight as always. We shall see you in the morning." The king exited as quickly as he arrived, leaving the two alone again.

Morgan looked at Lucious from the bed. "It seems you have your work cut out for you tonight. I could just hold a pillow over your head until you pass out to move things along." She gave him a devious grin.

"No I think I'm good, I'll just try old fashioned concentration, or perhaps some sleep. I appreciate your devotion to helping though," he said with a chuckle.

Morgan sprang from the bed like a predator pouncing on its prey. She straddled Lucious on the chair facing toward him. *I almost forgot how physically strong she is, there's nothing I could do to get her off me even if I wanted to, and I did not want her to. It feels good to be helpless with her.* Morgan had her way with him, kissing his neck delicately with those amazingly soft lips. Her breath on his skin as she worked her way to his mouth. Lucious lost himself to the moment forgetting everything else except for her and him. He wanted her so badly and she him but right now it was more about the chase. She moved back slightly and stared in his eyes, as she ran a claw gently down his forehead to the tip of his nose. "I'll be going to bed so you can continue on with the task at hand undisturbed." When she posted up on him to get up from his lap, her left hand rested on his groin. Morgan gave a devilish smile and headed off to get cleaned up for bed. *She did that on purpose knowing it would drive me crazy, I know it. Figuring out this vision ability is the last thing on my mind right now!*

Taking a deep cleansing breath he stood and walked outside. The cool night air felt refreshing and helped him calm back down. Two of the skeleton guards blankly stared at their master waiting for orders. "Continue standing guard." Slowly they turned to face straight ahead. Lucious put a hand to his face and scratched his short stubble before heading back inside. Morgan had already gotten into bed with her back facing him. She draped the blanket in a manner that revealed parts of her he had never seen before. He had to hand it to her, she definitely knew how to entice a man. Over to the table he went, seating himself so he could watch the light from the lanterns dance off her body. Quietly Lucious sat at the table while the chamber stove fire gave the occasional crackle. Many hours passed as he tried to make the connection with Arain. Letting out a deep breath, "No luck, maybe it's something I can't control." Something about these attempts bothered him, like a puzzle piece that just didn't fit. Looking back at Morgan it finally clicked. Maybe it's not working because deep down I don't want it to. He sat for some time thinking about that realization. Every time this vision has shown me something more horrible than the last. The monstrosities we will be forced to face, the ruthlessness of the battlefield, the absolute and total evil of my flesh and blood. Again Lucious looked over to the woman in bed he cared for so deeply. I have to do it for those I love, so that maybe what I see can give us just enough advantage to save their lives.

Sitting there he closed his eyes and relaxed placing his palms down on the table. Inhaling deeply as the runes encircling his head slowly lit to form his crown. His body felt light floating through the ether. Images flooded his mind of so many places and things he had never seen before. The past, the present, and even the future all in one head splitting moment. Ahhhh!! he screamed from the pain, standing upright he knocked the chair backwards to the floor. Lucious held his head in his hands as if he was trying to keep it from exploding. His skeleton guards ran in weapons drawn looking for the source of the screams.

Morgan woke, startled and disoriented. Her eyes fixed on Lucious collapsing to his knees holding his head. The light from the runes faded and went out. Simultaneously he vomited while falling forward, blood spewing from every orifice of his head. Morgan cleared the bed and grabbed him before his face connected with the floor. Lucious' body went limp, his skin felt hot and covered with perspiration. After a quick assessment she could tell he still lived but was unconscious. Morgan picked him up and laid him out on the bed. Gently slapping his face, she tried to rouse him. "Lucious, wake up your scaring me. Come on please wake up," she pleaded. But there came no response, just the shallow breathing and the name Pengeran being whispered repeatedly.

CHAPTER TWENTY-SIX

A TOUGH CROWD

E zra, Ulandra, and Trisk looked over the rise to see the town of Balderas. Not a huge place as towns go but busier than one twice its size. Three of the king's cargo ships sat tied up to the pier, gently swaying to the faint ocean swell. Seagulls with their high pitched calls floated on air currents waiting for anything to be dropped by the humans below. Ezra turned to face his companions. "Alright, I will head down to Balderas and deliver the king's letter. Once that's taken care of I will talk to whoever is in charge and see about getting your friends freed. Any questions?"

The Draconian's looked at him dumb founded. Ulandra chimed in, "So what's plan B if they decide the letter is fake and you're just a crazy old man?" Trisk nodded his head in agreement with Ulandra.

Ezra was appalled that they had so little faith in his plan. "I'll have you know I am not that old, and if they disregard the king's instructions then I will need to persuade them." The mage pondered the situation for a moment. "Alright if something happens, come in with Piercer and get me out of there. But whatever you do, try not to kill anyone or else we'll never get their cooperation, understood?"

That plan they could agree on. Ezra brushed off his robes and made himself as presentable as he could before heading down to the town. Ulandra and Trisk watched while trying to keep Piercer quiet and out of sight. "Ulandra, you really trust this human?"

She never took her eyes off Ezra. "Absolutely, he is the human that raised our creator Lucious Drake. I have seen first hand how noble and honorable humans can be. Now shut up and keep a lookout for trouble." They laid there on their stomachs like a pair of assassins watching for their next kill. Piercer kept preoccupied with a whale bone he picked up from the shore earlier. He looked like a giant winged dog chewing on it.

Ezra reached the town's gates and greeted the two pikemen standing guard. "Good day gentlemen, I have an urgent message for the town mayor from King Elrick himself. Could you be so kind as to point me in his direction?"

The pikemen looked at each other and then at the mage. "Where did you just come from?" asked the man on the left.

"I thought that would be evident seeing as I'm holding a sealed letter from the king."

Their pikes dropped towards Ezra. "What I mean is how did you get here? We were on roaming patrols yesterday up the main road and never saw you, so either you ran really fast or you sprouted wings and flew in! Either way, somethings not quite right here."

A chuckle slipped out when the mage heard the accusation of flying in. "Gentlemen, I know you're doing your duty so please escort me to the mayor so he can read this letter and then everything will be sorted out." Ezra held the letter out to the guards.

"Alright then," one of the guards approached and took the letter while at the same time clamping a shackle around his wrist.

"What is the meaning of this, unchain me this instant or I will force you to release me!"

The guard with the letter had the other end of the restraints shackled to his arm. "The mayor is terribly busy at the moment trying to decide what to do with those lizard freaks we captured the other day so you will need to wait in a holding cell until you're cleared."

With a motion of his hand, the mage cast a binding breaker spell on his restraint but nothing happened. The pikemen laughed, "I put that on you for a reason old timer. You're obviously some sort of magic user and it just so happens these bindings syphon the wearer's magical energy. To an ordinary person like me they're just bindings." Ezra's eyes burned with rage. *How could I have been subdued so easily? Good thing I made a plan B.*

The guards escorted Ezra to an old granite and steel building where the holding cells were located. With a loud click from the key turning, the cell door creaked open. "Here you are, get comfy you may be here awhile until you're dealt with." The pikemen pointed to a darker cell toward the end where the Draconian's resided while he uncuffed the mage. "Now no funny business, you here? These cells have the same enchantment as those shackles, so no magic." The man turned around and headed off with the letter in hand.

Ezra pressed his forehead against the bars in defeat. "I can't believe this is actually happening to me right now." His eyes panned over to the Draconian cell. The figures inside sat silently awaiting their fate. "This is not how I planned my day going." A few more spells were tried ending with the same result. The pikemen had been right, no magic worked in here. Reluctantly he walked over and had a seat on the old wooden bench that occupied each cell.

Trisk looked on in disgust. "See what I mean, the humans in that town cannot be trusted. We need to go to plan B." Ulandra couldn't believe that the mage didn't even make it past the front gate. She couldn't wait to rub an, I told you so in his face.

"We should probably wait until night before attempting the jail break, fewer eyes to be seen by. Come, let us go back to camp and prepare." The three of them made their way back to the bluff where they stayed the previous night. "Why don't you go ahead and get some rest and I'll take the watch."

"Alright but make sure you wake me in time so you can get some rest as well." Trisk used Ezra's patched tent for his nap.

Ulandra sat down next to Piercer while she contemplated the best plan of attack. "Head on would work, but the odds of having casualties on both sides is very high. It needs to be simple, low profile, and quiet." She would never forgive herself if something happened to Piercer or Ezra. Ulandra took count of her weapons and their condition. A few passes on the whetstone gave her blades a razor sharp edge. She cleaned her boots and light armor as best she could so she didn't look like a complete slob, before heading out on a patrol. "I think it best if I shifted to human form lest some-one see me." Back to the fiery redhead she morphed. "There, now that's better." Off she went to have a look around the area. The gryphon seemed more than happy to lay down and chew on its bone.

It remained a pleasant day until a swift gust started blowing off the ocean inland. The seas gained a bit of chop as small whitecaps formed. Dark clouds were soon ushered in on the winds insistence. Ulandra returned to camp just as the first rain drops fell from the sky. A flash and delayed rumble reverberated in the distance. Reaching into Ezra's tent she shook Trisk's leg. "Get up it's your turn, wake me in a few hours."

Still half asleep, Trisk exited his warm tent only to be greeted by cold rain drops hitting him in the head. "Well this sucks!" Glancing over at Piercer he could see the mighty beast preparing himself for the storm. His massive wings were a perfect place to put his head for protection. The rain pelted down and simply beaded off his water proof feathers. "I could use some of those right about now." Trisk thought it unwise to try and pluck them. "It's definitely safer to just deal with a little rain." As if on queue, the clouds unleashed their watery cargo. Sheets of rain were propelled by the gusting wind causing it to sting exposed flesh. Miserable was the word that kept coming to mind. For the next couple of hours, he sat there in the open doorway of the tent, waiting. He didn't see much sense in patrolling the area with this weather, who in their right mind would be outside wandering around. His eyelids were starting to get heavy, and before long Trisk dozed off.

Crack!! Ulandra's fist connected with the side of his face sending the young Draconian sprawling backwards into the tent. When he collected himself he cautiously walked out of the tent holding his jaw. "What did you go and do that for?"

She looked his way with fire in her eyes. "You were supposed to be on watch while I slept, instead you decided it wasn't needed and went back to sleep. What if somebody or something found us, we could be captured or worse, killed! If you ever fall asleep while on watch again a sore jaw will be the least of your problems."

Still enraged, she prepared for the task at hand. The storm had blown itself out a short while ago and the twin moons could be seen peaking through the broken cloud cover.

Trisk thought it best to remain quiet and let Ulandra cool off. Piercer just woke up and started shaking like a dog to rid himself of any lingering water on his feathers and fur. Walking over to the beast, she stroked the soft beautiful feathers on his neck. "Piercer, I want you to stay here and remain out of sight. Under no circumstances do I want you to attack the town if something should go wrong." He signaled his acknowledgement with a string of eagle like chirps.

"Do you think he actually understands you?"

She took a deep breath in order to not explode at him. "I think this gryphon is an extremely intelligent creature and can follow orders better than some humanoids." Trisk looked to the ground as he knew it was a dig at him. "Lets get going." On the way, she explained her plan to use him as a captured slave. She would be in human form and pose as a hunter. Just out of sight of the city gates, Ulandra loosely bound Trisk's hands behind his back before placing a rope leash around his neck. "There that should do it. I will do all of the talking so keep your mouth shut, understand?" He nodded. "Alright lets go." Ulandra held the opposite end of the rope and ordered him to walk onward.

As they reached the gate they were greeted by the usual pair of sentries. Their attention being fixated on the reptilian thing in front of them. "Good evening gentlemen, I found this thing caught in one of my snares earlier and decided it would be best to hand it over to the proper authorities. I heard a couple other ones were captured the other day, maybe I can throw it in with them?"

One of the guards, a woman turned and headed in past the gates. "That sounds like a good idea, we don't want these hideous things wandering around, who knows how dangerous they are."

Trisk just started opening his mouth to respond when Ulandra silenced him with a punch to the side of the head that dropped the Draconian to his knees. "You don't speak unless spoken to boy!"

The two guards burst out laughing. "Way to put it in its place," commented the woman leading them to the holding cells. The townspeople had mostly retired to bed by this time so few onlookers and only three patrolling soldiers were seen as they crossed town. They proceeded inside the jail to deliver the captor.

Nobody stood guard, the locked steel bars were sufficient. Walking over to the one that held the other Draconians, she produced a ring of keys and slid one into the door lock.

Ulandra used the rope to strangle the woman from behind. Caught unprepared, the rope found its mark cutting off blood flow and oxygen in seconds. As the woman collapsed, Ulandra and Trisk grabbed her and gently laid her on the ground. The jail door swung open as the other Draconians walked out to their freedom. "Quickly bind her hands and feet, I'm going to get Ezra." Trisk and the others did as they were ordered. Once bound, she was gagged and locked in the previously occupied cell. A short ways down the hall stood Ezra waiting to be released. It took a few tries until she finally picked the right key. Click! "There you go Ezra, and by the way how well is your plan working out?" Ulandra had the biggest toothy smile on her face.

"Very funny, very funny indeed. Would you mind unlocking these dreaded shackles so I can use my magic again?"

She tried all the keys but none opened his bindings. That is until a Draconian the size of Selim walked over. "Let me have a try." With inhuman strength he pulled, and in seconds the shackles broke apart releasing the mage.

"Thank you very much, my friend. My name is Ezra and this is Ulandra. We have been sent by Lucious Drake to gather your people and bring them to the City of Knowledge.

The massive draconian looked puzzled. "What for?"

"To help fight a WAR!"

CHAPTER TWENTY-SEVEN

LEARNING

H er eyes slowly opened and she blinked repeatedly to clear her vision. It felt familiar laying in this bed, staring up at the roof of the royal barracks. Panning downward the massive gray wolf came into view. Timber laid curled in a circle, fast asleep. "What happened?" Just as before when she died, Arain had quite a bit of fuzziness in her head. Luckily the effects were temporary and soon she would remember everything. "My werewolves, so many of them were killed, but how? They are immune to any kind of permanent damage." The queen sat up to focus better on those events. They had some sort of wire mesh that sliced clean through, then the arrows, and that glittery dust. Timber woke when he heard her voice and immediately stepped closer to express his affection for her. A couple big toothy licks to the face later and the pleasantries were over. "What's this?" Arain could see multiple patches of new fur on the wolf's back and sides. "Is this from that dust?" she questioned knowing there wouldn't be a reply.

The queen got out of bed and quickly dressed. She wanted answers for the failed attack right this second. Turning from the dresser to leave, something caught her eye. The armor on her rack looked a bit different. She ran her left hand across the breastplate and stopped when she felt the imperfection. "This entire section must have been damaged and repaired." She shook her head side to side in disgust. "This unacceptable display of blacksmithing will not go unpunished!" Arain closed her eyes and grabbed the armor in both hands. Her crown blazed for only a second before opening her eyes and stepping back. The imperfections were completely gone, in fact the suit of armor looked better than it ever had.

Timber jumped off the bed and gave a long full body stretch. "Lets go boy, time to get some answers," and out the entrance they went. The two soldiers standing guard outside her tent snapped to attention. They were pretty much useless as Timber inside would easily kill whoever was stupid enough to break in. Not saying a word she headed off to find Seget. His tent as always had been setup close to the queen's. No warning had been given, she just walked right into his tent throwing the entrance flap wide open.

Seget sat across the room at a square table eating some type of stew from a wooden spoon. Instinctively upon seeing her he sprang from his seat and bowed his head. "Greetings my queen, it's good to see you up and well again."

Arain walked over to the table in front of him. "Enough with the pleasantries, you may sit general." Following orders he sat back down but did not show disrespect by eating. "Seget, I would love to know what the hell happened to my werewolves on the battlefield!" She felt too aggravated to sit in the open chair.

Good thing Seget was an intelligent man because that's the very first question he wanted answered two days ago. "My queen, your mages and alchemists have thoroughly examined the dust and arrows from that instance and have come to the same conclusion that it's pure silver, nothing more."

The queen slammed her balled up fists on the table, sending the rest of his meal to the ground. "How could something as simple as silver kill my immortal beasts?"

"I assure you that it has been tested on no less than a dozen of your lycanthropes. All have the same reaction. The dust burns the skin and lungs while the arrows prevent any form of healing. That wire mesh trap must be made of the same material. Somehow Malik figured this out and had enough time to prepare before we arrived."

Arain pulled out the chair and sat down, quietly evaluating this new information. "Why silver?" Leaning back over the chair to face the entrance, she called out for the guards. The two outside came in immediately. "One of you go and fetch Ori, and be quick my patience is very thin at the moment. As fast as possible, one of the guards went outside and over to the training grounds where Ori and Vermillion spent most of their time with the special group of pack members.

He let out a sigh of relief seeing their target straight ahead. "General Ori, please forgive the interruption but I have orders to deliver you to her majesty immediately." Just being around these werewolves made the humans very uncomfortable. He nervously waited for her response.

Thud, thud, thud. Three throwing knives embedded into the wooden target some fifty yards away. All of them made a triangle around the center bullseye. "Doing that at fifty feet used to be impressive as a human, but with this enhanced strength and vision from the lycan blood in my veins, everything seems so easy. Are you sure you don't want me to turn you?" The guard swallowed hard, a bead of sweat ran down his right cheek. "Hahaha, I'm only kidding, lets not keep the queen waiting." Quickly they worked their way through the city of tents and arrived on Seget's doorstep. "Your majesty, I am here as requested."

"You may enter Ori," called out the queen. Inside she could see Arain and Seget still sitting at the small dinner table with Timber laying on the floor.

The assassin walked over to the table and bowed while keeping her gaze averted to the floor. "How may I be of service, your majesty?"

"General, don't you use silver arrows?"

"Yes your grace, I prefer the silver as it is softer, causing it to fan out when it hits bone. The end result is more internal damage of the target and a greater chance of death before any means of healing can be used."

"Wasn't it silver arrows you used to kill Timber?" Just those words coming off her lips brought up all the emotions of that terrible moment. It seemed odd to most under her command that she would keep Ori alive, but eternal servitude gave the assassin a long time to pay back the queen for her transgression.

"Yes your majesty, in fact it was. Do you think that has something to do with our weakness to it?"

Seget looked across the table to Arain. "It's the only thing that remotely makes any kind of sense."

Arain stood from the table looking down on her officers. "We must be cautious from now on, who knows how far this information may spread. Any silver we find must be confiscated and destroyed immediately!" Arain walked towards the door." Come Ori, we have another matter to attend to." Outside and in the direction of the blacksmiths she headed with the general and Timber in tow.

The tanging sound of hammer on steel could be heard from a considerable distance. Six blacksmiths took care of arming and outfitting all of Arain Drake's soldiers. They worked rotating shifts so three smiths were always at the forge tending to the military's needs. The three arrived to find one man hammering out red hot steel while another stoked the fire. A woman blacksmith worked on repairing a damaged suit of chain mail at the far end of the shop. All of them stopped immediately upon seeing the queen and bowed obediently. "Who can tell me the name of the person responsible for fixing my damaged breast plate?"

They looked at one another not sure if she asked to give praise or to inflict punishment. The burly fellow that had been feeding the fire in the forge spoke up. "I am the one responsible, your majesty."

Arain looked over at Timber. "Would you be so kind my dear and relay my dissatisfaction to this charlatan." The wolf transformed with amazing speed, grabbing the man with his massive hand wrapping around his throat. Struggling and gasping for air the blacksmith fought back with utter futility. Timber strode a few steps forward before slamming the entire man into the forge. A cascade of red hot ash shot out from the force of the blacksmith. Screams and cries of agony and mercy roared from the inferno. Timber still held onto him to make sure there would be no escape from this fiery death. The charred body shook and twitched on the white hot coals as the internal organs cooked and popped inside the man's stomach. Stench of burning flesh billowed from the forge now as the wolf removed his hand from the flames. His skin and fur obviously damaged healed and regrew right before their eyes. Arain smiled and rubbed her hands together in front of her. "I hope this lesson will be passed on to your counterparts that shoddy work will not be tolerated." Both of the remaining blacksmiths nodded vigorously that the lesson had been learned. "Now which one of you wants to do a special project for me?"

The husky smith now traumatized just stood there afraid to respond. "It would be my honor to handle the queen's special project," announced the woman smith. Hardened and confident in her abilities, she stood proud before the queen.

It always delighted Arain when woman surpassed men. "Very well, what is your name?"

"Dalia, your grace."

"Dalia this is General Ori, she is one of the many lycanthropes in my army. Due to the recent discovery of their kinds weakness, we find it necessary to come up with a new type of armor that will allow them to shift freely while wearing it. Ori here will be the first to experiment with it. You two brilliant women should be able to come up with something amazing. I grant you both free reign to use whoever and whatever you need to accomplish this task." Without another word Arain left Ori and Dalia behind so they could get to work immediately. The queen headed back to Seget's barracks for further discussion of their battle plans.

Just as before, Arain entered without warning. "What's the current status of Valin and my ogres?"

Seget snapped to attention. "I have just recently been given word from our scouts that they should be arriving by nightfall, your grace."

Arain's face lit up upon hearing the great news. "Excellent, now we will crush Malik with brute force! I'm heading out to see if a plan I'm thinking about will work. Send word to me as soon as Valin arrives, I can't wait to see my horde of ogres."

"Yes your majesty, may I inquire where you will be headed?"

"Me and Timber are going north to get a better view of that mountain Castle Kragg backs up to."

"Very well my queen, and please do try to be careful." Seget worried that Arain might one day come to find she has a vulnerability that ends up killing her. Up to this point it was obvious that massive amounts of physical damage weren't an issue, and even death couldn't hold her in its icy grasp. But from his experience everything had a weakness, and finding it usually happened at the worst time.

The two left Seget behind as they disappeared into the forest to the north. It felt weird being just the two of them. *For so long, most of my life actually, Valin or one of my many mentors had always been there. Training, teaching, guiding my extremely focused development. Now we are alone and it feels so freeing. Nobody watching, critiquing, scolding and most of all no judging.* Arain exhaled a deep cleansing breath. "Do you hear that, Timber? Nothing but quiet." The massive wolf, now completely preoccupied sniffing the surrounding area for possible threats paid little attention to his master's chit chat. About an hour passed until they reached the tree line and the base of the enormous mountain. *No trails or paths over this of any kind. Sheer cliffs on the north and south sides. East and west looked just as daunting, deep ravines and impassable gullies trail up the mountain's sides.* Lost in thought, Arain contemplated her attack options once the ogres arrived. Timber snarled from behind breaking her concentration. A young man ran straight towards her. From the look of absolute fear on his face she knew this not to be an attacker.

"Run milady, there's a ravenous wolf who's determined to have us for dinner!" He stopped just long enough to grab her hand and drag her onward. Timber barreled after the couple with ill intent.

A strange feeling gripped Arain for the very first time. This man's touch, so warm, comforting feeling that it caused her to not fight his pitiful attempt to save her. She looked back at the wolf long enough to signal his pursuit to cease. Timber slowed and disappeared from sight into the brush. "He's gone, I think you scared him off kind sir," relayed Arain as she pulled his speed down to a walk.

Out of breath and sweating profusely, the young man stopped and released his grip on her. "Are you alright miss?" He asked while looking back for the wolf.

Arain looked at this man's face and felt bewitched. He stood just barely taller than her with a moderate build. His blonde hair cut short, and his eyes a deep hazel color. "Yes thanks to you," she said without even thinking about it. *What's going on, this man must have cast a spell on me. I don't need his or anyone's saving!* This internal conflict being totally foreign to her confused the queen. For the first time ever she had no idea what to do.

The young man outstretched his hand in greeting. "Sorry about grabbing you so roughly, my name is William Fiddlemen."

She shook his hand, getting that tingling feeling as they touched again. "Nice to meet you mister Fiddlemen, my name's Arain Drake. What brings you here?"

"Brings me here, I've lived here my entire life. I'm a reagents farmer for the castle, been doing it for about twenty years now I guess. The king gives me a decent little home and everything I need to live and all I have to do is grow and collect the medicinal and magical plants in this area for him."

"Sounds like an extremely boring life, Mr. Fiddlemen!"

He shrugged his shoulders. "It isn't a very glamorous job but it's an honest one, Miss Drake."

Arain could see two of her soldiers approaching through the forest. Instinctively she punched William in the stomach, hard. A loud groan came from all the air being forced from his lungs at once, and his body fell limp on the ground. *I hope I didn't kill him.* She knew with her strength that she very easily could.

The two soldiers ran up moments later. "Your majesty, are you alright?" one of them asked.

"Yes perfectly fine. I want this man taken and placed in one of my holding cells for interrogation. He is not to be harmed or there will be severe consequences." The queen's demeanor as she said that sent chills down the men's spines.

"He will be taken care of, your majesty." Quickly one grabbed his feet while the other picked William up by his arms. "Your grace, General Seget sent us to inform you that Valin and your ogre army have started arriving back at camp."

Timber walked out of the shrubs silently and sat down next to Arain. "Excellent, I can't wait to have my revenge on King Malik for that embarrassment he caused me earlier. Come Timber, lets go see what wonderful things Valin has brought me." The small group headed back the way they came, only stopping long enough to reposition how they carried their prisoner. Night time had set in by the time they made it back to camp. The bonfires danced and played off of the mass of ogres before her, making their already horrific appearance that much more disturbing. Arain couldn't help but smile at the sight.

CHAPTER TWENTY-EIGHT
THE EVIL MEN DO

R usty sheers cut through the Veassel's flesh only stopping slightly as they hit the bone. "Ahhhhh!!!" Bobble screamed in agony and fear, his left pinky finger falling to the floor, bouncing once before coming to a stop. Warm blood flowed from the severed vein and pooled next to the freshly removed digit. Bobble cried and whimpered as he squirmed in the chair he was bound to. "Please don't do this, I have done nothing wrong. Please just let me go, I won't tell anyone you did this."

The sailor grinned evilly as he taunted Bobble by opening and closing the blood soaked sheers. The metallic sound they made would be burned into his memory. "Awww come now rat boy, we're just getting started. You still have nine thieving fingers to pay with!"

Bobble struggled to get free. "I haven't stole anything. There must be some kind of mistake. Please no more." Frantically the Veassel tried to keep his hands balled into fists as the man pried the next one straight.

"Are you ready for the next one rat boy?" Placing the sheers up to the second knuckle on his left left hand the sailor severed it slowly leaving just a small amount of bone holding it attached. The Veassel continued screaming and crying as he fought the bindings. Only when he calmed down did the sailor put the sheers down and snap the finger off the rest of the way by hand. Bobble passed out from the pain slumping back in the chair. The sailor turned and threw the finger to his friend who stood by quietly enjoying the show. "Hmph, you can't quit already ratty." The man teased while giving Bobble a few slaps to the side of his face. "Come on, wake up!" Bobble came to and lunged forward in the chair burying his teeth in the sailor's right hand. Caught off guard, the man stumbled backwards while reflexively pulling his hand back. The force combined with sharp teeth and a powerful bite easily separated the sailor's pointer finger from his hand. "Ahhh you stupid rat, look what you've done," holding up his maimed hand.

Bobble with a bloody grin spit the finger onto the floor. Ironically it landed next to the Veassel's own pinky. "Let me go now, you piece of shit!"

Robert followed the trail of blood from the main deck to the lower levels. "Come on Bobble, where are you?" On the third level he caught up to Selim and Bibble who by the looks of it just picked up on the blood trail. "Good were all together. Whatever happened to our friend started on the main deck at the stern. Looks like the trail continues onto the next level, shall we?"

Selim and Bibble gave a nod before descending the creaky wooden stairs. The blood drips were getting smaller and spaced further apart. Selim sneered showing his teeth, "Our trail is disappearing." Bibble continued sniffing the air. The blood spots didn't matter anymore, he had his brothers scent.

"Hurry you two, he's got to be on this level, the scent is strong this way." This level looked like it was primarily used for storage and not very populated with humans. Quickly the three of them worked there way forward towards the bow. Crates and barrels neatly stacked were lashed to the walls down both sides of the corridor. A layer of dust coated everything giving Robert and Selim footprints to follow on the floor.

A man's scream could now be heard up ahead. Selim charged through the door in front of them sending it splintering to little pieces from the impact. There stood a human with his back turned and his arms folded. The Draconian's massive hand engulfed the man's head as Selim slammed him into the hull. The force knocked the sailor out with ease. The man butchering Bobble stood up startled, holding his bloody hand. Robert didn't hesitate to bury his dagger in the man's throat from the side and rip it out through his windpipe. Blood gushed out in massive amounts as the body fell with a thud to the floor. The man's heart quickly pumped out what remained of his lifeblood.

Bibble sprinted over to his brother and quickly cut his bindings. "Thank the maker you're alive," he professed as he hugged him as tight as he could. "I'm so glad we found you, Bobble." Gently he helped him from the torture chair and out of the room.

Robert and Selim looked at blood and urine pooled in the seat of the chair and then the amputated fingers on the floor. Selim shook his head in disgust. "Why would they do this, Robert? Is this what non humans can expect from your species?"

Robert's head hung low in shame. "This man here is the same one Bibble and myself had a run in with earlier. I should have known something like this might have happened. I forget sometimes how cruel mankind can be. But not all of us condone these blatant acts of savagery. Most of us are good, Selim."

A sneer is all the Draconian gave in response before heading above deck with Bibble and Bobble. Robert wiped the blood from his dagger on the corpses sleeve before returning it to its sheath on his belt. He gave the area one last look and then left to catch up with his friends.

Above deck they immediately caught the attention of the captain. He rushed over to see what had happened. As he drew closer he could see the injured Veassel holding a bloody hand up to slow the bleeding. His fur matted down with dried, sticky blood, and a large lump on the back of his head looked like a second head trying to pop out of the first one. The captain needn't even ask, he knew this had been the work of someone under his command. "This way to the infirmary," he directed. They went underneath the bridge and into a small room that had partitions separating it. A bed then a wall, then another bed. The other side of the room held the exam table and various cabinets filled with items to treat injuries. "Have him sit on the exam table right there. We have no healer on board so about all I can offer is some basic treatment for your injuries." Heading over to one of the cabinets he pulled down a bottle of antiseptic and a jar of salve. Over to the next cabinet he found clean bandages and dressings. Bobble sat on the exam table exhausted, not only from the blood loss but the extreme stress the torture placed on his body. A couple clean blankets were pulled from beneath the counter. "Why don't you get him out of those soiled clothes, he can wrap in these until we clean them."

Bibble looked up at the captain who tried his best to help. "I will take care of my brother from here captain. Leave him with me and go tend to the business of running this ship."

Shocked, the skipper stepped back, his own sailors didn't talk to him like that, but he knew that Bibble was right. His assistance being no longer needed, the captain left to deal with his crew. Robert stopped him for a moment on his way back to the bridge. "Captain, we found two of your men on the fourth deck down torturing Bobble. One of them has already seen his justice but there is still one we left unconscious."

"Very well general, I will see to it that this matter is taken care of, and my sincerest of apologies for this unforgiveable act." The captain knew that he himself held the responsibility for everything that happened on his ship. He may very well find himself demoted or thrown in a jail cell. For the moment though he grabbed a few of his crew and headed down below to clean up and shackle the other man in irons. The ship didn't have a cell as this kind of thing never happened under normal circumstances. Typically they loaded cargo, sailed down the coast and unloaded before loading again and sailing back north. Not exactly an exciting or relaxation filled trip. The prisoner would have to be locked in one of the store rooms until they could make it back to port.

Robert headed into the ship's infirmary to find Selim standing guard while Bibble tended to his brother. "How is he?"

Selim didn't turn around when he spoke. "He'll live but there may be deeper wounds we cannot see. Only time will tell how badly this effects him." They both just stood in silence guarding the doorway while Bibble finished wrapping Bobbles bloody stumps where his fingers used to be. The warm blanket wrapped around his naked little body as Bibble helped him to one of the beds. He laid down and closed his eyes not saying a word.

Bibble gave his brother a kiss on his forehead and left him to sleep. Walking over to Selim he looked up at his friend. "Do you think you could stay in the infirmary with us incase someone else tries to do something?"

The Veassel staring at him made his big Draconian heart melt. "Sure thing Bibble, nobody is going to bother either of you without going through me first!"

Bibble reached forward and hugged Selim at the waist. His little furry arms barely reached around the sides of the thick muscular waist of his friend. "Thanks Selim," is all he said before going to sit by his brother's bedside.

It saddened Robert that this instance drove a wedge deeper between the humans and non humans. He took his leave to help on the bridge while mulling over everything. We're just at the beginning of the changes about to come and already there's conflict. Humans have had no problem killing one another, and now we have new races to hate and discriminate against. I fear there will be many more wars once this current one is concluded. Who knows, maybe humanity will find itself snuffed out because of its lack of ability to change...

CHAPTER TWENTY-NINE

STRANGE DREAMS

V alin stood conversing with Seget when Arain emerged from the tree line with Timber and two other soldiers carrying an unconscious man. "I will catch up with you later general, I must go greet my daughter." Valin headed off to meet the queen. "Ahh, Arain you look well," as he embraced her with a hug. Not very often did he show affection, but when he did she soaked it in.

"Greetings father, I hope all went well gathering the ogres." The sea of giant humanoids stretched out before her. Just looking at the horde caused Arain to get goose bumps.

Valin sort of half shrugged, "It went as well as can be expected. We lost Grumm in an ambush as we tried to exit the Forest of Abadon. He fought valiantly right up until his demise. A few others had to be taught a lesson in obedience the hard way and just yesterday two of them fell into a tar pit. So you're down five total during the trip." Valin looked over at the two soldiers carrying in an unconscious young man. "What's this, a new pet?"

Arain paused for a moment choosing her words carefully. "No just some reagent farmer I ran into. I didn't have time to interrogate him properly when I heard the news of your arrival. I can deal with him later, he's of no concern."

A red haired mage Arain had never seen before walked up beside Valin. "Seems you've picked up a new pet of your own, father."

Valin placed his hand on Talia's shoulder. "This woman is indeed worthy of mentoring, my queen. I present to you Talia Fine, a loyal deserter from Malik's regime."

Talia bowed, "It is an honor to meet you, Queen Arain Drake. I humbly seek to join you on your conquest of these lands. My skills and my life are yours."

The queen took her time examining this mage. "She is quite beautiful, Valin. Are you sure she hasn't bewitched you?" Her and Valin exchanged smiles knowing full well there wasn't a soul on this planet that could do that. "Very well Talia, I accept your allegiance. Valin, I leave her to you until she is fully trained or dies trying."

Talia raised her head. "Thank you my queen, I will not fail you."

"It's not me you have to impress. I've been through Valin's training, and somedays death seemed like a better choice." Valin grinned an evil smile at Talia. "I'm headed back to my room to get cleaned up. Have the officers ready in the war room for a briefing in thirty minutes."

Valin nodded, "I will take care of it my queen. Would you like me to have the ogre chieftain Adlin Bonecrusher attend as well?"

"Yes indeed, this new plan has the ogres at its core." Arain left Valin and Talia behind as she headed for a warm bath and some fresh clothes. Timber gave the new mage one last sniff before following the queen to her chambers. As Arain moved through the crowd of ogres, they instinctively bent down on one knee and uttered the word, goddess. Elation welled up inside her as she looked out across her creations. "Nothing can stop me with such a formidable force under my command, nothing!" Arain left them all and went back into her room.

Valin met up with General Seget, relaying the queen's orders. He immediately dispatched soldiers to notify the other officers. "It looks like you have everything under control here, Seget. I'll go over and collect Adlin." That didn't bother Seget in the least, he preferred handling the more human sized troops anyways.

The camp bustled with energy now that Valin had returned with such a large group of warriors. Arain's recent set back was already fading from memory. King Malik and Castle Kragg would soon fall, everyone knew it except those in the castle.

Thirty minutes had passed and all were assembled in the war room. Modifications to the tent needed to be made so Adlin could enter without tearing the whole thing down. The southern wall received a cut from floor to ceiling and acted as the entrance for larger than human sized soldiers. Arain scanned the crowd before her. "I think we are going to need a bigger tent for future meetings, wouldn't you agree Valin?"

"Yes indeed your grace," he responded with a chuckle.

"In case any of you hadn't noticed, the ogre horde from Fenrir Mountains has arrived and their chieftain, Adlin Bonecrusher will be my newest officer to join our cause."

The ogre chieftain knelt, "It is a great honor to be able to serve you my goddess."

"An honor indeed as you will spearhead the fall of Castle Kragg!" The room erupted in cheers, which the queen allowed for but a moment before continuing. "I currently have the deep ones scouring the perimeter of the castle disarming anymore of those nasty little traps we ran into. Once that's clear, we must deal with the artillery of silver dust. Until those are disabled no werewolves are to join in the assault. There will be some silver weapons and arrows to contend with so I have the blacksmiths and Ori working on a solution as we speak. Glub and Seget, I want the Krillox and human cavalry to form up outside of the Kragg's west entrance and wait for my signal to attack. Valin, I need you and the other mages to come up with a countermeasure in case that silver dust does get dispersed. Vermillion, have your archers focus on the wall defenses. Malik will have plenty of his own archers and ballista men raining down hell on us. We need to thin their numbers quickly. Adlin, you and only your warriors will scale the cliffs above the Kragg and attack from above while your ogre mages and the void will support the cavalry and foot soldiers. Are there any questions?"

Seget cleared his throat. "How will the ogres scale those cliffs? From all the reports I've been given they are impassable."

Arain stretched her neck from one side and then the other. "Seget, don't you know nothing is impassable to a God!"

Seget bowed his head, "My apologies your grace. I will try to remember that next time I have a doubt. Please continue."

Arain went on laying out the exact placement and soldier type on the castle map. The whole briefing took little more than fifteen minutes as very few objections or questions were ever asked. It was safer that way. "Adlin, make sure that the horde is ready to travel soon. We need to be back to where I had been scouting earlier as soon as we can."

"It will be but a moment my queen, we are ready to serve." Adlin took his leave, heading straight into the throng of ogres outside. "Our time has finally arrived for us to be the mighty hammer the goddess will use to smite her foes!"

Roars of excitement erupted, as they raised their weapons in the air. Adlin pulled aside the void and the mages so they could be used on the frontal assault, while the rest marched north with Arain and Timber guiding them.

Arain held up a hand calling the horde to stop. "From here on out we must be extremely quiet so we don't give away our advantage of surprise." Ogres by nature are large, loud, in your face types of creatures. Silencing them would be like trying to make thunder quiet. But they would try their hardest to please their master. As they drew closer to the mountain, Arain made them walk in single file to try and limit the snapping of tree limbs and sticks on the forest floor. They were at the point now where the cities walls ended against the side of the first cliff. "Just a little further and we will be out of the sentries field of vision." The only thing they could see now was the mountainous cliffs shooting straight up hundreds of feet in the air.

A few of the ogres slung their weapons over their backs and set upon the task of scaling the cliff face. Only a handful made it higher than sixty feet before losing their grip and falling back to the ground. Arain stood back with Timber enjoying the show for a few moments. "They sure are determined, and with a few days time might actually make it to the top. But we don't have that kind of time." She looked to Timber. "I'll need you to take me back to camp when I'm done here alright?" On cue the wolf transformed into his werewolf form. Patiently he stood waiting as he looked down on Arain. "Good boy. Now all of you step back to the tree line while I work." Like a silent rhythmic dance Arain closed her eyes and held her hands up high. Her crown of runes blazed to life, blinding the onlookers. Her hands made their way downward and to the front as she continued crafting her invisible sculpture. A few more movements and her creating came to an end. The light faded as she collapsed to her knees. Next came the fatigue and blood pouring from her nose and mouth she had become accustomed to. The throng of ogres looked on not sure what had just happened. Timber instinctively helped her to her feet and remained there steadying her. At first it seemed like nothing had happened but soon small chunks of rock started to bounce down the cliff face. A faint chittering sound grew louder by the second until three enormous spider like creatures landed in front of Arain. Adlin who already stood beside her and Timber, readied his weapon to strike. "That won't be necessary chieftain, they are what I have just created." The upper half looked almost like a human woman with the body of a red and black spider. They stood roughly twelve feet tall with eight sword like legs, and a pair of two foot long mandibles that looked like they could easily pierce the thickest of armors.

All three bowed before Arain, while the largest of the three spoke in a soft raspy voice. "We are here to serve our creator. What will you have us do?" Arain staggered a step forward. "Look at you my beautiful cryptids. How magnificent I have made you." She took a few moments to bask in the glory of what she had accomplished. "You will see to it that this army of ogres is on the top of that mountain by daybreak."

No question, no rebuke, and no excuses. If the goddess commanded it then it would be done. The cryptids immediately began spewing streams of white webbing onto the rock. Up they went, sticking to the wall as if it were made of glue. Not once did a leg slip or falter as they continued making the web ladder. Arain watched for a short time as the ogres again attempted to climb, but this time they did not fall. The cryptids made the white web amazingly strong, and sticky enough to grip onto. The ogres climbed to the top with ease. Satisfied, Arain weakly grabbed onto Timber. "Take me home now boy." With absolutely no effort, the massive werewolf cradled Arain in his arms and headed back to camp. She snuggled into the safety of his warm furry chest and fell into a deep sleep.

Arain dreamt of her brother Lucious and his reptilian girlfriend marching towards the forest city of Hemshir. *What a large army of human mortals you've amassed or are they not yours to command? Ahh at the head of the column, this must be King Elrick of Westlin. My brother somehow managed to persuade you to aid him in his futile cause. Oh well it matters little, you can bring ten times that number and the only thing it will do is swell my ranks.* Arain floated like a ghost taking in everything this vision could show her. *Oh how I wish I could strike them down from this ethereal form.* "Arain!" came a deep toned voice. She quickly looked around wondering if somehow somebody could see her, but there wasn't anybody looking in her direction. "Arain, come here!" boomed the voice again. This time however it distinctly sounded like it came from above. Looking skyward she began to rise, slowly at first but then so fast everything raced by in a blur.

"What is happening?" Arain lost all control of everything around her and travelled by some unseen force pulling her faster and faster. Just as she felt she would be torn apart, everything stopped. "What is this? I feel like I'm standing on solid ground but everything is cold and black and I can't see where anything begins or ends." Off in the distance, two ancient wooden doors creaked and groaned open revealing a gigantic doorway with white light pouring through it into the darkness. *I don't like this, but I have no other choice than to walk toward the light.* As she drew closer, the pitch black somehow started to be diluted by the white making everything look gray. Eventually all the black and gray was gone, replaced by only white. Reluctantly Arain stepped past the blinding white threshold and into what looked like a throne room. Magnificent sconces of magic light illuminated the largest room she had ever seen. "Either I'm the size of an ant or someone unbelievably huge lives here." Arain continued on walking further into the room.

After walking for some time she came up to what looked like a humungous winged lizard sitting on an equally large throne. In perfect symmetry the lizard and the throne were colored half white and half black straight down the middle from nose to tail. The sight of its grandeur made her feel small indeed.

To her absolute surprise the winged lizard moved, leaning forward towards her. "There you are," came that same deep voice, except the creature's mouth didn't move.

It's speaking directly into my mind.

"Yes Arain Drake that is correct, speech through thought is much safer. I'm afraid the sound of my voice would destroy someone even as powerful as you."

"What do you want with me, and where the hell am I?"

"Hahahahaha..... So fierce and determined you are even without your abilities.

She hadn't thought about it until now but try as she might nothing worked in this realm. *No magic, no special gifts, nothing. For all intents and purposes I'm just a normal human.* That realization made her head spin and her stomach tense. "So now what, I have no weapons physical or otherwise."

"Oh dear, weapons are not needed, as I have not called you here to battle. I simply wanted to meet you up close like I did Lucious."

Arain's blood boiled and rage built at the mention of his name. "You have summoned my brother as well? Who or what are you and why do we interest you so?"

The being seated in the throne sat back, not taking his gaze off of Arain. "Who I am is easy, Pengeran is my chosen name. What am I is a bit more difficult to explain, and even if I did your human mind could not handle such knowledge. Let's just say I'm a bit of a creator like yourself."

That was the last thing Arain heard before shooting bolt upright from her bed. She landing in a crouched position on her floor. Her eyes slowly panned around as she stood up. Timber sat there watching her with his long pink tongue sticking out slightly between his two lower canines.

Looking over to where she just laid she could see trails of blood streaked down the pillow and soaked into the sheets. Her mind raced trying to remember everything that just happened. "Was it a dream?"

Chapter Thirty

MY TURN

Inside Arain's barracks her two chamber maids aided the queen with donning her armor. The breastplate was lowered over her head and arms ever so gently as the two maids went to work. This wasn't the first time doing this nor the hundredth, it literally could be closer to the thousandth time the two have prepared her for battle. These same two women have been with Arain since she was just a baby, and they were the only ones entrusted with tending to the queen's needs off the battlefield. Once they finished suiting her and the last buckle had been fastened, the two middle aged maids went directly onto cleaning her chambers. The bloody linens were stripped away and the stain on the mattress was scrubbed out with warm soapy water and a thick bristled brush. Quietly they worked their way around the room, cleaning and straightening as they went.

Arain and Timber exited her abode and headed for the blacksmiths. She looked over at her gray protector. "I do hope that they've come up with something to protect your kind from the weapons of silver. We can't afford to loose anymore lycanthropes today." The tinging of hammer on steel grew louder as they approached. Ori stood half naked, waiting. She wore a type of chainmail the queen had never seen before. It had a dull blue hue to it and it moved like fabric hugging the assassin's curves of her chest. Ori turned when she smelled Arain and Timbers scent. Reaching out with her hand, the queen felt this new material. "It's so light and warm. Is it strong?"

Ori nodded, "Yes my queen, it is extremely protective." Pulling a dagger from her hip she plunged it into her own stomach. What should have been a terrible wound amounted to nothing. "See your majesty, the blade cannot penetrate."

Arain held out the material looking for any sign of damage but could find none. "Truly amazing, how is it forged?"

Dalia set down her hammer beside her anvil and stepped closer. "I used mithrite which I had enchanted with a elastomeric spell by one of your mages. It took a few attempts but I think we have the combination just right now, your highness."

"And what about when they shift?" the queen asked.

Ori took a couple steps away from the two women before turning back into a werewolf. To Arain's delight the armor stretched to accommodate her new form perfectly.

"Does it restrict any of your movements?"

Ori leapt onto the roof of the blacksmiths hut and over to the mess hall before flipping back down to the ground where she started. "No your majesty, I have completely free, unhindered movement. It's unlike any armor that I have ever worn."

Arain hugged Dalia and then Ori. "Splendid work you two, I knew I picked the right women for the job. Now how quickly can these suits of armor be made?"

Dalia's smile faded away at the question. "Forgive me my queen, we only have enough mithrite left to make two more suits. I'm afraid the ore is fairly rare. I was surprised when I found that we had any at all."

"Hhhhhh," Arain exhaled displeased. "Well then we will just have to find more. Ori you keep the set you have on and lets have Timber and Vermillion outfitted first." She looked down at her friend. "You do as the smithy says and shift when she requests it." The wolf sat down and waited to be instructed. "Good boy, Dalia he's all yours. Send him to find me as soon as you're done with him."

"Yes your majesty, I will get started immediately." Dalia grabbed a long thin length of leather that had numbers written along it in specified increments, and took Timber's measurements. Arain seeing that her wolf was in good hands excused herself and headed to the war room. Ori took her leave as well to go and get Vermillion for his fitting. Timber, Dalia, and the petrified smith were left alone with only the forge and the cool night air to accompany them.

All over camp, Arain's soldiers prepared for the up-coming battle. Everyone knew their role and nobody want-ed to disappoint their queen. Humans, Krillox, and ogres donned armor and sharpened weapons. The excitement in the air felt electric. The second moon had almost reached the horizon signaling that dawn would soon follow. Entering the war room, Arain could see Valin, Talia, Seget, and Glub waiting for her arrival. Last but not least came the deep ones Elder worm, protruding from the ground by at least three feet. "Excellent, the time is almost here for us to dethrone King Malik and take over the Kragg!" Her excitement fueled her generals who erupted in cheers. "You all have your or-ders, now let us go bathe in the blood of our enemy!" The deafening cheers continued as one by one they filed out of the war room and headed to their designated posts. "This is truly what I have been put on this planet for." The feeling of excitement and anticipation flooded her senses. As Arain rode to the front lines, she surveyed all who would die for her. "Wonderful."

Across the open field and out of arrows range stood rows upon rows of cavalry, foot soldiers, and archers. The city walls, were now packed full of mages, archers, and ballista. Mechanical war machines were dispersed throughout the ranks. These heavy constructs made of wood and steel were propelled by steam engines and housed an assortment of death dealing devices. Catapults loaded with silver dust munitions sat ready to deliver there payload with a pull of a lever. Malik stared down from his balcony high up at the castle. "There's no need to be down in the fray, we outnumber them ten to one, and with her werewolves out of the picture she poses no real threat." Talo Gray and Pogo stood with the king.

"As you say so shall it be King Malik. We have the last bit of silver being melted down as we speak and almost a fourth of your soldiers have been outfitted with silver weapons of one form or another."

"That's good to hear Pogo," responded the king. "Let us wait and see what this charlatan brings to the battle field today." The king's tone conveyed little interest in the current proceedings. Talo Gray had pretty much become the king's right hand man after he saved him from Hortus, and gave them the key to defending against the lycanthropes. Now he stood by silently waiting to aid his king in whatever way he could.

"General Yuni is in charge of the forces on the battlefield, while Corwin and his mages will be concentrating on magical attacks that have a large blast radius. Clink is leading a tank regiment to flank the enemy from the right. The battle should be over quickly you two, so don't blink," mocked Malik. He had planned the defenses himself and left nothing to chance.

Arain Drake pulled her horse to a stop next to Seget, Valin, and Talia. "Let us begin, general." She raised her outstretched hand in front of her, "Emolate" left her lips and a flaming red ball formed around her hand. With a flick of her fingers the ball shot skyward at incredible speed and soon disappeared in the clouds that had formed at the top of the cliffs.

"It looks like her aims a bit off today," shouted Yuni to her troops. They burst into laughter alongside the general. As the first boulders fell from the clouds smashing into the castle and city below, their laughing quickly turned to gasps of horror. "No this is not possible, nobody could scale those cliffs."

With Malik's troops distracted and caught off guard, General Seget gave the order, "ATTACK!!" The first wave included the void ogres out front with berserker ogres behind. With inhuman speed, the monstrosities known as the void clashed with the enemies first line of cavalry. Ogre clubs met with human plate mail. Riders were knocked clear off their mounts and were sent flying in a multitude of directions.

The clangs and dings of steel on steel drowned out some of the screams from the soon to be deceased. Swords and lances did little to no damage against the voids armor like skin. Arrows were launched in massive volleys, in hopes that at least one would show a weak spot, but every arrow bounced off uselessly.

Nothing could have prepared Malik's forces for the extreme brutality of the alchemist berserkers. With their special potions consumed, the berserkers went into a blind rage smashing anything and everything in their path. The front line of cavalry being dispatched so easily caused a paralyzing fear of futility to grip some of Malik's troops. Yuni demanded obedience as she shouted orders. "Archers, aim for their eyes and mouths, they can't be that tough everywhere. Mages, concentrate on shielding the castle and city from those boulders. Constructs, focus your attacks on the crazed ogres. Lancers and second cavalry, assist the constructs. Third cavalry and swordsmen, attack the black ones with bolos and nets. If we can't hurt them we can at least immobilize them!"

Wave after wave of massive rocks fell from the sky in an endless bombardment. The mages did quite well at destroying the incoming projectiles at first but soon their magic reserves waned. More and more made it through to their intended targets. Homes and businesses were wiped out in seconds. The castle held up much better but it soon began collapsing under the assault.

Crash!! a rock the size of a bull smashed into the balcony where Malik, Talo and General Pogo had just been standing. A huge chunk of the floor and railing ripped off and tumbled to the courtyard below. "Damn that woman, she'll leave nothing but rubble by days end! Pogo, let's get down there. Talo, I need you to survive and bring word of what we've learned to King Elrick in the City of Knowledge. If for some reason we fall here, seek asylum under Elrick's banner. He is a fair ruler and you would serve him well. Now GO!!"

Seget ordered the next wave to commence their attack. "Krillox, assassins attack their archers and mages. Mages, concentrate on destroying those constructs, they've already slain two berserkers!"

Arain just sat atop her horse smiling as the battle unfolded. The amount of life lost mattered little to her. She only needed enough people to replenish her werewolf forces and to manage the town and castle while she continued her conquest. *Right about now the deep ones and lycans should be past the city's walls, turning as many humans as possible into more soldiers.* A small chuckle escaped her lips at the thought.

Inside the city and out of sight of the wall archers, the ground gave way in a large circle, as werewolves started pouring out into the city. The deep ones were ordered to stay with the lycans as extra protection. House by house and store by store they went turning everyone unlucky enough to be found into werewolves. The lucky ones died unable to bond with the lycan virus. Deep ones injected their larva into anyone the wolves missed. Quickly the city turned into a huge slaughterhouse. Arain's werewolf numbers had returned and then some. No matter which way the city sentries turned, they were met with death. Krillox warriors bounded over the city walls while at the same time they snatched up their prey for a quick meal. "All that silver being wasted on everything but werewolves, how comical wouldn't you say Seget?"

Looking over to Arain by his side still, "Yes it is your majesty, King Malik underestimated you and soon it will cost him his life."

Pogo and Malik mounted their horses and headed to the wall with great haste. "Pogo, have your artillery strike into the city, we need to...." SMASH!! a massive rock fell perfectly onto the alchemist and his steed. Both died on impact, and no trace of them could be seen. "Dammit!" His teeth clenched tight in anger. "That son of a bitch is going to suffer for these transgressions!" Onward the king raced, twice he ran into werewolves only to quickly take their lives with his silver etched sword. Still he raced on until he finally reached the western gates. Without a second thought he jumped into the fray. Malik's swordsmanship allowed him to score kill after kill. Werewolf, Krillox, and human, it mattered little to the thirsty blade. Blood in a multitude of colors spattered his armor and the ground. A deep one emerged behind him firing a needle. Malik's agility let him evade the parasitic attack. He lunged forward bringing his sword in a downward arc. The blade split the worm strait down the middle so that both halves flopped over in opposite directions. Whack!! a sticky pink tongue wrapped around his waist, knocking him off of his horse. Quickly the tongue retracted towards the toothy maw, dragging the king with it. "Oh no you don't." His sword flashed in the early sunlight as he chopped the tongue off with ease. Green liquid sprayed from the severed end as it raced back to its owner some twenty feet away. Malik hauled back his weapon and launched it at the giant toad creature. Thud... the sword buried up to the hilt stuck from the Krillox head. A second later the beast fell to the ground dead. On he ran, grabbing his sword from the downed opponent as he passed by.

For the moment, no more rocks fell from the sky. They were replaced with Ogre's and Drider's repelling down the cliff face above the castle. Malik's heart sank as hundreds of those abominations descended on his home. "We cannot hope to defeat such a force, there's only one chance." Sonic BOOM.... His fists struck one another releasing a devastating explosion around him. Bodies flew in an outward direction from his center point. For just a few moments a thirty foot diameter circle around the king stood clear. Holding his sword out he pointed it at Arain, challenging her to a duel.

Arain focused on the king. "Well, well it's about time I have some fun. Seget call a cessation of hostilities." The signal horn bellowed across the battle field, signifying an all stop. Arain rode down from her vantage point to accept the king's challenge. Both sides stood waiting and watching, a duel of this magnitude demanded attention. Once the queen reached fifty feet or so, she dismounted her horse.

"Arain Drake of the Moorlands, I King Malik challenge you to a duel."

Arain paced back and forth with her right hand resting on her sword. "Very well, what are your terms Malik."

"If I claim victory then you leave my lands and my people in peace."

"Very well, and if you lose it all belongs to me."

"Agreed," pledged Malik for he knew the only way to win now was to defeat her in a duel.

The warring all stopped as man and beast waited for the outcome. An entire legacy hung in the balance, Malik being the second royal to survive the king wars. The only other person was King Elrick who ended the brutal conquest of kings so many years ago. Malik started with a series of lunges and sweeps trying to get Arain off balance but she reacted like she knew his every move. Their swords crossed causing sparks to fly and a deafening metal on metal clang rang out. Even though her size and weight amounted to only half of Malik's, Arain pushed her sword against his until it cut the side of his face. *I can't believe how fast and strong such a small woman could be. My best assaults and not once has she faltered. I fear that the rumors are true and indeed she is a goddess.* The doubt began to creep in.

"What's wrong oh great King Malik? You seem so slow and weak to a young woman like myself. Are you really trying or is this just how pathetic you truly are?"

Her taunts enraged him to madness. "Vicious blades," he called forth. That special ability increased his speed and accuracy ten fold. A lunge, parry, and upward arc were made before he finally contacted with her flesh. His sword caught her in the left armpit, cleaving it to the shoulder bone. Blood shot forth across Malik's face and ran down Arain's armor. *At last I will defeat this bitch and reclaim what is mine,* thought the king.

Arain recoiled in pain at the exchange. Blood flowed like a river both inside, and outside her armor. It felt so warm, and sticky. But already the wound started healing "Is that all you have King Malik? I certainly expected more seeing as your life and all of those under you are at stake."

Malik rushed forward swinging his sword with ill intent, but nothing even came close to landing on the queen. "You will die by my hand, you unnatural freak of nature!"

Attack and lunge with no connection on Malik's side. Although Arain managed to connect every time in even the slightest way. Within minutes Malik looked a mess bleeding from a dozen or more wounds. Heavily winded he stood with his sword on his shoulder. Arain had for the most part completely healed from his only successful attack. "I have a special place for you in my legions Malik. You will be my general of death. Are you ready to end this pitiful excuse for a duel?"

Malik caught his breath and readied for his final winner takes all attack. "Cosmic divergence!" He called out creating a focal point for ten meteors to strike. Bam! Crash! Bang! the interstellar rocks slammed into Arain's location. Debris flew hundreds of feet in the air as the rocks hit their mark with lethal intent. Malik stood winded as the dust began to settle from the attack. *Surely no creature on this planet could have survived that!*

To his amazement she stood in defiance of his best offense. "I think it's time to end this charade, obviously you haven't the power to challenge me!" His forces looked on in disbelief. How could their king fall to an eighteen year old girl! Arain walked forward as if time had stopped altogether, her crown blazed white hot. Placing her hand on his head she recited the words, "eternal life." A shockwave went out knocking everything down in a hundred yard radius. Malik's body distorted as his flesh now blew away like dust in the wind. His body being separated from his soul until all that was left was a life sucking envoy of death. "I give to this world the Lich King Acererak! He will be my trophy for liberating the western legions of Tauro."

Acererak still knelt before Arain. "I pledge to serve you for all eternity, my queen."

"Rise my lich king, you will tend to the spiteful souls that I send to the afterlife, while spreading fear into the living. You are the total embodiment of death and evil!"

Acererak stood before his queen. A green aura emanated from his body in all directions. Like a creeping fog, it snaked across the battlefield seeking out the recently deceased. Upon its evil touch the bodies quivered and then stood back up with weapon in hand. The fog not only re-animated the dead humans, but the dead Krillox, and ogres as well. These lower level undead didn't seem to retain their minds to the extent Acererak did. Sure they could move and fight but the power of speech and reasoning were gone for good. They served the lich king and in turn served Arain. Those who once served Malik threw down their weapons and surrendered. Raising her sword skyward she addressed everyone in attendance. "The battle for Castle Kragg is won!" Cheers roared from her soldiers as they raised their weapons and chanted her name.

Seget bowed to Arain. "I would like to be the first one to congratulate you on this momentous victory. Valin and his prophecy were indeed correct that you would rule this world."

Arain stepped closer to Seget placing her hand on his shoulder. "Thank you for your expert leadership general. The tactical training you have given me will be invaluable in the upcoming battles. For now I need to rest and regain my strength." Blood ran from her nose and she looked like she was about to collapse.

Seget reached out and steadied her. "I will take over from here my queen, go and leave the rest to me." He signaled over two human soldiers. "Escort her majesty back to her barracks immediately."

"Yes general," replied the two before assisting Arain to her room. Timber as always stayed next to his master as they walked.

Seget did as he promised. Orders were given to imprison all of Malik's surviving soldiers in the castle dungeon until Arain decided what their fates would be. Fires were extinguished and the dead were reclaimed by Acererak. Effectively between the undead, werewolves, and deep ones the queen's army grew ten fold this day. What citizens remained had been corralled into the city square for educating. Cleaning up and restoring all of the damage would take months to repair so Seget setup a city council to run things in the absence of the queen. He would also leave one of his trusted officers and a handful of soldiers behind to oversee that everything ran smoothly. Ori and Vermillion were ordered to go on ahead to the City of Knowledge and begin weakening the enemy from within.

Valin and Talia raided the castle seizing all of the riches and magical items left behind. A treasure trove of goodies awaited them. The coffers were overflowing with gold and jewels of all shapes and sizes. "Now Arain has everything she needs before continuing on with her campaign," voiced Talia while examining an emerald the size of her hand.

The black mage looked at her. "Material things matter little to her, power is what she seeks. Power and absolute control of everyone and everything. I must say she is off to a stellar start, don't you agree, Talia?"

"An amazing start indeed, Lord Valin. Her enemies will cower in fear with just the whisper of her name. I can't wait to see what else she's capable of."

Talo snuck out the side of the castle, away from the watchful eyes of Arain Drake's minions. As stealthy as he could, he grabbed his horse and stuffed some supplies into the saddle bags. Up on the steed he climbed and took off for the eastern gates. The noise from the battlefield faded in the distance once he left the Kragg behind. He rubbed the side of his horse's neck. "Here we go girl, I'm gonna need your best once again." The horse almost died last time and he didn't intend to push her quite as hard this time.

General Yuni and Corwin's body were recovered from the carnage and reanimated into something special, wraiths. Acererak it seemed had multiple abilities where death was concerned. Not only could he make skeleton warriors and zombies but also wraiths and possibly much more. Clink managed to survive the destruction of his construct and escaped the city before the enemy could find him. He too headed for the City of Knowledge. "What happened here must be shared with the high council if we are to have any hope of defeating her."

Arain made it back to her tent with some help. Her two chamber maids returned to remove the queen's armor and bathe her. Then straight into bed she went not saying a word. Arain fell asleep before her head hit the pillow.

CHAPTER THIRTY-ONE

MORE QUESTIONS

T he early morning sun chased away the last remnants of night at the camp. Lucious woke and stretched. "My body feels so sore this morning, I wonder if Morgan has anything to do with it?" Looking over to where Morgan usually slept, he could see she had already gotten up. "I hope she's getting us some breakfast, I'm absolutely starving." His stomach seconded the request with a string of growls. He sat up and swung his legs over the side of the bed. *What happened last night? Everything is a bit unclear at the moment,* he thought while scratching his head. The last thing he remembered was trying to project over to his sister and then nothing.

Morgan returned and let out a deep sigh of relief when she saw Lucious awake and moving. "I hoped the smell of food would wake you, or else I would have had to strap you to your horse again in order to travel." She smiled and brought over the tray of food to their little table. "Come now, you need to get your strength back, you're no use to us asleep."

"How long have I been unconscious this time? It feels like no more than an hour might have passed since I focused on Arain."

Now sitting at the table Morgan finished swallowing a mouthful of green grapes. "You have been out for almost three days now. That night you scared me to death when you screamed, and the blood. There was so much blood coming out of you that I thought you were dying for real this time."

Walking over to the table he pulled out the chair and sat down across from her. Confusion shown on his face as he tried to remember what he saw. "I'm not entirely sure what happened to me." He picked up a wedge of orange cheese and devoured it in seconds. "My apologies for scaring you, and thanks for not leaving me behind." Lucious gave her a playful grin.

"Well next time I just might!" She leaned across the table and kissed him. "The only thing I could make out is the word Pengeran, you repeated it over and over again for almost an hour before you finally stopped. The name is not one I recognize, do you?"

"Pengeran," as he said the word it triggered his subconscious to release the memories that it held so tightly in the dark. "I can see it now, the past, present, and the future were all laid out plainly for me to see. Pengeran is the name of the giant winged beast sitting atop it's massive throne."

"What did you see, Lucious?"

"I saw Arain at the Kragg. Malik and her had an epic battle but in the end she reigned victorious. There were more monsters now, ogres of all different sizes and colors, sentient psionic worms, and enormous spider human type hybrids."

Morgan looked more concerned than Lucious had ever seen. "So King Malik is dead?"

"If he isn't, he soon will be, and what he becomes is pure evil the likes of which this world has never seen."

Morgan reached across the table and grabbed one of Lucious' hands. "We must go inform the king right away. Hurry and finish eating while I get ready."

She didn't need to tell him twice. Like a starved person he gorged himself on the fruit, nuts, and cheese she so graciously picked up for him. The whole time though he kept repeating that name, Pengeran in his head. *That thing definitely has something to do with all of this.* By now the tray only held small crumbs and Morgan had finished getting prepared for the days ride. "Come Lucious, we should probably catch King Elrick before he leaves." Like an obedient dog Lucious followed closely behind. He would follow her anywhere.

They arrived just in time to catch the king as he left his tent. "Lord Elrick, can we please have a moment of your time? Lucious has some urgent news I feel you must hear."

Elrick gave a courteous bow of the head to Morgan and Lucious. "By all means my dear, come let us inside." The king held open the door for them to come in. "It warms my heart to see you awake and alive my friend." A much nicer and considerably larger dining table and chairs were stationed in his barracks. He pulled out a chair for Morgan, "Come, come sit and tell me news."

Lucious recounted everything he saw in his vision while Elrick sat back in his chair with his right hand supporting his chin. Only after Lucious finished did he stand and pace. "This certainly is troubling news to hear that Malik and the Kragg have fallen with such ease to your sister. I had hoped that he could defeat her or at least buy us more time to prepare. We still have more than a day until we reach the City of Knowledge and she may very well be marching there as we speak." Elrick's mood changed quickly as the first seeds of doubt began to take root and grow. "We need to hurry, there's no time to waste. Prepare yourselves for a long day, we will not make camp again until we reach our destination."

Elrick showed the two of them to the door and dispatched a squire to fetch his officers.

Just when Lucious thought the king couldn't push his soldiers any harder, he did just that. The atmosphere in the camp felt frantic as all personnel rushed to break down camp. Everyone pitched in including Morgan and Lucious. They loaded their tent and belongings onto the wagons themselves. Stormy would have helped if he could but the best thing was for him to stay out of the way and out of trouble. The fur ball sat in his special position on Morgan's saddle and oversaw the work being done. The entire regiment had been packed and moving within an hour. Lucious wiped the sweat from his brow with his shirt sleeve. "It's unbelievable that this many people could work together so fast."

Morgan riding next to him smiled. "It truly is, imagine if we can all join together to stop your sister."

He pondered that thought for a moment before responding. "I hope we can for all of our sakes."

The two rode for a short time in silence knowing that very soon they would be facing Arain and her horde of monsters. Word of Lucious' visions spread through the ranks like the black plague, chipping away at the troops morale. These things of nightmares they would soon meet in the flesh. The days extended march didn't help either as it gave them all plenty of time to worry and dwell on these new revelations.

Lucious and Morgan could only watch as this happened. A few soldiers couldn't take it and tried to desert rather than continue on, but they were dealt with swiftly. King Elrick had no room in his military for cowards and deserters. "Morgan, whatever happens in the days ahead, promise me that you'll survive. I don't think I could do this without you." He stared into her eyes as he spoke leaving no doubt in her mind that he meant what he said.

"I will not leave you Lucious, no matter what happens." She reached out and held his hand in hers. Her touch calmed him and gave him strength. They rode for most of the day this way while conversing occasionally. The king held true to his word and stopped only a few times all day. Night began closing in and they still marched on tired and weary. Torches and light orbs were used to light their way. Their pace slowed only slightly with the darkness, yet onward they went. The sense of time eluded them now and it felt like they would never see the beautiful lights of the city. Every hill held hope that on the other side would be their destination. Time and time again though one hill just led into the next one and the one after that.

It must have been some time after midnight that they finally saw their destination in the distance. The towering white spires stood like beacons of hope in the dark. A renewed vigor filled everyone as the pace quickened and the city drew closer. Morgan and Lucious were totally stunned by the size and beauty of this place. The Westlin castle paled in comparison to the grandeur of this city. Even at this time of night, the streets were crowded with people from all walks of life. Merchants, healers, scholars, mages, and so on went about their business like it was just a normal day. Elrick gave the order to set the encampment on the border of the city. "Thank you all for the hard work, now get some food and rest. Only the essentials need to be setup tonight." After addressing his soldiers, the king headed over to Morgan and Lucious. "Why don't you three get cleaned up and have some food. I will send for you shortly so we may have a meeting with the high council tonight." Elrick left for his tent to prepare himself and to send word of an emergency council meeting.

Stormy jumped to the ground and stretched, letting out a big yawn. Morgan laughed at him, "Rough day?" The Arabis payed her no mind and relived himself. "Stormy, where are your manners?"

Lucious walked over chuckling, "When you have to go you have to go!" He received a smirk and a raised eyebrow from Morgan for his comment. "I suppose we should get these poor horses unloaded. Here we are complaining we're tired and sore all while these two carry three hundred pounds of gear and rider all day and night." One of the squires made her rounds and collected the two horses so they could be taken care of. Not everyone's horses received such treatment only the officers and higher ranking. It's not to say the other animals were treated badly but their care fell to each and every rider. Lucious handed over the reins to the miniature soldier along with one shiny silver piece. "I want you to take extra special care of my two friends, understand?"

The four foot tall blue eyed girl looked up and smiled. "Thank you so much Mr. Lucious I will see to their care myself." With a skip in her step she vanished into the sea of tents that were being erected all around.

Looking back to Morgan he could see her just standing there with her arms crossed watching him. "You will make a wonderful father someday Lucious, you're so good with children that aren't even your own."

Stepping over Stormy he held her by the waist and kissed her. "I'm going to get us some food. Why don't you go help get our tent in order, and I'll be back soon alright?"

"Alright, come Stormy I see our wagon over there." Morgan, Stormy and the four skeleton sentries headed towards the wagon. The sentries weren't much good at helping setup camp but they were fierce fighters that Lucious bound to Morgan as protectors. It gave him some comfort knowing that she had extra protection when he wasn't there.

CHAPTER THIRTY-TWO

PREEMPTIVE STRIKE

T he jail cells lay quiet now that its only occupant laid unconscious on the floor. Ezra and his new Draconian escapees used the cover of night to work their way back towards the city gates. Kneeling down in the shadows, the mage called them closer so he could whisper his plans. "Alright, I'll go first and create a distraction for the guards. Once they leave their post, Ulandra here will guide you out of town and to our camp."

"What if they don't leave, then what?" asked Trisk with a shaky voice.

"Trust me they'll be out of your way, just wait for the signal." Ezra said nothing more and headed closer to the guards and the open portcullis. "Alright let's see," as he scanned the surroundings looking for something to blow up. "Ahh, there it is." Two wagons that had been unloaded during the day now sat side by side empty. "Perfect." Before he could ready the spell a fireball came out of nowhere striking the wall behind the two wagons. Boom!! Wood, fire, and stone showered down from the explosion. "What the," his sentence cut short as a fireball slammed into another building, again sending rock and flame everywhere. Looking behind him towards the ocean he could see where the attacks originated. At least five ships floated off shore lobbing the flaming spheres. There silhouette perfectly outlined with each shot. Ezra could also see something strange happening on the shore. With every shot fired more of whatever it was showed up on the beach coming into town. Only when they drew close enough could Ezra make out the Draconian forms. "Oh no this isn't good, they must have known that their companions were imprisoned and came to free them by force."

By now sections of the town were engulfed in flames illuminating the surrounding area. The soldiers that had been sleeping now gathered in the courtyard to receive their defensive orders. Ulandra and the other Draconian's raced over to Ezra. "We have to stop this now before it gets out of hand," pleaded Ulandra. Trisk and the others agreed they didn't wish to see any of their family injured or worse, killed.

"Alright go and see if you can stop the assault and I'll go see if the humans can be reasoned with." Ezra rushed over to the courtyard to try and get the attention of the officer in charge. The flash and intense heat was the last thing he would remember as a fireball landed directly in front of him. He flew like a rag doll from the impact and landed on the ground some twenty feet away. The volley incapacitated the mage and would have surely killed a lesser man. Blood streaked down his face as he laid there at the mercy of whatever would come next.

The Draconian's ran towards the beach and their advancing brethren. They waved their arms frantically, "Stop!" screamed Ulandra but the impact of fireballs pelting the city drowned out her voice.

Trisk searched the attackers but couldn't find the Alpha Draconis that orchestrated the assault. "Stop, please, there has been a huge misunderstanding!" Him and his companions were pushed aside as the humans rallied to attack. Arrows rained down into the bulk of the Draconian attackers accompanied by chain lighting from the few human mages. The air crackled with electricity as it fried the Draconian warriors. Still they rushed forward at their prey closing the distance inhumanly fast. A second volley from the city soldiers never came. Like a reptilian wave, the Draconian's swept through the town killing ever human combatant they found. All of the townsfolk were gathered and bound together in the courtyard. The assault on Balderas was over just minutes after it started. Forty seven humans and twelve Draconian's lost their lives in the battle.

Nearly one thousand lizard men and women engulfed the town. Some were Selim's size while others had a more sleek figure like Morgan or Ulandra. All of them brandished their weapon of choice. A favorite that many wielded was a long sword with jagged serrated teeth on one side, perfect for cutting and tearing flesh. Axes and lances were also plentiful throughout. The Draconian mages arrived on shore last as they stayed on the ships laying down the barrage of flaming artilleries for the others. They wore scarlet red robes and pendants depicting their god, Lucious Drake.

Ulandra rushed over to the last place she saw Ezra. Chunks of rocks and wood laid scattered all around. She found him partially buried. "Come on Ezra, you better be alright. I'm not going to be the one to tell Lucious you died!" Franticly she lifted away the chunks of wall until she could pull him to a clearer spot. Kneeling down Ulandra tapped on his cheek. "Ezra wake up."

Still rattled with his ears ringing, he opened his eyes. "Ulandra, what happened?"

She grabbed hold and helped the mage to a sitting position. "It looks like my brethren decided to rescue their comrades themselves. Unfortunately they killed all the soldiers stationed here."

A look of horror washed over his face. "No, it didn't have to end like this. What a senseless waste of life." He shook his head in disgust. "Not exactly how this was supposed to go." Standing up he brushed himself off. Dust puffed out of his robes every time he patted them. "Ulandra, we must find out who is in charge so we can talk some sense into them."

Ulandra nodded in agreement. "Come, but let me do all the talking Ezra." As she led the way he did as she suggested and played the mute. Without the exploding fireballs they could finally hear each other talk. Ulandra approached Trisk and his recently released friends. "I need to speak with their leader, can one of you take us to him immediately?"

Trisk eagerly wanted to help. "Sure right this way," he waved on. They all headed for the mass of Draconian's. Ezra followed at the rear as not to incite any problems.

Ezra's companions entered the Draconian crowd with no issues. He however did not receive the same treatment. One of the larger Draconian's stepped directly into his path and pushed the mage flailing backwards with the face of his axe. Boom!! Crash!! Piercer slammed to the ground from above and with one devastating move used his beak to send the axe wielding Draconian flying into the crowd. The gryphon wailed, deafening those close by. His posture showed the masses that he meant business. Ulandra burst through the crowd waving her arms. "Everyone calm down! This mage and this creature mean no harm to any of you." Ulandra walked backwards to Piercer so she could keep an eye on the angry Draconian's. She only slightly turned away when she reached her friend. Gently she stroked the soft feathers of his head. "It's alright Piercer, nobody is going to hurt us ,I promise. Shh, Shh, Shh, they are not out enemy." Slowly the agitated beast calmed as she continued to soothe him. Eventually Piercer folded his wings and stopped clawing the ground.

Ezra now walked up besides Ulandra and placed his hand on the gryphon trying to help calm him. "Thank you my friend, you protected me and now I'm alright. You can rest now and calm down." Piercer finished with a little chirp as he sat down. "Thank you as well Ulandra, this could have turned out badly."

"Anytime, you would do the same for me." Ulandra stepped away and addressed the crowd. "My name is Ulandra, and this is my human friend Ezra, and my gryphon friend Piercer. We have been sent by the creator Lucious Drake himself to summon you to the City of Knowledge. He needs all of you to aid him in defending against his evil sister, Arain Drake and her unholy hordes. The fate of this world, your world, depends on it!"

The crowd whispered amongst themselves, not completely convinced in this Draconian's story. A moment later the throng of lizard warriors started to part making way for a single Draconian to pass. The three companions watched as the biggest and meanest looking one of them all approached. "I am the Alpha Draconis, Slade Hunter. Why has the creator not come to us himself? Why send you?"

To say Slade is intimidating is an understatement, he towered over Ulandra and Ezra. His scales on his chest and stomach were light blue and transitioned to a dark almost black color as they reached his spine. His eyes were a light gray and his head shaped like that of a dragon. The males of the species typically had the more Draconic features while the women looked more human. Two large dark blue horns twisted from his head backwards. Ezra stepped forward standing defiantly. "He sent us because I am his father and Ulandra is his friend, he trusts us to see his orders carried out. As we speak, Lucious is marching with the human King Elrick and a massive army to the City of Knowledge. It is there that the battle will be fought, it is there that we stand the best chance of winning. But Lucious needs the help of all his creations if there is any hope of victory."

Slade paced for a moment thinking about the mage's words. Facing the human prisoners he shook his head. "How do you expect us to side with the humans when the first thing they do is treat us with distrust and hold us against our will?"

Ulandra now stepped forward and bowed her head. "I have traveled with the creator for some time now and have seen the cruelty humans possess, yet I have also seen their ability for kindness and compassion. There will be those that hate and distrust but they are few. Should we condemn a species to annihilation because of it? What happened here today is a tragedy, such a loss of life when cooler heads may have prevailed and prevented all of this. Let us show the humans how truly great and noble the race of Draconian's is!"

Stepping forward Slade placed his massive clawed hand on her shoulder. "I see how truly wise the creator is to have sent you to us. We will heed his call and go with you my sister. Ezra, we will need some time to unload our horses and supplies from the ships. We shall also bury the dead before moving on."

Ezra walked over to the townsfolk sitting on the ground huddled together and scared. "With no military presence what do you wish to do? You are all free to stay and we can inform the soldiers in the next village of your needs, or you can all come with us to be relocated to Addleberry or Belrose. The choice is yours, but let it be known that we leave at first light heading north." Slade motioned for his soldiers to release the humans and begin digging graves. Everyone worked in the early hours before dawn cleaning up the mess from the battle as best they could. The Draconian's made a new graveyard on the outskirts of town where humans and Draconian's were buried side by side. Wooden markers with names scrawled on them served as makeshift tombstones.

Small larder boats were used to ferry the supplies and horses from the five ships anchored in the bay. Ulandra stopped for a moment and looked out across the water in the direction of her homeland. It stung being so close to seeing her place of origin yet having to turn around and head north again. "I suppose it will still be there when all of this is over. I'd rather see it with Selim for the first time anyways."

CHAPTER THIRTY-THREE

DEFENSIVE STEPS

"Queen Victoria, the outer walls have been scoured for weak spots and possible breach points. The ones we did find have already been repaired and reinforced. Messengers have also been dispatched to the southern towns, those who wish the protection of the castle will be returning over the coming weeks." General Cappell knew what needed to be done, but just as he would report to King Elrick he now had to report to Queen Victoria. His calm and stern demeanor is exactly what the occupants of Westlin needed right now as they prepared for the worst. "I have the blacksmiths working on reinforcing the steel gates around the city and sealing the ones we do not need. After that, they will transition to making extra weapons and armor for spares. The fletchers are focusing on making a variety of arrows and bows as well as installing extra ballista on the walls. Mages are busy enchanting as many of the weapons as they can. By no means are they creating hero worthy magical weapons, but every little bit helps."

Victoria sat in her chair in the war room as the officers relayed their completed tasks. Gone were the fancy dresses of royalty, she wore a battle ready suit of enchanted green and tan leather armor. A short sword hung on her left hip and a long dagger on her right. They all knew that at any point Arain could send some horrible things to attack the city. They would not be caught off guard, until the threat was eliminated this is the way things would be. "As always, exceptional work general and officers. How is the collection of food, water, and livestock going?"

One of the newer officers by the name of Shane spoke up. "We have escorts at every farm and plantation from here to Addleberry, your grace. They are protecting the supply routes allowing goods to arrive uninterrupted. At last count our siege store rooms are just over half full your grace."

The queen tapped her pointer finger on the heavily lacquered table. "Sounds like we have a lot of work ahead of us then. A half empty store room will not do us any good in a siege. Have the efforts doubled on collecting resources and supplies. We will not leave our enemies a buffet of free food and drink when they arrive. General, I want you to enact a draft. Those sixteen and older who are able to fight need to be enlisted and trained as quickly and efficiently as possible. Tell them they may return to whatever work they choose when the dog Arain Drake is put down. Has there been any word from the expedition east or south yet?"

Cappell cleared his throat. "The expedition to the east led by General Robert has made it to the port town of New Haven and is currently sailing to the Veassel stronghold of Dennar. No word yet on Ezra, Ulandra, or the gryphon but it is expected that they should have reached the southern shore by now. The speed of the gryphon has made it challenging to gauge their daily range your grace."

Victoria understood, these times presented special situations that they have never had to deal with before. Sliding her chair back from the table the queen stood up. "Keep up the good work everyone, you do your king proud. Let us reconvene here tomorrow, same time." All in attendance bowed to the queen before exiting the room. She left last and stood looking out the window to the courtyard below. Uniform rows of soldiers practiced their training in nearly perfect synchronization. Victoria couldn't help but wonder how many of them would loose their lives before this ended. She hoped it wouldn't be many but knew it very well could be all. Conflict between men and women she could deal with, rationalize with. Not what might be coming, monsters and minions of pure evil that had no fear and could not be swayed. Their sole purpose was to kill, no matter what. The thought made her heart sink knowing her love would soon be facing such things without her. A tear streaked down her left cheek and dripped onto the window sill. Wiping it away she let out a cleansing breath. "I must be strong for my people, this is no time for weakness," Victoria scolded herself. Standing tall and proud she straightened her tunic before heading off to oversee the remaining preparations of Westlin castle.

Erin and her soldiers reached the bottom of the Vesper and entered into the mining town of Tellium. Meeting with the city guard, the general laid out the objective of the town from this day forward. "Shipments of ore will continue to Westlin castle for a few days longer. After that the portal must be sealed to prevent Arain Drake access to its materials. If the forward defense at the City of Knowledge fails, we must be ready to stop their advance here. Fortify the walls with waste rock from the mine and clear out the trees a hundred yards back." The troops and miners worked hand in hand to complete the tasks laid out by the general. "Blacksmiths, your sole purpose from this moment on is to make ballista for the city walls. After that, weapons and armor will be your focus." It would take at least a week to complete all the preparations, they only hoped they were going to be given the time to do so. Erin called for a meeting with all of the civilians in the town square. "Every one of you must make a choice, either you stay and continue on with your daily duties or you leave tomorrow with an escort to the capital city of Westlin. The choice is yours but be warned, those who stay may end up being called on to fight. The escort leaves at noon tomorrow. That is all." Erin convened with her officers about guard rotations, scouting parties, and the most important, siege rations. Just as with the capital city, the local farmers and herders would be gathered along with all of their crops and livestock to be used in case of a siege. All were assured repayment for items used for the war effort.

Throughout the night barracks and triage tents were erected as the city hadn't the facilities to accommodate such a large force. The town slowly transformed, looking more and more like a full fledged fort every hour. As noon approached, more than half of the town's citizens were lined up with horse and pack, ready to cross the Vesper for the protection of the capital. With a final glance back, they left their homes and livelihoods behind and headed forward to an uncertain future. The town's mood had changed to somber and serious now. With all of the children gone the town laid quiet. Leaving only thoughts of war and monsters in everyone's minds. It would surely be a long tense wait for news from the frontlines to arrive. Work and worry were all that remained for the town of Tellium.

CHAPTER THIRTY-FOUR

DENNAR

General Robert peered through the captains telescope scanning the horizon for any sign of land. It looked like there could be something far off in the distance just a few degrees to their port. He handed the telescope over, and pointed in the direction. "Captain, have a look. I think I see a landmass over there."

A few minutes of readjusting the scope and rubbing his eyes passed. "I do believe you are correct general, it does indeed look like land."

Robert slapped his hands together and smiled with excitement. After the recent incident below, crew spirits were pretty dismal but this would get everyone amped up especially the two Veassels. "Full speed ahead captain!" was the last thing Robert said before heading off to the infirmary. He surely had a jump in his step when he opened the door. "Selim, Bibble, Bobble there's land in the distance. Come up and have a look for yourselves."

Bibble and Bobble gave each other a big hug. Selim made the mistake of stepping closer as he soon got sucked into the hugging session. "Alright you two, are you feeling well enough to go up and have a look?" Selim just wanted to be out of the Veassels clutches as soon as possible. The Draconian would easily carry both of them but he figured they wanted to walk out on their own two feet. A matter of pride to not show weakness to the other humans that would surely be standing on the top deck watching the new discovery. The four of them made their way to the ship's bow. A light breeze and warm sunshine greeted them. Gulls squawked overhead as they quickly approached the landmass.

"Would you look at that Bobble, we're almost home." The two Veassels almost couldn't contain their excitement. Closer and closer they sailed until smells and sounds from the bustling city ignited more memories to fire in their minds. Nobody on the deck had any idea how beautiful Dennar actually was. Two level cobblestone buildings supported on large square wooden stilts were the first things they reached at the ports entrance. Flower boxes full of fresh blooms adorned the outside of most of the windows. The city actually spanned and connected two islands that sat about fifty feet apart. It's a marvel of ingenuity not seen in human cities and towns. Two long wooden peers stretched out into the bay like welcoming arms. A handful of different sized vessels were tied to the pilons that held the docks to the ocean floor. Everyone on the top deck stood in awe as they marveled at the new city. Veassels freely walked around going about their business. That is until the strange ship in their harbor drew their attention. A calm normal day in Dennar quickly turned to one of tension and unrest. The civilians scattered quickly making the city look deserted.

Robert signaled the captain. "Let's tie up to the pier over there. Everyone remain on the ship and do nothing to provoke the indigenous people. Me and my companions will go and make first contact." All the deckhands gave one type of grunt or another in response.

The captain at the wheel shouted out his docking orders. "Drop the sails and stow the jibs! Get ready to dock and prepare the bow and stern lines!" Deckhand's ran this way and that. Some were on the masts securing the sails while others walked to the port side with coils of large rope. The captain gently eased the massive vessel up to the dock pilons. Two men heaved as they wrapped the rope around the pilon and fastened it to the bow and stern cleats, pulling the ship in. It took only a matter of minutes until their ship floated securely with the dock. "Alright you sorry excuses for seamen, let's get this ship ready for our return voyage." Aye, Ayes could be heard from around the deck. "General, it's safe to disembark now."

"Very well captain, and please make sure nobody leaves the ship!" Robert climbed over the rail and onto the dock followed by Bibble, Bobble, and of course Selim. "Maybe it's best if we leave all our weapons here for now, just so we don't scare the locals." Robert's eyes fell on Selim as he said those last words. There would be no way to prevent that with his Draconic looks. Everyone placed their weapons up against or on top of a row of old wooden crates that lined one side of the pier. Some held extra dock ropes while others contained crab pots and fishing nets. "Alright you two you're in charge now, lead the way."

Bibble and Bobble happily bounded down the wooden pier and past the buildings that were built over the shallows. Wind battered cobblestone buildings and streets sprawled out before them. The occasional waft of dead fish and seagull squalor slowly faded into the distance as they walked down a wide street named, Kingsway. Movement could be seen flittering past windows as their occupants hid from the strangers. Shutters snapped closed as they approached. Bibble cupped his hands around both sides of his mouth making his voice carry better. "Hello..... We mean you no harm..... We are unarmed and wish to speak with the person in charge here....." His voice echoed around the densely packed homes and buildings. Walking a little further down the street they came across the first of what looked like many suspension bridges that connected the two islands together. Unguarded carts of food, trinkets, and supplies lined the sides of the street in this area. The companions being so mesmerized by their surroundings were less than focused on threats. Nobody noticed the Veassels closing in from behind, below and above them until it was too late. Two bolos struck Selim from behind, one around his ankles and the other around his arms and waist. It happened so quick that he lost his balance and fell face first onto the road in front of him. Robert turned around just in time to see him fall before a weighted net dropped from the top of the second floor above, pinning him to the ground. "Wait! Stop!" Yelled Bibble to the attackers closing in. In front of them a sewer grate flipped open as four Veassel soldiers emerged. They were adorned in dull silver colored chainmail armor and brandishing two long daggers.

Robert struggled under the weight of the net trying to get free. His efforts totally wasted as the Veassels roped down from above and quickly cinched the draw line. *Caught like a helpless fish, how embarrassing,* he thought. Selim on the other hand had much better success freeing himself. With a dose of adrenaline, the already strong Draconian doubled his strength letting him easily snap the bolo ropes around his waist and arms. In a matter of seconds, he ripped the ones off around his legs and jumped up to face his attackers. Another bolo hurtled towards him but he dodged it with ease. "Not so easy from the front, is it?" Lunging forward, Selim reached the first guard with ease. In one fluid motion his giant hand wrapped around the Veassel's entire head. He threw the poor guard like one would throw a ball in a game of catch. The small body sailed almost thirty feet before coming to a stop with a bone shattering thud against a wall of one of the houses. Either dead or unconscious were the only two outcomes from such a brutal assault.

Bobble ran in front of Selim waving his arms above his head. "Stop, everyone stop! We mean the inhabitants of Dennar no harm, we come in peace." More soldiers ran down both ends of the street until the group of four were completely outnumbered and surrounded. Bobble placed a hand on Selim's arm, "Please no more." The Draconian acknowledged and took a much less intimidating stance.

Bibble worked at the net trying to free his friend. Peeling a corner of the net clear he reached out a furry hand to Robert. Taking it, the general finally pulled himself clear. "Thanks Bibble, I was beginning to feel a bit helpless there." He chuckled at the situation as he brushed himself off. "Well between the first incident on the ship and now here, I would say our introductions aren't going so well my friends."

A taller well dressed Veassel pushed through the crowd. Being almost a foot taller than the rest of her kind she stood out quite badly. Her regal blue clothing also set her uniquely apart from her brethren as well. Taking a moment, this Veassel royalty studied the four intruders before her. Finally settling her gaze on Bibble and Bobble, she spoke. "I am the matriarch of Dennar, Helena Tildi. What happened to your hand my child?" Obviously the bandages on Bobbles hand had not gone unnoticed.

Holding up his hand he looked at the backside and then the blood spotted palm. "This was an accident your highness, one that has been resolved with the harshest of punishments."

Her eyes drifted accusingly over to Robert and Selim. Then back to the Veassel brothers "What are your names? I don't recall seeing you two before."

"My name is Bobble and this here is my brother, Bibble your highness. Pointing to the others, this human here is named Robert and the Draconian is Selim."

"Why have you brought these outsiders to our home, my young Veassels?"

It quickly started to feel like an interrogation or a scolding from their mother. That is if they could remember her. Bobble again took it upon himself to answer the question. "Please forgive us for our indiscretion your highness, but we are in desperate need of your help. Well, not just your help but the help of all Veassels. An evil the likes of which this world has never seen is quickly sweeping across Tauro from the west, and if left unchecked will engulf the world in very little time. The creator, Lucious Drake has sent us to gather the citizens of Dennar and bring them to the human city of Tellium to aid in its defenses."

Helena silently paced in front of them weighing what she had just been told. "You say the creator sent you, was this in some dream or vision?"

Bibble chimed in. "No he sent us shortly after we freed him and his friends from King Elrick's dungeon in Westlin."

Helena stopped in front of him. "You're telling me the creator is alive and in the flesh?" The Veassel community when created all had the visage and teachings of Lucious imprinted in their memories even though they technically were all just created. It seemed strange that such an all powerful being walked this planet with them.

Bibble nodded, "Yes your highness, Lucious and an enormous army of humans is currently marching to face the enemy. Will you heed his call and join in the fight?" Not a sound could be heard as everyone held their breath, and waited for Helena's response.

The matriarch smiled and nodded in agreement. "We will answer the call of the creator and join him in this battle." Raising her arms high she slowly turned in place looking out at the hundreds of Veassels surrounding them. "People of Dennar, prepare for WAR!" Cheers erupted from the crowd as everyone filled with righteous purpose. Helena let them go on for a short time before dolling out a laundry list of orders to her subordinates. As quickly as they arrived, the citizens dispersed back into the cobblestone city to prepare. Helena and a small contingent of soldiers stayed with the visitors as the Matriarch had quite a few questions. "Bobble, did Lucious create the human and lizard people as well?"

Selim chuckled, "I'm a Draconian your highness, not a lizard, and no Lucious did not create the humans. In fact he's a human himself."

So much information in such a short span of time gave Helena a headache. "I take it that the massive ship docked at the pier will be our transportation to this human land of Tauro?"

Robert stepped forward with a kind of half bow. "Yes your highness, it will take us across the ocean to the mainland and the human port city of New Haven. There we will travel west past the capital city of Westlin and over the Vesper mountains. Just past the mountains base, we will reach the mining town of Tellium which as we speak is being fortified and garrisoned by General Erin and her soldiers. If the weather holds good and we don't have any issues, we should make it to our destination within a week.

Helena laughed as she shook her head. "To think this morning when I woke, I thought it would be another boring day!"

CHAPTER THIRTY-FIVE

ALMOST THERE

Traveling after working most of the night isn't what any-one wanted to do but they knew time was against them. Just as the sun started its skyward ascent, Ezra, Ulandra, and the legion of Draconians left the battle worn town of Belderas behind. None of the townsfolk wanted to leave, especially not with the creatures that just sacked their town. It would be quite some time before they would be wel-comed back. Ezra, Ulandra, and Slade led the legion north by north-west towards the City of Knowledge. "Ulandra, how about you and Piercer fly ahead and look for possible trouble in our way. We certainly don't need any extra surprises now do we?" Ezra stroked his beard as he gave the gryphon a scratch. "You take care of her now you hear me?" Piercer rubbed his giant yellow beak up and down Ezra's arm to show that he understood.

A moment later and Ulandra climbed into the saddle and gave the gryphon a command. "Fly." Piercer bolted into the sky with a few mighty flaps of his wings. Holding onto the saddle horn with an iron grip, she pressed her body closer to his so the wind wasn't so violent. He leveled off a few moments later and set into a calm glide. Ulandra could now sit erect without fear of being ripped off the saddle by the wind. "Another calm beautiful day to be up in the sky, isn't it Piercer?" The gryphon let out one of his ear piercing calls in agreement. Being almost a thousand feet high gave them an excellent field of view, it also kept them safe from archers and mages that might attack from below.

By days end, they had made it considerably further than Ezra thought possible. Upon further inspection and talking with Slade, he found the reason why. "Our horses are much larger and muscular than your human variety. Their legs are longer as well allowing them to cover more ground per stride, and besides that, they have three lungs. All of that extra air feeds their muscles incredibly well, allowing them to run much farther before becoming tired."

Ezra walked over to Slade's horse to inspect closer. He hadn't payed much attention until now and could clearly see the differences. "His white and blue steed is massive. Look Ulandra, I can't even see over this horses back it's so tall. Heck I don't think I could get up in the saddle of one of these, haha."

Ulandra walked over to pet the beautiful horse. "We call them Clontiss horses, Ezra. They are named after the Draconian Clontiss Surly. He's the one that first domesticated them." She gave a couple quick side to side shakes of her head. "Don't even ask me how I know that!" Off she went to get the gryphon's saddle off for the night.

Ezra headed off as well to tend to his poor under sized steed. *I feel so bad for my horse having to keep pace with these Draconian mounts. Maybe I can make it easier by giving my packs to Ulandra to carry on our winged friend.* Without much more thought, he brushed out the horse and gave it some fresh feed and water. "That's a good girl, you rest up now." With a parting pat on the muzzle, the mage headed off to find Ulandra and Piercer.

"Thanks for such a wonderful day of flying." Ulandra placed her forehead to the gryphon's as she gently pet him on the side of the face. She realized how truly special it was to be gifted the ability to fly with such a majestic creature. As long as she held the reins, her food would stay safely in her stomach. A thought back to Ezra controlling their flight made her instantly queasy. She could see the mage approaching and released the animal to its own devices. The Draconians had made a makeshift pen for the griffon so bystanders would give the creature its much needed space.

"Hello Ezra, how was the ride today? Uneventful I hope."

"That it was Ulandra. After flying so freely in the sky it's plain boring to ride a horse on the ground. All in all though there weren't any issues to contend with. How was your day? Not to cold up there I hope."

She shook her head. "Nope not cold at all, and I didn't even need to throw up once!" A sarcastic smile stretched across her face. "I'm done here, how about we go grab some dinner and discuss tomorrow's agenda?"

Ezra nodded, "Sounds like a fine idea. I think I saw the mess hall open when I walked over here." The two headed over and waited in line with all the other Draconians. Ulandra had been welcomed immediately but Ezra still received the occasional look of discontent from those around him. *I'm sure nobody would try and hurt me but I can still feel the air of uneasiness.* Once given their food, the two headed back to their tents to sit besides the campfire and eat. Slade and a handful of his bodyguards joined them. Most of the food they ate came from the supplies that were brought over from the Draconian homeland. None of it looked indigenous to the foods of Tauro. The mage held up an odd looking fruit that resembled a red banana with perfect circular black spots on the peel. It smelled faintly like strawberry and tasted exactly like a strawberry banana. "This is amazing, what's it called?"

Slade finished his mouthful before responding. "It's called a plantoon fruit. They grow on the tentacles of the carnivorous plantoon trees in Ruuk. Their aromatic smell attracts juniper moonks which the tree eats as their main source of food." Slade could see from the look on Ezra's face that his answer would require a bit more explanation. "Sorry, I take it you do not have these where you come from?"

The mage now finished, set his plate down on the ground in front of him, his interest now in overdrive to learn about this new flora and fauna. "Let me get my notebook out before you continue." Reaching into his robes he produced the red notebook and pen he used to detail such information. "Alright, now would you be so kind to explain what a plantoon tree and a juniper moonk is?"

Clearing his throat the enormous alpha Draconis began his explanation. "A plantoon tree stands roughly thirty feet tall with light green bark and dark green tentacles that would mimic branches of your trees. These tentacles are covered with plantoon fruit such as the one you just ate. Under the fruit however is a neurotoxic filled barb that shoots out when the fruit is removed. The juniper moonks are a six legged hairless mammal that lives high up in the trees on Ruuk. They absolutely love the plantoon fruit and take their chances picking it from these trees. Quite often a moonk gets a bit too greedy and is paralyzed from one of those poisonous barbs. When it falls into the trunk of the tree, it's then liquified and absorbed to make more fruit."

Ezra felt a bit woozy thinking about just eating a liquified juniper moonk as he finished writing the notes in his book. "Thank you so much for that visually disturbing depiction, Slade. I'm sure I will never forget it."

Slade and his bodyguards chuckled in response to the humans squeamish demeanor. Crossing his arms and leaning back, the Draconian leader quickly changed subjects. "How about we discuss tomorrow's travel plans?"

Ulandra pulled a map from her tent and spread it out on the ground next to the fire. It would give them a rough visual idea of their location but not much more. On her knees, Ulandra placed a small rock onto the map where she believed they were located. Ezra looked over and agreed that her placement looked fairly close. Ulandra discussed the plans. "The Clontiss horses are traveling at almost twice the distance we could normally travel in a day. By tomorrow we should just make it to the southern outskirts of Hemshir Forest. I'll switch off with Ezra and he can fly as over watch tomorrow. It will be mostly open grass fields between here and the Hemshir so our chances of running into people will be small."

"Slade do you all know how to shape shift?" asked Ezra. "If you can, then we shouldn't have to worry at all about being seen."

The alpha Draconis cocked his head. "Shape shift?"

Ulandra transformed into the red haired human form that she used. Gasps came from those seated around the fire followed by silence and some perplexed looks. Just as quickly, she morphed back to her Draconian form. "We should all posses this gift of transformation Slade, I will teach you how to use it." For the next few hours they sat by the fire practicing. Some grasped the technique quickly while others had trouble. Eventually though everyone could successfully do it. By Slade's command those in attendance were sent out to teach the others. By morning the camp looked quite different. It looked like they had been invaded by humans overnight as half of them were in human form mingling freely with the others.

Ezra and Ulandra looked out into the mix and smiled at each other. This is how they envisioned the real humans and Draconians interacting. "Someday Ulandra, this will be for real." He patted her on the shoulder. "We better get packed up or I fear they'll leave us behind, and I don't think our horses would be able to catch up if they did."

Ulandra agreed, her brethren were not the likes to dilly dally. They would be heading on for another long day of riding very soon. She could tell from Ezra's mood that he grew more excited by the minute as today he would be flying with Piercer. "I can finish this if you want to go get the gryphon ready. I don't mind."

His reaction belied his elder years. Giddy as a school girl, he dropped the chest that he just packed his tent in and rushed for the griffon pen. "Thanks Ulandra," is all she could hear as he disappeared into the crowd. His heart raced with anticipation. "This is the highlight of any day!" Rounding the bend he could see his friend just finishing some sort of medium sized animal for breakfast. Into the pen he went going straight to scratch his beautiful head. "Good morning Piercer, I hope you're rested because today we're going to have some fun!" One of his lower pitched chirps came out as Ezra rubbed him. Hastily the mage grabbed the special saddle and started the task of securing it to him. "I'm getting faster at this buddy, but it still takes a bit of time to do it right. Don't want me falling off now, do you?" A couple blinks of his beautiful eyes and another chirp would be his only response.

A few minutes later and they were airborne. Ezra inhaled deeply as if it was his first breath of the day. "The air up here is so clean and fresh, none of the smells from the ground make it up this high. It's so intoxicating wouldn't you say,

Piercer?" His ear piercing cry had returned this time but it didn't seem as bad from the saddle.

Ulandra stared skyward as the two quickly left the ground behind. It made her happy to see two spirits so alive and free, dancing on the wind currents above. It looked as if they hadn't a care in the world. *It's beautiful,* she thought until one of the many wagons pulled by a pair of Clontiss stopped next to her. Ulandra hastily loaded the three full trunks that held both their tents and supplies onto it. She rubbed the dirt from her clawed hands. "Well I suppose it's time to go," over to the makeshift stable she headed to collect her horse. The day progressed much like the day before with little in the way of excitement. Ulandra used this time to mingle with her fellow Draconians and learn as much as she could. More than a few of the males showed interest in her for a mate but she made it known that her hand and heart were taken. One of the suiters being quite smitten with her required a bit more convincing. No sooner did his hand touch her, he fell unconscious from the lightning fast punch she responded with. Ulandra didn't need to teach that lesson more than once. All of the men took note and focused their affections elsewhere.

CHAPTER THIRTY-SIX

DEATH IS

Acererak's disfigured body hovered just off the ground as he silently floated on a carpet of green mist. Bright green hued sockets scanned for potential victims, while his fog of reanimation flowed outward in all directions. Every crack and crevice being molested in search of creatures dead or alive so that they may be added to his queen's ranks. Mutilated rotting corpses stood silently ready for their creator's commands. Swarms of flies gathered drawn to the stench of carrion. The few remaining human soldiers gave them a wide berth as just the look from Acererak induced fear. It made them uneasy knowing that death would not be the end for them, and that they would be forced to fight on for an eternity.

Every minute that passed, Acererak's legion continued to grow. Now long dead bones of forest creatures started to move and reassemble, vaguely resembling their living counterparts. Bears, wolves, and moose were the largest of the reanimated but all were required to answer his call. A throng of skeletal rabbits looked absolutely terrifying with their glowing green eye sockets and long teeth. Remnants of what used to be cute noses twitched mimicking their habits when they were alive.

The Cryptids skittered about the upper levels of the castle webbing large broken sections back together as a temporary repair. In a never ending procession they slinked down their steel like webs from the mountain tops to the castle below. The entire scene made it look like the castle had the worst spider infestation possible. Everyone did their part whether it be the cooks supplying the food and mead or the ogres collecting wood and materials for the blacksmiths and fletchers. Seget had instructed them all that Arain would be recovering for a few days and everything better be ready for when she wished to continue on. Arain's recent show of power cemented their loyalties even deeper. None of them wanted to disappoint their god and creator. Human's, ogre's, Krillox, and lycans all worked together seamlessly.

Seget and his officers attended long planning meetings to lay out their next possible moves. Scouts from each of the factions were sent out to the west towards the City of Knowledge. Their goal being the collection of information on the enemies defenses only. No engagement was to be made without the queen's consent. Similar small contingents of soldiers were sent out to gather food and supplies from the surrounding farmlands. Seget knew that keeping enough rations would be one of the more difficult aspects of this campaign. More troops with bigger mouths to feed.

For two days they labored and prepared. On the third day, Arain awoke from her deep slumber. As she had so many times before, her eyes opened to stare at the roof of her red tent. "This is becoming old, maybe I'll have one of my artisans paint a mural on the ceiling next time. What do you think, Timber?" His massive gray tail wagged side to side on the blankets. Lovingly she stroked the fur on his head. Sunlight streamed in from the small openings of the tent's entrance. "Looks like it's morning, we should get up and start heading for the City of Knowledge. I can't wait to crush my brother!" With a much renewed vigor, Arain dressed while she sent one of her chamber maids to fetch Seget.

He had been waiting impatiently for her to awake and felt elation upon seeing her maid heading in his direction. "Commander, the queen is awake and requests your presence immediately."

Rushing past her, no reply was given. Directly to the large red tent he headed, stopping only when he reached the doorway. "Your grace, may I enter?"

"You may, Seget."

The commander entered and immediately bowed his head when he greeted her. "It warms my heart to see you up and well rested my queen. How may I serve you?"

Arain slid on the left bracer of her new armor. "Is everything ready to continue onward, commander?"

"Yes your grace, we have been preparing since you took your leave three days ago. Repairs have started on the castle, supplies have been refilled, and scouts have been dispatched. We are just now starting to receive the first reports back from the city."

She walked over to her dining table and picked up a cup of water. "Well what has my pathetic brother done to defend the city?"

"It looks like King Elrick and your brother have just recently arrived at the southern outskirts of the city. They have brought with them a considerably large contingent of human soldiers. No new breeds except for the Draconian woman and her pet are present. As expected, the city is preparing its defenses for our arrival."

Setting the empty glass back down, Arain stood silent for a moment before issuing the next set of orders. "Good work,

I think defeating my brother will be easier than taking Castle Kragg from Malik was! Hahahahaha. What else Seget?"

"As you instructed, all prisoners have been put into the dungeons until you see fit to deal with them. Valin and Talia haven't left the castle's treasuries since they went in days ago. They have been sending out a catalogued arsenal of magic armor and weapons though, which have been placed in our armory. The blacksmith, Dalia has put the mithrite ore we found in the castle holds to good use, outfitting over half of the werewolves with the new armor you requested."

"Excellent, I want to be underway in two hours. I have to tend to the captives first, and depending on how receptive they are it may take a little while before I'm ready to leave."

Seget again bowed his head. "I will have everything ready for when you're finished my queen." The commander took his leave. He knew she would want to leave quickly so he had the camp being packed for travel starting at first light. Another twenty minutes and nothing but loaded carts remained where the various tents used to be.

Arain rode the short distance to the castle entrance where she left her horse. Valin and Talia stood waiting for her arrival so they could escort her to the dungeons. "Good morning your grace, it's good to see you well." Talia stood behind Valin, head bowed and silent.

"You two as well, father. I hear your treasure hunting is going quite well. Malik had a considerable stash here that he kept all to himself. What a waste to not even use these items for his final stand. Oh well, you may distribute these items to those you deem worthy Valin. Now how about you show me to the prisoners?"

Talia took the lead. "Right this way, your majesty." She led them to the staircase that descended into the bowels' of the castle. Unlike Westlin, this location looked more like a proper dungeon. The cold black stone steps sprawled out before them. Every flight they descended the colder and more damp the air became. Lit sconces cast a gloomy yellowish light throughout. As they reached the bottom, many voices could be heard now coming from the captives. Valin had taken the liberty of interrogating a handful of Malik's officers as evidenced by the blood covered rack and the two men caged in the hanging coffins. A Judas chair in another cell still had its victims split corpse adorned on the metal pyramid. A horrific way to go for sure as the poor mans weight gradually split his rectum and pelvis from being lowered onto the pyramids point.

"Were you able to gather any good information, Valin?"

The black robed mage just shook his head. "Nothing of much use, my queen. We found everything this castle held secret by using simple discovery spells. These volunteers did serve for some amusement though while we waited for your arrival." Valin had a devilish grin on his face as he spoke the words.

Just past the interrogation rooms is what she came to see. Row upon row of citizens and soldiers packed into dungeon cells as far as the eye could see. Talia bowed and gestured forward with her outstretched arm. "Here are your prisoners as requested, my queen."

Arain walked past the red haired mage to take in the sights before her. The cells were packed full enough to prevent any sort of comfort or rest. As ordered, the soldiers and the civilians were separated. Arain peered through the bars at the tired and hungry prisoners. "Valin, see to it that these first four cells are turned and added to the lycan regiments. I don't see much need for any of these human soldiers to be spared, I want absolute loyalty not empty pledges. Let the deep ones and the lich have the next four cells.

Valin stood by Arain's side as she doled out orders. "What would you have done with the last cell of soldiers, your grace?"

She thought for a brief moment with her hand on her chin. "Feed them to the ogres and cryptids!"

The men and women in their confines cried and pleaded with the queen to spare their lives, but her decision remained their death sentence. "Come now, you will be of great use nourishing my monsters. Is that not the ultimate show of allegiance?" Arain's words were colder than the wet stone walls of the dungeon. All hope faded from the prisoners in the last cell as she walked away to inspect the civilians. At least twenty cells stood packed full of men, women, and children. Arain turned to Valin and Talia. "Release them, I wish to have my subjects out in the daylight for my inauguration."

Both of the mages bowed at her request. Snap, the sound came from his fingers and all the civilians cell doors creaked open. "Her highness would like to welcome her new subjects in the courtyard above for her formal inauguration as queen of Castle Kragg. Any who do not wish to attend are free to remain in their cells until the ogres return for feeding." Arain had already left to head upstairs, and the crowd followed with great enthusiasm. To nobody's surprise the civilians cells were left completely empty. Valin and Talia followed last to make sure nobody had any ideas of running away.

Amazingly some thirty thousand civilians crammed into the massive courtyard in less than thirty minutes time. Timber with a group of lycans and ogres headed into the castle and down into the dungeons to carry out their orders. Many onlookers watched in horror as the procession of death walked by. The sight below would be unbelievable by any standards. Arain walked up onto a makeshift wooden podium to address the crowd. No one dared make a sound as they stared intently at the evil before them. Valin stepped behind her and placed Malik's forfeit crown upon her head. "Kneel before your queen and goddess, Arain Drake!" roared the black mage. As a wave curls before running ashore the people all bowed and knelt before her.

"People of the Kragg, I Arain Drake stand before you as your new and rightful ruler of the late King Malik's entire domain. Everyone here owes me a debt of life. I will allow you to live and prosper fully protected in this city. All I ask in return is your total and absolute devotion. You will make this castle and city the envy of the land. It will be a place fit for a god! Anything less will be paid for with the lives of your children, wives, and husbands." Arain pointed to long table to her left where a dozen of her soldiers sat. Large empty tomes with ink pots and quills were laid out before them. "Everyone here will make their way to this table where you will give your name, status, and skill to be recorded for duty distribution. Anyone knowingly falsifying their identification will be executed immediately!"

The crowd nervously looked around at one another upon this revelation. Trust would not be placed so easily among neighbors so telling the truth would be the safest course of action. Everyone being on edge not to mention hungry and tired just wanted their feeling of safety restored. Over the past few days their entire scope of the world had been torn down and replaced with the one provided by Arain and her monsters. Being protected by these beasts is far better than being eaten by them, the majority thought.

Without incident the people formed uniform and or-derly lines in front of the table. The processing of the entire courtyard began. Seeing her subjects obey filled her with overwhelming satisfaction. Walking down from the stage Arain, Valin, and Talia headed out of the courtyard towards the assembled procession lead by Commander Seget.

A small detachment of humans and cryptids remained behind to act as the city stewards. They were tasked with delegating jobs to restore the city and castle as well as maintaining order and discipline. Any failures would fall squarely on this groups shoulders so being strict would be the first course of action. With backup from the cryptids, nobody would be foolish enough to challenge their ruling.

Ahead of schedule, the motley procession headed westward for the City of Knowledge and beyond. The enormously long formation looked like some grotesque snake patched together with so many different sections as it made its way across the land. At its tail, a green mist radiated from the passing of Acererak and the undead legion. Arain figured it to be wise and have the lich behind the living so that his aura of fear wouldn't cause any problems.

Seget pulled his horse besides Arain so he could speak quietly. "Your majesty, I had your special prisoner placed on a horse just a short ways back with Glub guarding him. I hope that is to your satisfaction?"

Arain blushed just briefly, up until now she had all but forgotten the young man she had met in the forest not so many days ago. "You have done well Seget, as always." With an approving nod, she gave the commander the lead as she fell back to find her special prisoner.

CHAPTER THIRTY-SEVEN

THE RED ROOM

O ri and Vermillion made it to the outskirts of the city in record time. The thrill of their previous battle and the anticipation of the one before them acted like an intoxicating drug that neither could get enough of. Changed back to humans, the two dressed with clothing they had brought in their lycan sized packs. Once fully clothed and armed, the two disposed of their bags as they would be of little use in their current form. The two posed as a married farming couple to cause as little suspicion as possible. They exited the forest and headed for the long line that already formed outside the western gates. As seamless as ever they blended into the crowd. Nobody was the wiser, not the other citizens nor the guards checking everyone who entered the great city. Ori nudged Vermillion's arm to get his attention. "Look over there," she gestured to the massive encampment of King Elrick's army.

Vermillion acknowledged with a slight nod. "We have much work to do before the goddess arrives." Past the giant portcullis they proceeded. Before them sprawled the majestic City of Knowledge. The sheer spectacle made even these two hardened killers pause for a moment.

Ori took Vermillion by the hand and lead him from the crowded main street towards the quieter side streets. Like a blood hound on a scent, she weaved through the streets until she found what she seeked. A small, quaint, totally obscure home stood before the couple. Even the door looked unremarkable, just plain wood with a wrought iron handle, and a small slot about eye height. Ori outstretched a hand but before she could knock, the latch on the door clicked, before slowly swinging open. Without hesitation she entered with Vermillion close behind. The door slid silently closed making only the sound of the latch catching. They now stood in a small black entranceway. No light, no sound except for their shallow breathing. "Ori, what is this place?"

"Don't be alarmed Vermillion, it's one of hundreds of assassin dens scattered throughout Tauro. I have agents in almost every city, town, and village of the known world." Ori reached out in the blackness and depressed a switch on the wall in front of her. A click followed by a low whirring noise and light began flooding into the room. The section of wall in front of them slid to the right revealing a much larger and well lit chamber. A smaller framed and completely garbed assassin approached. The bright green eyes of the person were the only thing visible.

Stopping in front of them the person bowed, "Welcome to Ni-sec General Ori and Vermillion. To what do we owe this most welcome visit?"

Ori having trained each and every one of these assassins personally, could remember their names from just seeing their eyes. "It's good to be here Raksha, we have come with news from the west. King Malik has been slain and the Kragg has fallen to the goddess, Arain Drake. Vermillion and myself now serve her, as will all of my assassins. Do you have issue with this, Raksha?"

Placing her right fist into her left hand Raksha again bowed her head. "We serve you, the leader of the dark brotherhood above all else general. If you wish it, we will serve Arain Drake as well."

"Good Raksha, gather the others so we may share Arain's message with everyone."

With inhuman quickness, the assassin left to complete her task leaving the two generals to their own devices. The room they stood in had all manner of death inducing devices. Against the far northern wall a rack containing small different colored vials spanned from floor to ceiling. Some were black as ink while others looked to be filled with honey. Vermillion surmised the contents weren't anything so benign. Ori walked over to him. "Be sure not to touch, some of those cause quite gruesome deaths."

Vermillion cracked a smile, "I wonder if any of them would have an effect on us?"

Ori picked up one of the red filled vials and faced the archer. "Let's play a game, take your shirt off." He gave her a sideways look as he started unbuttoning his shirt. His thin muscular physique and the possibility of death aroused Ori immensely. She stepped forward and caressed his warm firm chest before pouring the red liquid down his right shoulder and arm. Immediately steam rose from his flesh accompanied by a low sizzling sound. Vermillion winced in pain as Ori pulled him down to her level kissing him passionately. These two have always had a certain chemistry but never had it gone this far. Aggressively they embraced each other kissing. Seconds later the burning stopped and the archer's arm remained unblemished.

"Now it's your turn," Ori seductively removed her top exposing the most perfect breasts he had ever seen.

Ori grabbed a greenish vial and handed it to him. "Try this one," she said just as seductively. Popping the cap he dumped the contents down her spine, and within seconds lesions and blisters formed. With clenched teeth Ori jumped on Vermillion knocking him onto his back. They kissed and bit one another drawing blood occasionally. Their game of pleasure and pain went on for over an hour. Many more poisons were applied during that time with all of them having minimal, temporary injuries. Now completely naked, they enjoyed each other until both participants dripped with sweat and were breathing heavily. When they finally stopped they noticed the small group of assassins standing silently watching. Ori looked into Vermillion's eyes giving him the most evil smile, "I'm starving."

Without warning the two burst into their lycan forms, pouncing on the spectators. With no time to defend, the first four were dispatched in a bloody whirlwind of violence. Raksha and one other were quick enough to evade the initial assault but their skill only prolonged their lives by a couple of minutes. Useless attacks with steel weapons sealed their fates. Once the seven had been slain the two blood soaked generals reverted to their human forms. The death and carnage all around threw them into a mating rage. Ori licked the warm crimson from his neck as their moment of passion commenced on the now slick floor.

The masses of flesh quivered and contorted around them. This now red room looked like the village slaughterhouse. When everything had finished only the eight of them remained. One unfortunate soul did not survive the transformation but his sacrifice was not in vane. They consumed him as a snack without a second thought.

"Welcome my brothers and sisters, embrace your queen's gift as she welcomes you to her fold!" Ori spoke with such conviction and allegiance to her queen that nobody would have guessed just a short time ago she tried to kill her. The lycan venom induced complete obedience to its creator.

Raksha walked to a door on the western wall and grabbed the handle. She looked back at the group. "Come, let us get cleaned and dressed so we may discuss what needs to be done for the queen's arrival." With a click she pushed the door open and walked inside. The small quaint exterior of the house disguised the massive underground network the brotherhood had built. Exits and escape routes by the dozen were connected to various locations around the city allowing their movements and plotting to remain concealed from magical and nonmagical entities.

The small group gathered around a black oval table in one of the underground rooms. Vermillion, while waiting inspected a bookshelf in one section of the room. It contained all manner of literature on how to kill, maim, and torture in the most effective ways. Next to those were volume upon volume of books about herbs, poisons, and salves. The archer's brow raised as he fingered various tomes. "I never realized how much one needed to know in order to be an assassin. The level of knowledge about the human body bordered on that of a healer or shaman." Coming back over to the table, Vermillion caught the werewolves up on important aspects of their new condition, regarding their heightened strength and senses as well as their ability to spread the lycan infection. The most important of all being that silver could end their immortality for good. In fact one of their key tasks would be to have as much of the substance collected and disposed of as possible.

Raksha spoke up. "The brotherhoods far reaching connections throughout this massive city will prove extremely useful in accomplishing this task. We can start gathering immediately."

Ori just now walked into the room while fastening the last button on her black tunic. "Above all we must keep our infiltration secret as we always have. Queen Arain's brother has just arrived with King Elrick and a enormous military force. They are here to stop the queen and all of her minions from conquering the world. Make no mistake her brother Lucious has the same powers and could easily destroy us. That means nobody can know werewolves are already here! Myself and Vermillion will handle lycan recruitment while everyone else works on gathering silver. Do not reveal your beast side to anyone outside of this room! Now if there are no further questions let's get started." The six pushed back from the table and headed out of the room in multiple directions. Each one heading to meet up with their connections throughout the city.

CHAPTER THIRTY-EIGHT

THE MEETING

"**M**r. Drake, are you in there sir?" came a young man's voice from outside the tent. Lucious, Morgan, and Stormy had all fallen asleep while they waited for the meeting with the council of elders. "Mr. Drake, King Elrick sent me to request your presence in his tent."

The flap on the tent flung open revealing a shirtless and exhausted Lucious. "Alright, let Elrick know we'll be there in a few minutes please," he requested while wiping the crusty junk from the corners of his eyes.

"Will do Mr. Drake," replied the young soldier before leaving.

Looking back at Morgan lying across the comfortable bed with Stormy curled up beside her, made him wish for just a little more time to sleep. "Morgan it's time, we're to head over to Elrick's immediately."

She just groaned and moaned in protest at the request. "Does King Elrick ever sleep?" Morgan questioned as she sat upright facing Lucious. Stormy barely moved through all the commotion. The Draconian gently scratched his belly. "If I have to get up, so do you fuzzy!"

Lucious pulled on a clean tunic and then sat down at the table to put his boots on. "I know we're all beat but the meeting with the council is the single most important thing we need to do right now. I promise there will be time to sleep afterward."

His speech did little to console his companions. Morgan being the next one out of bed walked over to the table where a mirror and brush rested. In no time she had tamed her wild hair which now laid sleek and straight down her neck. Last thing she donned was her weapons belt which she cinched down tightly. "All set, are you ready Lucious?"

He walked up close to her. "I'm as ready as I can be. I just hope they don't throw us into any more dungeons." Morgan let out a little laugh at his joke before giving him a kiss. Lucious exited the tent leading the way with his two companions following. As to be expected, the camp bustled with soldiers in all directions, performing all manner of tasks. It would all be temporary until preparations are complete to welcome such a large force into the safety of the city.

The moons were already heading downward for the horizon signaling morning to be on its way. Just ahead of them stood Elrick exiting his barracks with a group of his officers in tow. Upon seeing them, Elrick smiled and waved them over. The king gave Lucious and Morgan each a welcoming hug. "It's good to see you three, I hope you had enough time to eat and get cleaned."

Both nodded that the amount of time had been sufficient. "We're ready to go when you are Elrick," declared Lucious as he put his hand on the small of Morgan's back protectively.

Elrick took a deep breathe and exhaled. "Here we go," as he turned towards the city and headed off to the council hall. His pace as usual remained brisk. "I'm amazed every time I come here Lucious. This city is the birth place of so many different things we take for granted every day.

Magic, engineering, alchemy, and so much more is studied, perfected, and taught within these walls. You could spend the rest of your days here and never run out of new things to learn."

Morgan and Lucious' heads swiveled about trying to take the enormity of it all in. The Draconian asked the first question. "Is this city in your kingdom, Elrick?"

He shook his head. "Not entirely, you see when Malik was defeated at the conclusion of the King Wars I used this city as a gesture of peace. It allows everyone from anywhere to come and learn or share their knowledge. This city sits on neutral land that isn't owned by any one person. That is why we're here to ask for their help instead of demanding it. His reasoning and logic for doing what he did with this city is quite smart they thought. Advancements can be achieved much faster when everyone can work together.

Their walk brought them to the base of one of the many massive white spires. Looking all the way to the top really gave the companions a proper perspective of just how huge these towers are. A young man in gray robes walked out from the doors at its base to greet them. The man bowed and introduced himself. "My name is Oleg Streep and I'm one of the apprentices here. I will be taking you all up to the high council hall if you'd be so kind and follow me."

Morgan could see the surprise on Oleg's face when he noticed her. *I hope there won't be any issues here.* Oleg ushered everyone onto the platform and up they went to the up-permost floor. Looking around made it clear that this form of transportation didn't sit well with everyone. Stormy leapt into Morgan's arms so fast it even startled her, and one of the king's officers looked a bit green as he tried to hold the vomit back. Oleg however didn't miss a beat, off the platform and through the doors to the high council room he walked. "Here we are King Elrick, it looks like the elders are all here. I will be waiting outside the doors when you're finished." Without wasting time Oleg exited the room closing the doors behind him.

Before them stood the most beautiful white marble room with a large table at its center. Around the table were seated the elders, a group of older men and women who were the pinnacle of their craft. One of the women stood from the table. She had long peppered hair and she wore bright red robes. "Welcome everyone, we have been anxiously awaiting your arrival, please feel free to take a seat at the table." Elrick and his companions found their places and sat down.

Morgan and Lucious were among the last to be seated which allowed them to clearly hear some of the gasps. Lucious pulled out her chair and gestured for Morgan to sit. He looked into her eyes. "Never mind them, it's your beauty that makes them do that." His support made her feel better. Lucious sat beside her holding her hand in his.

One of the oldest looking gentlemen stood now that everyone was seated. He wore dark green silk robes with silver stitching that matched the color of his beard. "Welcome everyone and good morning. Most of you know me but for those of you that don't, my name is Bishop Alder, and I am one of the high council patrons. We are called here today to discuss the threat to the west. King Elrick of Westlin and his companions have traveled here in hopes to help defend the city. I personally received your sealed letter from the messenger, Sebastian whom arrived just a few days earlier. Preparations to defend the City of Knowledge have been under way since then. I will now turn the meeting over to you, King Elrick." Bishop gestured to him and then sat back down.

Elrick pushed his chair back and stood up to address the council. "Thank you all for joining this most important of meetings. We are all facing a wave of evil that threatens to wash humanity from the face of this planet. A woman by the name Arain Drake leads an army of nightmares to this city as we speak, and nothing has even slowed her progress. King Malik and castle Kragg have fallen!" Shocked gasps broke out among the elders who evidently did not hear this latest news. Panning around the table Elrick continued. "From all the information we have gathered, Arain is nothing short of a god. She can create life through sheer will, and she has yet to be permanently killed. Her magical ability rivals that of anyone here."

A woman with brown hair and glasses questioned the king. "If this woman is so powerful, how do you suggest we beat her?"

Elrick looked over and pointed to Lucious. "We beat her with him!" Silence fell upon the room as the council stared at this somewhat unremarkable looking young man. "This is Lucious Drake, Arain's twin brother, and my friend. He possesses the same godly abilities as his sister and has created new life as well. Right now emissaries are bringing his armies to aid us."

"What kind of armies are we talking about," came another question from across the table.

The king looked to Morgan. "An army of warriors like her... Ladies and gentlemen I would like to introduce to you the lovely Draconian, Morgan Hunter." With an outstretched hand, Elrick motioned for her to stand.

Nervously she stood in front of everyone. She could almost feel their eyes analyzing every inch of her flesh. Morgan bowed to the council. "The Draconian people will aid you in this fight against the approaching evil. Our creator will not fight alone." Morgan again took her seat.

Lucious thought the shock of Morgan may have killed some of these elderly council members. Jaws hung wide open in awe at this new sentient species, and it took a few minutes before anyone spoke. Lucious now stood. "Council I know this is a lot to take in, but you better adjust quickly because my sister is bringing horrible beasts that will not hesitate to kill each and every person in this city. They will not stop, they will not show mercy." Lucious hated having to be so cold but he knew they didn't have the luxury of time. Arain would be there in a few days at most. He took his seat, again holding Morgan's hand in his for all to see.

The mood in the room changed as if someone had flipped a switch. All of the gawking looks were gone, replaced with stern faces of determination. One of the council cast a spell in the center of the table that made a giant floating render of the entire city. With a swipe of his finger the image could be turned any way they wanted. The next six hours were spent in a tactical deliberation the likes of which Lucious and Morgan had never seen. Ideas came from every person at the table, and nobody stayed quiet for long. Every detail they approved instantly appeared on the cityscape floating in front of them. A few minutes later an apprentice would be given a parchment with instructions on how to begin and complete each phase. Each page had a list of names and their required task listed on it. In an almost constant stream these young acolytes would show up only to disappear again once they received their parchment.

Elrick leaned over to Lucious. "What an amazing system they have, isn't it?"

"Indeed it is, and so efficient. For the first time in awhile, I feel like we're prepared to take on my sister!"

CHAPTER THIRTY-NINE

FRAYING AT THE SEAMS

S ebastian sat in the chair next to a woman lying in bed, barely recognizable as Seline. Her black streaked hand now gently held in his. The mighty Uluck sat on the opposing side with his head hung low in defeat. They both knew it wouldn't be long now until their companion was dead. Healer Fennil entered the room to administer another dose of salmisine for the pain. All they could do now was ease their friend's pain.

Sebastian looked up at Fennil. "Thank you so much for all your help. I'm sure Seline would thank you if she could."

Fennil shook his head slightly up and down a couple times. "The amputation was too late, just too damn late." He stood there for a moment looking down at the once vibrant woman now streaked from the black poison coursing through her veins. "I'll be back later to give her another dose." Fennil placed his hand on Uluck's shoulder. "I'm sorry," is all he said before leaving to attend to his other patients.

Using a damp cloth, Sebastian wiped the perspirations from Seline's forehead. Her body still waged a war on the invading death even though in the end it would be for naught.

In a voice just above a whisper, Sebastian spoke to her. "We're here for you Seline, and we will not leave you alone." The messenger kissed her gently on the head before placing the cloth back into its bowl. "Uluck, I need to go get some fresh air can you stay with her for a few minutes?"

Uluck raised his head. "I'm not going anywhere my friend, take as long as you need."

Sebastian gave a nod and headed for the hospital exit, and the open air of the city streets. The magic of the cities grandeur had all but faded when Seline's condition relapsed a day ago. Not leaving the hospital for so long, he completely missed the arrival of King Elrick. My mission has been complete for days now. I should really check in with his majesty for further orders, but I just can't leave Seline right now. A battle brewed in his head over what he should do. His heart knew the right thing would be to stay with Seline even though he had a duty to the king. The conflict made his stomach knot as tears welled up in his eyes. "Life used to be so easy just a few weeks ago. I hadn't a care in the world besides myself and my job." He wiped the tears and snot away when through the crowd he could see Elrick approaching. His heart sank, the decision it seems would be made for him in just a moment.

Elrick's face lit up when he saw Sebastian standing outside the hospital. Arm's spread wide the king embraced the messenger with a bone cracking hug. "Sebastian, it's so good to see you. I knew you were the right person for such an important task." The two separated, and now the king could see the his subject looked distressed. "What's wrong lad, you look awful. Are you sick?"

"No, I'm fine your grace, and thank you for your praise. It's just that one of the soldier's you sent to aid me is in here on her death bed right now."

Elrick placed his hands on Sebastian's shoulders. "Is there nothing that can be done for Seline?"

With so many under his command, it amazed him that the king could remember every one of their names. "No your grace, the hell hounds venom is fatal."

The king cocked his head to the side at the messenger's response. "Hell hound? Do you mean Arain Drake's Morlock's?"

"Yes, I believe that's what they were."

Elrick stepped back. "It just so happens that I have brought Arain's twin brother with me. If anyone has a chance of helping her it will be him." The king turned to the small group of the men accompanying him. "I need all of you to go find Lucious Drake and bring him here immediately! Tell him it's a matter of life and death! Now go!" His soldiers dispersed, heading towards the most likely places he would be. "Sebastian, would you be so kind and take me to see Seline?"

"Certainly your grace, follow me." Back into the hospital they went. Even though the city resided on it's own land the citizens still showed their respect when addressing him. "Welcome King Elrick," and a few bows were exchanged between the hospital staff and his majesty. Sebastian paused outside the door to Seline's room to prepare himself once more. "I must warn you your grace, her condition is severe."

Elrick gave the nod to proceed. Sebastian opened the door, and let the king in. "Oh my dear, what have they done to you?" Elrick felt his heart drop, weighed down with so much sadness. He walked into the room and went straight to Seline's bedside and sat down.

Uluck, unaware of the king's arrival leapt to his feet to greet him properly. "It's alright Uluck there's no need for formalities in here. Please sit and act as if I'm just a regular person." Elrick could see the clearly haggard look on the brother's face. A look that only the lack of sleep and crying can cause. "I'm so very sorry for Seline's current condition, Uluck." The king took up the task of holding her hand so she would know somebody is there. "How long has she been unresponsive?"

"Since yesterday, your grace. She went to sleep and never regained consciousness," informed Sebastian.

The three of them sat with her and waited in silence.

Lucious, Morgan, and Stormy had decided to explore the city a bit after the council meeting had concluded. It would have been impossible to sleep after such an intense planning session anyway. Just a few streets away from the hospital they walked, enjoying the sites and smells of the city. Vendors and shops of all kinds were open peddling their wares. One in particular caught Stormy's attention. The sign out front read, Peony's Pastries, and the smell coming from its open doors made all their mouths water. They both looked at each other and then down at Stormy. "We better check this place out," commanded Morgan. With authority they entered the bakery.

In front of them were six clear glass cases filled with the most delicious looking baked goods. Pastries and desserts of all kinds just begging to be eaten. Stormy's little nose twitched frantically as he pressed it against the glass. A rather plump fellow broke their concentration when he spoke from behind the counter. "How may I help you folks?"

It felt like they were hypnotized and somebody just broke the trance. Lucious wiped the drool from the corners of his mouth. "Everything smells wonderful in here, what do you suggest we try first sir?"

The baker pulled out a parchment like bag and proceeded to fill it with a couple things from each case. He handed the bulging sack over to Lucious. "That's what I like to call the sampler, it gives a good mix of the delicacies we make here. That will be one silver even."

Lucious gladly reached into his pouch, and produced a shiny silver coin. "Here you go. Thank you so much for the food, we can't wait to dig in!" Morgan now starving rushed Lucious out of the store so they could eat. Like ravenous buzzards the three went to work sampling the contents of the sack. Thirty minutes later and everything was gone. The sweetness overload made them all a bit sick feeling but the overall consensus was that it was so worth it. "I don't think I have ever tasted food that good, ever."

Morgan walking with a hand on her stomach agreed. "Amazing, that's all I have to say." They walked hand in hand a ways further down the street as they continued exploring. The mood in the city had changed just in the few hours since the council meeting. More and more Westlin soldiers could be seen inside the city walls as preparations on different phases of their defense were under way. At the same time, visitors by the hundreds were leaving to head east, away from the fighting. In fact a large number of the populace were scholars with no useable skills on the battlefield. Instead of becoming casualties or slaves, many decided to leave as well.

Lucious stopped and looked around. "I suppose we should go get some sleep while we can. There will be plenty of work for us to do later."

"You're right, and after eating all that food I'm ready for a long nap." Morgan let out a yawn. "We should head over to the main thoroughfare, and then go south. That should take us back to the tent." Lucious followed her lead with Stormy in the middle. The three of them worked their way through the thinning crowds and back to the encampment. Sleep being the only thought on any of their minds.

That's odd, thought Lucious when he saw one of Elrick's soldiers standing outside the tent's entrance. "Is there something you need soldier?"

The person bowed his head before speaking. "I have an urgent message from King Elrick to Lucious Drake. Your assistance is needed immediately at the city hospital. It's a matter of life and death."

Lucious' adrenaline started to flow, waking him instantly. "Is the king injured?!"

"No Sir Lucious, his need is for someone else but I know not who."

"Morgan, you and Stormy stay here and get some rest, and I'll be back as soon as I can."

She quickly kissed him. "Good luck, I hope you can help whoever it is."

Lucious gave his skeleton warriors the command to guard Morgan before he raced off towards the hospital. He burst through the front doors sweating and breathing heavily as he approached the front attendants. "I'm her to see King Elrick!"

One of the women came from behind the long counter, "Follow me this way, sir." Off the two walked down the hall and to the right. She stopped outside of the room. "King Elrick is inside."

Without a moment to lose, he opened the door and walked inside. What he saw startled him. There were the three men and one very sick looking woman. "Elrick what's going on, are you alright?"

The king nodded his head. "I'm fine Lucious, I requested you for her." Going around the room Elrick introduced Sebastian, Uluck, and Seline to him along with the sad tale of her current condition. "I believe she was bitten by a Morlock a few days past, and now the monsters venom is killing her. The healers have gone to great lengths to stop it but to no avail." Elrick motioned towards the missing leg. "Her only and last hope is with you Lucious." The king kissed the back of Seline's hand before standing to face him. "All I ask is for you to try Lucious, please." Elrick said nothing more and left the room.

Uluck kissed Seline on the forehead before standing to shake Lucious' hand. "Thank you for anything you can do to help my sister." He took his leave next following the way Elrick had gone.

Sebastian just sat there beside her holding her now almost completely black hand. "If it's alright with you, I'd like to stay with her."

Lucious nodded. "By all means stay with her as long as you wish, Sebastian." Sitting down in the free chair Lucious could feel the enormous weight the three men had heaped on him. *I honestly don't know where to begin,* he thought anxiously to himself. I've just begun learning to use these powers to create new life, who knows if they'll work to save someone that already exists. Taking a moment to compose himself and clear his mind before rolling up his sleeves. Standing up, he reached down and removed the black stained sheet that covered her. The sight and smell almost made him spew his recently eaten pastries. A hand went instinctively to his mouth and nose to try and block some of the stench. Despair and doubt crept in a bit further as he looked down at the horror.

Come on Lucious, you have to do something! The voice screamed in his mind. He knew that until he calmed the chaos inside his head he would be useless. Looking over to Sebastian and then back to Seline, he felt like the answer laid in front of him but he just couldn't see it. That is until he closed his eyes and thought of Morgan. Suddenly he didn't feel so lost. His mind cleared as his doubt's faded away to nothing. *Morgan is my clarity,* he repeated to himself. Slowly he opened his eyes and focused on Seline. His crown of runes blazed to life with the intensity of the sun. Sebastian fell off his chair as he tried to shield his eyes from the light. The door of the room burst outward releasing some of the illumination into the hallway. Lucious placed his hands upon Seline's motionless body. The energy he now produced made her body shake and contort.

No matter how hard he tried, Sebastian couldn't see anything other than the searing white light that flowed from Lucious.

Lucious continued using Morgan as his center while trying to focus everything on saving Seline. "You still have so much good to do in this world, now is not your TIME!!" Immediately the surge of power in the room ran fractures up the walls, and then just like a switch, the room went dark.

Elrick and Uluck tried to enter the room but were met by Sebastian stumbling out coughing. His hair now singed and his clothes steamed like it does when taking a nice hot bath. He collapsed to his knees. "I need water, please water."

One of the apprentice healers who came by to see what all the commotion was about, quickly ran down the hall for help. Now more than half of the hospital personnel stood outside Seline's destroyed room. The apprentice healer returned with a pitcher of water and a metal cup. "Here you are mister," handing over a full cup to Sebastian. The messenger grabbed it and drank the contents violently. Repeatedly the apprentice filled the cup and just as quickly he emptied it.

Elrick knelt down. "Sebastian, are you alright?"

He stopped just long enough to catch his breath. "Hot, so very, very hot."

Uluck stared into the dark room unable to see anything. "Lucious, Seline, are you alright?"

Lucious stumbled through the doorway soaked in sweat from the exertion. He didn't talk. He didn't stop. He just walked past everyone heading towards the hospital exit. *Elrick, Uluck, Sebastian, their all here with there mouths moving but I can't hear anything. I just need to get back to Morgan, and everything will be alright.* That's all he kept telling himself as he stumbled like a drunk to the entrance.

"Uluck, stay here with Sebastian, I need to go make sure Lucious is alright." As soon as he stood up, a concentrated beam of light hit him smack in the face. Reflexively Elrick's arm went up to block it. With clear vision still left in one eye he could see the light came from inside the room. The small crowd that now amassed went silent as everyone waited for whatever would come next.

"Seline, is that you?" called out her brother. More shards of light now sprang forth from inside the room. A clank sound followed each new beam of light. It sounded like ceramic hitting the floor. "I think it best if we all backed up now," warned Uluck as he helped Sebastian to his feet. Faster and faster came the new streaks of light and the clanking sound until a deafening pop sent shards of some rocklike substance shooting out the door like shrapnel. All in attendance shielded themselves from the blast. Slowly Uluck lowered his hands, and what he saw made his jaw hang. In the doorway stood a woman in a regal white hooded cloak with gold symbols adorning it. At first it looked like a human face but as Uluck stepped closer he could see it was a beautifully crafted mask. The eyeholes radiated that same white light they were all just witness to a few short moments ago.

A familiar voice cut through the silence. "Hello brother." It sounded like Seline but just a bit different. The woman in front of Uluck stood a bit taller and a bit wider than he remembered his sister being as well.

The massive warrior stepped cautiously forward. "Why do you wear the mask, sister?"

She stepped out of the doorway and stood directly in front of Uluck. "I wear this garb and mask for your protection. Just as one would not gaze upon the sun directly, neither should you look at me. I am not human anymore brother. I retained a similar shape, and have memories of my human self but I also have new memories of my people. The Seraphim."

In all of the commotion, Elrick had momentarily forgotten about Lucious. "Dammit, I'm going to find Lucious. Fennil come with me in case he needs aid." The two of them rushed around the corner and down the hallway towards the entrance. As they exited the building, they could see Lucious along with every person on the street looking skyward. "What is it now?" Elrick and Fennil looked in the same direction. What they witnessed defied anything in their wildest imaginations. An enormous island hung in mid air just a short distance from the city.

Lucious stood wobbly with streams of blood running from his mouth, nose, and ears. Unable to support his own weight, he fell down to his knees as he desperately fought to stay conscience. Elrick and Fennil rushed into the street to aid him. Carefully each grabbed an arm and picked him up. "Take me to Morgan please," being his only request.

Fennil wanted to just take him back into the hospital but Elrick knew better. "No, we need to get him to her as soon as possible."

"Alright, let me at least go and get a stretcher and someone a bit stronger." Off the healer ran back into the hospital. He came back out with a stretcher and Uluck. "Here we go, lets put it out like this, now lay him gently down the middle." Elrick and Uluck did as instructed.

"I think we have it from here Fennil, thank you so very much for you help," thanked the king. With ease the two picked up the stretcher with Lucious on top, and started walking for the tents just outside the city walls. Many soldiers tried relieving the king but he would have nobody take his place. Elrick always tried to set a good example for his soldiers to follow rather than hide behind his royalty.

Just as they reached the southern gates, a strange but somewhat familiar sound could be heard. Lucious pointed to the horizon. "Piercer," was the last word he said before he succumbed to his exhaustion and passed out.

There came the sound again but just a bit louder this time. Elrick and Uluck looked skyward and could see what looked like a giant bird coming towards the city. The king smiled, "Yes!" he shouted with excitement. Uluck you are in for a treat, soon you're going to meet a gryphon and a Draconian! Come, let's get Lucious tended to." Elrick now walked double time as the sight of Piercer invigorated him.

Weaving through the tent labyrinth they arrived outside Lucious' barracks. The skeleton warriors drew their swords and blocked the entrance. "We better set him down here Uluck while I get Morgan to call off her guardians." Uluck looked on in disbelief at the animated bones in front of him. This day would surly be remembered as the craziest day he had ever had. Elrick walked over to the entrance just shy of the skeletons swords. "Morgan, I have Lucious here, we need to get him inside. Can you call off your guardians please?"

The flap burst open as Morgan raced outside nearly knocking over her protectors. "I'm safe, go back to your posts," she commanded. Sheathing their swords, both skeletons stepped aside for her to pass. With unreal speed Morgan went to Lucious' side and picked him up before either of the men could offer assistance. Inside she took him and laid him on the bed. From the mass of old blood streaked down his face and tunic she could tell he had used his power, and a lot of it. Systematically she placed an ear to his chest to confirm his heart beat nice and strong. Then opening his mouth she made sure there wasn't any blood to choke on. Satisfied she looked over to the two men standing there. "What happened? I've only ever seen him this bad when he created Veassels and Gryphons on the same day."

Uluck stepped forward. "I think it's because he created something more powerful than both of them. Outside and just off in the distance a massive island floats that shouldn't be there. He also saved my sister, but she's no longer human. She called herself a Seraphim."

Morgan stood up from the bed and walked over to Elrick and Uluck. "Thank you so very much for bringing him to me, I can take it from here. He is going to need a lot of rest, I just hope he recovers in time to help defend the city."

Elrick nodded in agreement. "You let me know if you need anything, anything at all. I will have someone stationed outside day and night. All you need to do is call out your request."

"Thank you for that your grace, but right now I think I have everything I need. I will let you know if there's a change in his condition." Uluck and the king departed with a smile. Morgan however went straight to work caring for Lucious. She placed a kettle full of water over the fire before heading over to the dresser for some wash cloths. Without a second thought she stripped Lucious down to nothing. Using the wash cloths and hot water she went about the task of getting him clean. Gently and carefully she cleansed every inch of his body. Lastly Morgan put him under the blankets, and fluffed up a pillow for his head. He looked eerie lying there not moving and barely breathing. She sat next to him on the bed and cried for just a moment. "Seeing you like this makes my heart ache Lucious. Please come back to me quickly." Stormy had already laid claim to the other side of his creator where he curled into a ball with his head resting on Lucious' chest. Morgan even more exhausted now laid down beside Lucious, and held him until she fell asleep.

CHAPTER FORTY

LOSS AND REBIRTH

O ff just a little ways in the distance, Ulandra and Piercer floated up high on the wind currents. It was another beautiful day as the City of Knowledge came into view in front of them. Ulandra leaned forward in the saddle to be closer to the gryphon's ears. "Look Piercer there it is, we made it. I can't wait to see our friends." Excited, he let out the loudest call she had heard yet. Sitting back in the saddle her stress just melted away, they would make it to the city in time. A smile wider than any before was permanently displayed on her face. They flew closer and closer with every minute that passed. *Even at this distance the city looks massive. I wonder how long it took to build this place?*

Ulandra started getting impatient, it seemed like they had been approaching the city for hours now yet still weren't there. "Come on Piercer, I can't wait much longer!" Her slight whining didn't make things go any faster however. All she could do was wait, and wait, and wait. Finally the tent camp and people on the ground came into view. The expert craftsmanship of the city towers and walls could now be seen and enjoyed as well.

Once they reached high over the city, Ulandra gave a tug on the reins to land. Piercer followed her direction and began flying downward in slow wide circles. Landing this way took longer but it kept her from becoming sick. They flew low enough now that Ulandra could see King Elrick standing there waving at them from the ground. They reached the height of the spires when something went terribly wrong. Searing, burning pain shot through her abdomen the likes of which she had never felt before. "What..." is the only word she got out before spewing blood all over the back of the gryphon's mane. *I can't breathe.... I can't see....* Everything went black as she slumped forward and slid off the saddle.

Elrick and the crowd of onlookers watched in horror as Ulandra plummeted three hundred feet to the ground. "Nooo...." Elrick screamed as he ran in vane to catch her. THUD... echoed when her body slammed into the ground breaking most of the bones. Elrick reached her seconds later. "No Ulandra, no," the king wailed. He knew from how mangled she looked that the impact had killed her. It didn't matter, he would try anyways. Elrick scooped her up in his arms. He burst into tears when her body felt more like a sack of meat than a person. The majority of her skeletal structure in her torso had failed making her body bend in disturbing ways. The crowd parted as the king headed for the hospital. Trails of blood dripped onto the stone road with every step, leaving a macabre scene behind him. His boots felt like lead as time seemed to slow to a crawl. Elrick's muscles burned from the weight of his Draconian friend but he would not stop until he reached the hospital.

Out front the healers and attendants rushed a floating gurney over to the king. "It's alright, place her down here and we'll take care of her," came the comforting voice of Fennil. Gently as laying a baby in it's cradle, Elrick put Ulandra onto the table. Immediately they rushed her into the hospital and vanished. The king just stood there blood soaked and weeping in the street. It wasn't until one of his officers spun him around and pointed up to one of the spires.

Piercer attacked the highest point with an unimaginable fury. Large white marble blocks came crashing down on the streets below as the gryphon desperately tried to reach Ulandra's attacker. An arrow narrowly missed him and sailed down landing in front of Elrick. Rage boiled up inside the king, "Lock down that tower and find me the bastard that killed my friend!!" The onlookers dispersed rather quickly as the situation escalated. A battalion of soldiers surrounded the spire while another group disappeared inside. Piercer finally stopped his rampage and flew down next to Elrick. Blood soaked his once beautiful feathers on his mane. His side and claws had multiple cuts either from the attacker or the sharp stone. Elrick examined the distressed animal but could not find any life threatening injuries. After he calmed down, the king felt comfortable to approach the gryphon. "It's alright my friend, it's alright. Whoever that coward is they won't make it out of that tower alive." With extreme care he stroked Piercer's beak and head, trying to comfort the animal.

Seline and Uluck ran over to offer aid. The gryphon started getting agitated as they approached. Elrick held out his hand motioning them to stop. "I think introductions at this moment would be unwise," said the king as he continued stroking the creatures head.

The Seraphim ignored his warning and stepped beside Piercer. Seline removed her left glove, revealing a hand made of white light. "It's going to be fine," she assured him as she placed her hand on the side of his neck. Piercer shuttered for a moment like he had been chilled. Seline's hand blazed brighter, making his wounds heal. Right in front of everyone the lacerations disappeared. Clink, came the sound as an arrow fell to the ground from the belly of the griffon. Elrick and Uluck looked at the arrow wondering where it came from. "That arrow was lodged deep in his abdomen, and may have killed him," Seline informed them. "There, our friend is completely healed now." She removed her hand from his side and put the glove back on.

Elrick seeing her extraordinary healing powers wondered if she could heal Ulandra. "Seline can you please try and heal our other friend in the hospital?" he asked in desperation.

"I am truly sorry your majesty, while my gifts are powerful, they cannot resurrect a being once they have died."

The king hung his head as the grief washed over him. "It is a sad day indeed." Elrick looked back at the tower when a man screamed, while falling to his death from one of the many windows of the spire. A moment later a dead soldier came crashing down on top of the first. "It seems our assassin isn't going to surrender. Very well, I'm up for a good hunt. Seline, Uluck you two stay down here with Piercer and back up my soldiers. I'm going to deal with that murderer." Walking to the entrance, Elrick unsheathed his sword and went into the spire.

Methodically he went room to room working his way upward. He moved incredibly quiet for such a large man as he stalked his prey. A man's scream rang out for just a moment before being silenced. *Must be another one of my soldiers*. The scream at least gave him an idea of how much higher the assailant resided. Elrick skipped the next two floors entirely before continuing the search. Papers and debris were scattered around on the floor, along with little droplets of blood leading off to another room. *It could be a trap,* but continued to follow the droplets anyway. They brought him to a room with at least a hundred bookshelves full of scrolls. Elrick stopped when he saw where the blood trail ended some twenty feet away. One of his troops laid face down in a growing pool of his own blood. The hairs on the nape of his neck stood on end. *Something is about to happen,* nagged the voice in his head. His sword held defensively as he continued onward. The twang of a bowstring is the only warning he had to evade, causing the arrow to miss its mark, hitting his left arm instead. Blood trickled down his arm staining his white tunic. The arrow cut the outside of his bicep missing the bone completely. "Come on out and fight me up close, if you dare!" taunted the king. His eyes feverishly searching the room high and low for his attacker.

A woman's voice came from the shadows. "King Elrick, how arrogant to come in here all alone. My queen will be so pleased when I dispose of you."

Elrick kept his back to one of the scroll shelves while he tried to pinpoint the origin of the voice. His left arm started to tingle from the cut.

"Ha, ha, ha, ha, ha," came the voice again. "I can see you're starting to feel the poison in your arm, foolish king."

"Only cowards use poisons to beat their opponents, girl!"

"Ha, ha, ha, you will be dead soon anyways, I might as well have some fun."

From the other end of the giant room, a petite figure draped entirely in black emerged from the shadows. She removed her quiver and leaned it against the wall with her bow before walking over to Elrick. "Are you prepared to die, king?"

Hoping to catch her off guard, he lunged at her with a downward slice of his blade. Ching! echoed in the quiet room, and sparks flew when she crossed her two short swords to parry his strike. With substantial force, the king pushed his blade forward but the assassin gave no ground.

"Nice try king of idiots, but you have no chance here. I am death and her name is Ori!" She moved to the side and sliced the king's leg with one of her swords.

Elrick winced, his leg hurt and his left arm now hung almost completely useless. He agreed, how stupid he felt now coming in alone. Again he pressed forward offering up slashes from multiple angles, only to have each and every one of them blocked or dodged. Their exchanges continued on one sided, with Elrick receiving all of the injuries. He stood in front of her bloodied and breathing heavily. If I don't turn this around soon I'm done for. I must use my sacred sword technique. Elrick slowed his breathing and focused on activating his magical skill.

Ori bounced up and down like an excited school girl. "Ooooh, someone is going to use a special technique!"

The king's sword burst into bright red flames as he charged one last time. Up over his head the mighty blade came down with all of his force. "Sundering blade!" yelled Elrick.

Ori simply stood there smiling. The flaming sword cut her clean in two before it smashed into the floor. Elrick stepped back not taking his eyes off of her. The smallest droplets of blood wept from the split, however she did not fall. "I don't understand, you should be dead!"

The assassin didn't move until her healing fused her back together. That big smile froze on her face. "My turn." Ori shifted to her werewolf form. Her special chain mail now cut in half from the technique used by the king. She wanted to eat him, leaving nothing left to be turned. With blinding speed she leapt into Elrick, slamming him into the wall with his arms pinned up by her massive clawed hands. Fight as he might, he couldn't come close to her strength. Ori opened wide revealing rows of jagged white teeth. Caught up in her frenzy to feed, Ori didn't notice the other person until the arrow slammed into her back. A heat hotter than the sun burned inside of her. Ori released Elrick as she frantically tried to reach back and remove the arrow, but Ori's muscles were too big in werewolf form to allow such a maneuver. Tearing open her chest she frantically tried to reach the silver tipped arrow head and remove it.

Ori might have actually saved herself if she had a bit more time before a blade severed her head from her body. Down the body slumped as it quivered and devolved to a smoking husk. The head still alive looked up at Talo who smiled back in return. "This is repayment for that poisonous kiss you bitch!" He drove his magical silver blade through her skull and into her brain. The blade sizzled when it contacted the lycan flesh until her head melted into a unrecognizable black blob. Talo picked up a piece of Ori's shredded black uniform and wiped his blade clean before sliding it back into its sheath. Elrick looked on in shock at what had just transpired. "King Elrick I presume, my name is Talo Gray and we have much to discuss." Helping the king up he aided him down and out of the spire where Seline waited. Just as before, she removed one of her gloves and placed her hand onto Elrick's flesh. Her light blazed as the poison squirted from his arm before the cut mended back together.

It didn't take long for the king to be rejuvenated. "Thank you Seline, I owe you my life."

She just gave him a nod while putting her glove back on. Talo and Elrick dismissed themselves and headed off to his tent to talk, while Seline and Uluck took Piercer to get unsaddled and cleaned. Never had any of them been witness to a day like today. A day with such magnificent rebirth and heartbreaking loss.

CHAPTER FORTY-ONE

DECOMPRESSION

A rain pulled her horse besides the young William Fid-dlemen. As soon as their eyes met that strange feeling returned in her stomach, and her mind went blank. Quick-ly she looked ahead at the procession in front of them. William's hands were shackled to the horse's reins and a cloth gag had been put in his mouth. Arain reached over with her dagger and cut his gag. "Sorry about that, we don't normally take prisoners so they weren't quite sure what to do with you. If I hadn't taken such drastic measures, you would most likely be dead right now. Basically I saved your life, which means you are indentured to me."

"What kind of craziness are you spouting? The only rea-son I was in danger was because of you! I owe you nothing, release me immediately!"

The soldiers responsible for guarding William backed away as he spoke. Nobody, not even Valin talked to Arain Drake this way. They were sure he would be dead before they made camp.

Arain kept her focus forward until she could figure out what magic this man possessed. "I know not how you are effecting me but be sure that I will find the reason and snuff it out!"

"HAH!" he burst out loudly so everyone nearby could hear. "I'm just a simple reagent farmer, not a mage, not a powerful sorcerer, just a plain old farmer! Why are you having so much trouble with the concept?"

One of her soldiers smacked William in the face with his gauntleted hand. "You address the queen properly, prisoner!"

Blood trickled from William's split lower lip. Arain incensed slit the soldier's throat without even a second thought. His body slumped over gurgling on the blood filling his lungs. "I apologize for that William, it is not my intention to harm you."

William sat up straight in his saddle and just watched the soldier's life fade away. "That seemed a little severe, don't you think Arain?"

The way he said her name gave her goosebumps. *What is it about him that weakens me so? I feel powerless in his presence.* Sitting up in her saddle Arain tried to regain her powerful demeanor, that made man and beast obey her but she failed miserably. William chuckled as he watched her. "You don't have to impress me your majesty, I'm just a nobody you can have thrown away when you're finished with me."

Arain scowled, "I'm not trying to impress you! I don't have to impress anybody! I'm a god!"

"Alright your god ship, I apologize for any disrespect."

She could feel her blood boil at his insolence. The urge to smite him almost overpowered her, but Arain calmed herself in time. "You are free to go William, however I cannot guarantee your safety once you leave." Arain snapped her fingers and his shackles popped open. "Well go on, get back to your farming." She conveyed disinterest, though she desperately wanted him to stay.

William removed the restraints and threw them on the ground. "I don't imagine I have anything left to go home to, and where else could I get such engaging conversation?" Arain relaxed upon hearing his response. "So where are we heading?"

"The City of Knowledge is our next destination if you must know." These two young adults talked for a good portion of the day, discussing a little bit of everything from childhoods to prophecies. They genuinely enjoyed each others company in a way that Arain had never experienced before. Sure she got to know some of her soldiers and generals quite well but never so personal.

Valin kept a close eye on the two of them. "Look at them Talia. This boy, a simple farmer has my daughter so distracted. I may need to make him disappear if this becomes a problem."

"Hahaha, Lord Valin I wouldn't worry about him. He's just a passing distraction that she'll probably outgrow by the time we reach the city. This boy possesses no wealth, no power, or magic. His good looks will only keep him safe for so long." Little did Talia know that Arain thought of her as just a distraction for Valin to grow tired of and discard.

Regardless, Arain finally had someone her own age that could care less about her abilities or power. Just someone to feel normal with. Timber however did not wish to share his master with William, and more than once he walked over and snarled at him. Arain simply scolded the wolf and off he would disappear again. Eventually the sunlight started to wane and the chore of camp setup had begun. One of Arain's personal guards confronted the couple. "If you're ready, I can take the prisoner and shackle him down for the night, your highness."

"No that's alright, he's not a prisoner anymore. He can leave whenever he wishes." The guard stood completely stunned at her almost kind orders. He just bowed and fell back to his guard position. The queen looked back at William. "You'll be safe as long as you stay close to me." Just then three ogres walked past them on their way to assist with camp erection.

William swallowed the knot now in his throat. "I think sticking with you is a wonderful idea. Lead the way, your majesty." She blushed when he referenced her like that but hid it by quickly turning away to look for her tent. It being the first one always set up made it easy to spot. With a light spur, her horse headed forward. William followed right behind.

Inside her tent the two maids worked quickly to have everything prepared for her. "Ladies we will need a cot, and some clothes for Mr. Fiddlemen here, he will be staying indefinitely." A bow and off one of them went to fetch the needed items. William, feel free to get yourself cleaned up, and if you need something don't hesitate to ask one of these two wonderful women. I have a council to attend and then I will be back." Arain left the farmer behind, and headed for a brief meeting with Valin and Seget.

The maid readied a warm bowl of water and some wash cloths for William at the far corner of the room where the tub and vanity were located. She went straight back to work preparing the room for the queen. William walked over to the vanity and started the chore of cleaning himself up. He wet one of the cloths and put it to his face. "That smells wonderful, what's in this water?"

"It's simply warm water infused with lemon and orange. The acid from the fruit really helps get you clean, and the smell is just a welcome bonus," conferred the chamber maid while setting the nightstand by the head of the bed.

By the time William had finished, the second maid had returned with the requested items. She set down the clean clothes on the chair at the vanity and went back to her work. "Thank you," replied William before getting dressed. As he buttoned the last button on his shirt Timber entered and jumped up on the bed where he always laid. *That is the biggest wolf I've ever seen.* They stared at each other while William walked over to sit at the dining table near the fire. Timber's eyes glinted in the fire light making him look even more menacing. *I can feel that wolf's stare, I feel like at any moment he's gonna kill me.*

Arain came back shortly after and had her armor removed. Straight into the bath she went and a blind stretched across the bathing area to keep the farmer for stealing a peek. "Are you hungry William?"

"Yes your majesty, quite famished actually. Should I go get us something to eat?"

"Hahahaha," giggled the queen. No need, I already requested dinner for both of us. Are the clothes satisfactory, and the bed?"

"Very comfortable your majesty. The cot is nicer than my bed at home. Thank you for your hospitality, your majesty."

Arain now finished with her bath, dressed in a black robe before coming out from behind the blind. "You're most welcome William, and please call me Arain when we're in my barracks." She walked over to the bed where she gave Timber a good scratch behind the ear, then carried on to sit in the second chair at the table.

"Forgive me if I'm being rude, but why am I here Arain?"

The queen sat back in her chair with her arms folded. She shook her head just slightly side to side. "I don't know yet

William. You intrigue me I guess." Outside the food bearer called for permission to enter. "Come in." The man distributed the food between the two table occupants before taking his place by the door. Arain leaned closer to William. "Let us just be two people having a meal while trying to get to know each other better."

William smiled and nodded. "That sounds reasonable." They ate and conversed like two normal young adults. Childhoods and embarrassing moments were shared with almost no talk about Arain's prophecy or conquest. William figured it best to leave those discussions for a much later time. Timber watched vigilantly, waiting for his master to tire of this intruder so he could eat him. To his disappointment, that time never came.

CHAPTER FORTY-TWO

ENEMIES WITHIN

Rain came down ice cold on the City of Knowledge as Elrick's soldiers continued moving their encampment inside the city walls. The move needed to be completed this morning so the next phase of the defensive could be started. Lucious, Morgan, and Stormy were the last to be moved. It's almost been one full day since he slipped into a coma, and Morgan knew it would likely be one, maybe two more days until he recovered.

The council had the empty homes and shops on the east side of the city converted into temporary barracks for the Draconian army that would be arriving by days end. Elrick and Talo spent the morning hours with the council going over all the new information he presented them with. Everything from the lycanthropes weakness to silver to the deep ones ability to burrow under the ground was shared. Talo for his aid with General Ori and his information on the enemy secured a place for himself as advisor and body guard to the king. A city wide call out for any and all silver was issued, and received only minimal response. The collection point at the council's spire has barely enough silver to make a few dozen swords at most. Elrick and Talo looked at the small pile of metal. "Talo, I can't believe that this is all the silver in this massive city, somethings not right."

"Your highness, I think our shortage is directly connected to the assassin, Ori. It makes perfect sense to send a handful of her lycans ahead of the main force to sabotage us from within. It certainly fits with what I've heard of her conquest up the west coast."

Elrick put a hand to his chin. "This isn't good, Talo. That means we have more of those werewolves lurking around, building Arain's forces from within our very own walls. You mentioned yesterday that this affliction can be spread easily and without limit, is that correct?"

"Yes your highness. General Hortus turned from simply being cut on the face."

"Alright, we need to get what we have converted to weapons right now. Talo, I want you to take a small group of soldiers and this silver to the blacksmiths. Have them forge what they can and equip your soldiers. Then we will have a city meeting and try to flush out our infiltrators."

"Consider it done, your highness. We will return as soon as we're equipped." Talo picked his ten soldiers, five men and five women. The orders were repeated, and the small company of soldiers with the almost empty cart of silver headed for the closest smithy.

King Elrick didn't need to be at the noon council meeting for a while yet. *I have a little bit of time, I suppose I should go pay my respects to Ulandra.* He had been dreading this task all morning, but he knew it is something that needed to be done. His eyes watered just thinking back to yesterday. He could still feel her broken body in his arms. A deep cleansing breath, and off he traveled to the hospital where her body lay. The hall leading to where Seline had been reborn now showed a closed for study and repairs sign. One of the front desk attendants ushered Elrick to follow her to the opposite hallway this time. She stopped about five doors down and opened it before heading back to the front desk. With his eyes lowered to the floor, the king entered the room. Slowly he looked up until he could see the wooden box wherein laid Ulandra. From the neck down she had been covered by a beautifully embroidered blanket with flowers on it. They had done an exemplary job repairing the damage to her head and face so at least the casket didn't need to be closed for viewing. Elrick stepped up to the side of the coffin where he placed his hands. Tears returned, however this time the king let them flow freely. "I'm so very sorry Ulandra, I thought the city to be safe and secure. Instead I motioned you into range for Ori to attack. I know it's little consolation but she never made it out of that spire alive. I will inform Morgan of your loss today and Lucious whenever he wakes. Rest now Ulandra and be at peace." Elrick stayed with her for a while longer in silence.

Ezra and the Draconian army drew ever closer to the city, they could see it now way off in the distance. Ezra rode exhausted as he spent much of the night awake waiting for his friends to return. *I just can't see Ulandra not returning if everything was alright. Something must have happened to them, I sure hope they're alright.*

Slade worried as well. *What if the people they were racing to help were the ones that shot them down. Maybe the humans had changed their minds about Draconian aid.* Slade fell back a bit to ride next to Ezra. "You look terrible my friend, would you like to lie down in one of the wagons for a while?"

Ezra simply smiled at the alpha Draconis. "No I will be just fine on my horse, been meaning to loose a few extra pounds anyways."

"Very well, I will leave you to it. We should reach the city before nightfall." With that, Slade went back to the lead of his army.

Morgan watched over Lucious intently. Nothing would threaten him while he slept. "Morgan it's Elrick, may I enter?"

Morgan brushed her hair back and did her best to do a last minute clean up of the tent. "Give me one moment." Elrick patiently waited outside for the signal to enter. "Alright you can come in," she yelled.

The skeleton guards acknowledged her acceptance and let the king pass unhindered. Inside he could plainly see Lucious, eyes closed and asleep. Then his gaze met Morgan and he felt fear well up in his soul. Elrick walked up to her clearly showing signs that something was seriously wrong.

"What is it, King Elrick? What troubles you so?" Morgan held his outstretched hands in hers. "You're scaring me, what happened?"

Elrick already felt like he could break down at any moment. "I'm afraid I have some terrible news to convey.

Yesterday Ulandra arrived with Piercer when she was attacked by one of Arain's lycanthropes. She was shot with an arrow that killed her before she hit the ground. I'm so very sorry for your loss Morgan, I know she was like a sister to you."

Morgan shook her head quickly side to side. "No, it can't be her. It must be one of the other Draconians. Ulandra's not dead!"

Elrick dropped his head. "I'm sorry, it is Ulandra. Her body is in the hospital for now until everyone has said their goodbyes. You should go and I'll sit here with Lucious."

Morgan sobbed while holding her face in her hands. *Why, Ulandra? Why did you have to leave me?* Elrick consoled her as best he could but nothing would bring her friend back. Morgan composed herself, wiping the tears away. "I'll be back in a little while," is all she said before heading over to the viewing.

The king pulled up a chair beside Lucious and took a seat. "Come back to us soon, we need you creator."

Lucious' tent grew silent as they waited for Morgan's return.

Morgan reached the hospital quickly, and was directed to the room where Ulandra lay. In she went, her heart shattered to a thousand pieces as she looked upon her friend. Ulandra's color had all but faded leaving just the morticians makeup to give her the look of being alive. Morgan stumbled over to the coffin and wrapped her arms around her friend. "Why Ulandra, why did you have to leave me at such a crucial moment?" Tears of sadness rained down uncontrollably from the grieving Draconian. "I hope you're in a better place where evil can never again touch you, and don't worry I will take care of Selim until you two are rejoined in the after life." Morgan stepped back from her friend. "We will never forget you and your sacrifice." Leaning forward, she kissed Ulandra's forehead one last time. "Goodbye my friend, my sister." Finished, Morgan found her way back to the tent with Lucious and Elrick. "Thank you for watching him, you can go now."

Elrick followed her wishes. "If there's anything you need Morgan, anything at all just let me know."

"Thank you King Elrick, all we need now is time for Lucious to recover, and thank you for doing everything you could for Ulandra."

Elrick never felt so useless in his life as he nodded back to her. "It's the least we could do for such a heroic woman." The king took his leave heading back to the spire of the council members, anything to get away from the latest fatality of the war. The king had almost forgotten how terrible it felt when people died supporting his cause. It felt as if he had ended the person's life with his own hands. Of course he knew this to be simplistic thinking but it did little to dull the pain he felt. For now he would wait for the silver weapons to be forged so they could start a widespread werewolf purge. It would be imperative that all enemy combatants be found before Arain Drake arrived.

Noon time drew closer, bringing with it the officers and council members. They filed into the spire heading for the top floor. Elrick went up with the last group and took his seat at the table. They discussed the status of defensive preparations throughout the city. Everyone in attendance had been put in charge of one or more aspects of their overall plan. One by one they went around the table giving updates on their progress. In all, everything looked like they were going to be ready before Arain arrived. The fact that their biggest weapon still laid unconscious caused the most worry. That is until Elrick brought up the infiltration they had just uncovered.

Elrick stood at the table while discussing the issue. "General Ori is the name of the female assassin that killed my friend Ulandra yesterday. She had once been King Malik's general until Arain had her killed and transformed into a lycanthrope. Ori was sent with an unconfirmed number of enemy troops to infiltrate the city and cripple us from within. We have already seen their efforts from the lack of silver in the city. As Talo Gray has demonstrated, silver is the only known thing that can permanently kill one of these creatures. No silver, no weapons, no fighting chance. Efforts to collect more will continue but for now I had all the silver we acquired turned into weapons. I suggest we arm a group with these weapons and then call a mandatory city meeting where we can test every single citizen and soldier for this affliction."

Around the table votes to move forward with this plan came quickly. As before, a group of apprentices were called in and given instructions on what to do. Everyone still in the city would know about the mandatory meeting at four o'clock in front of the southern gates.

The second biggest problem they had to contend with being the burrowing worms, the Deep Ones. One of the white robed mages by the name Phillip stood to discuss a possible solution. "After further research, one of my colleagues discovered a way to use a large Ethereum crystal to amplify our barrier sphere spell to encompass the entire city. A complete three hundred and sixty degrees of protection. We have three such crystals that we are combining into one as we speak. Once it's finished we can set it up in the center of the city and cast our spells."

Bishop Alder now stood. "Excellent work everyone, are there any further issues that need attention right now?" No one spoke up at the question. "Very good, we shall reconvene at ten tonight. By then our Draconian military should have arrived, and they'll need to be brought up to speed on everything." Everyone filed out of the council room and down to the streets below.

Elrick could see Talo and his troops waiting near the collection site. The king walked directly over to him. A quick look around and he could see the newly forged swords that resembled the one Talo possessed. "Good, now we can start the lycan hunt." Elrick laid out his plans to Talo and his soldiers. "A checkpoint will be setup so that three groups of three sword bearers and one coin handler will go through and test each individual. Anyone that fails will be dealt with on the spot. We will start with our own men and women first, then we will move onto the citizens of the city."

Executing the plan went smooth at first with none of King Elrick's troops failing to pass the test. The citizens were a bit more difficult as the elderly and children proved to be uncooperative at times. However all the citizens that showed up were tested and cleared. Elrick watched the whole of the proceedings. "Thank you everyone for enduring these proceedings, none of you have the affliction. Now we must ask you to stay here for the time being as we go house to house in search of those who did not come. Once an area is considered clear, you will be allowed to go back to your homes." By this time, the silver sword count had tripled due to a hidden stash found in one merchant's possession. Multiple groups led by a handful of brave civilians fanned out across the city. The residents were invaluable at pointing out all the spots that otherwise might be overlooked by the soldiers. Slowly, homes were cleared for families to return to. By the time they were half done, only two werewolves had been discovered. Their brute force stood no chance against the lethality of the silver weapons.

Hour after hour passed as the sweep continued. Talo led his squad to the next door, but before he could knock the smell of death assaulted his nose. Looking to his resident helpers, "Who lives here?" Both shook their heads, they had never seen the door open, ever. "There's something definitely wrong inside this home, everyone be ready for anything." Talo signaled for the opening of the door as they all stood with weapons raised. The door swung open with ease and a low click. Three poison darts came flying from the darkness and through the doorway about stomach height. Lucky for Talo and his soldiers, they were all standing at the sides of the entrance and not directly in front. Nobody wanted to be run over if a rampaging werewolf came running out. Talo peered into the pitch black void. The smell intensified ten fold causing a few in the group to gag. "Alright were going to need a professional here." Talo picked one of his soldiers, a young woman named Astrid. "I need you to head back to head quarters and inform them that we've potentially found a group of lycans. Also inform them that we require someone highly skilled in trap detection and removal." Quickly Astrid departed, leaving the rest of them to stand around waiting and wondering what horrors lie inside.

Astrid reached the officers building which Elrick and his men had taken over as their head quarters. The city guard gladly relinquished their claim on it under the circumstances. "Whew," she bent over trying to catch her breath. *Running in chainmail is not the easiest thing to do.* Sweat rolled down her forehead. *Alright, let's do this.* Into the front door and up to the front desk she went. "Astrid Lumlas reporting with an urgent message from specialist, Talo Gray." A group of six officers occupied this area, each performing various tasks.

A black haired, middle aged man sat at the table in front of her. "I'm Lieutenant Doss, what's this urgent message?" Astrid quickly relayed Talo's situation and request. Doss slid back his chair and came around the desk. "Follow me," and out the door he went. Astrid followed as he led her to another building located just a stones throw from where they stood. Inside looked like the other soldiers barracks except with not as many beds. Against the west wall stretched a metal table from one corner to the other with chairs placed every two feet or so. Astrid walked over to inspect the various devices lying on its surface. Some of the items had gears, others had pulleys, and wire.

She reached down to touch one when a voice screamed from across the room. "Stop!! Don't touch that unless you want to die in the next thirty seconds." Instinctively her arm recoiled from the item, like a child with their hand caught in a cookie jar.

"Ahh, there you are Foster, I hoped to find you in here with all your toys of death."

A grumpy looking white bearded fellow about five foot tall came stomping over. "What do you need Doss, can't you see I'm busy?"

"Foster this is Astrid, she requires the help of our best trap expert. Naturally you were my first choice old friend." Astrid could tell by his tone that these two were anything but friends.

"Nice to make your acquaintance Foster, as Doss has said I require someone with your talents. I'm part of one of the special detachments searching for werewolves in the city. We have found a possible den but traps have been set to keep us from entering."

Foster's lips curled downward with a "Hmph. That does sound like a problem. Let me grab my tool kit and I'll be right with you."

"Well you should be all set now. I'll take my leave, good luck." Doss turned around and headed back to the headquarters.

Astrid patiently waited while Foster walked the entire length of the table picking up his needed tools. "I'm all set, lead the way Astrid." The two worked their way back to the suspect home. "Gast!, what is that smell?"

Talo pointed into the dark entrance way. "We're going to find out as soon as you give us the all clear, Foster."

Foster set down his pack of tools next to the doorway. From inside he pulled out something round about the size of an apple. Gently he rubbed the device with his pointer finger in a clockwise circular motion. Instantly it lit up bright white, and started to float. With a slight push it floated into the room. The blackness tried to extinguish the light, but its brightness persisted. Foster looked back at the waiting group. "You see there, someone has placed a blinding vail spell on the room. Pretty crafty for keeping triggers hidden." Turning back, Foster started his inspection on the door first. He meticulously scrutinized everything. The trap that already triggered could now be seen. An eyelet on the door itself with a hair thin wire tied to it at one end. The opposite end attached to the trigger of three small crossbows fastened to the opposite wall. Poor Foster had to keep taking breaks to get fresh air. The further into the room he went the stronger the smell became. "Alright the first room is clear, no more surprises waiting for you. The trap on the next door has been taken care of as well." Foster pulled a rag from his pack to cover his nose and mouth. "You go on ahead, I'll wait out here until you need me again."

Talo smiled with a nod of thanks. "Is everyone ready?" Reluctantly they replied with a guarded yes. The point man held his breath as he grabbed a hold of the door handle. Every inch he opened it the smell intensified. Flies by the hundreds came buzzing out on the warm putrid air. No force in the world could hold back the vomit. Everyone including Talo reflexively started to gag. The room looked like it had been used as slaughter house for the past twenty years. "What the hell happened in there?" Talo asked nobody in particular.

All the noise from the retching soldiers covered the sound of the two werewolves that rushed out to eat them. The massive beasts leapt into the two closest troops knocking them entirely off of their feet and into the others. Complete chaos descended on the street, as screams whaled out from the two men getting their throats ripped out. A wash of crimson now sprayed around the area. Talo getting his bearings, rallied his troops. "Get up and defend yourselves, they cannot escape!" Talo's blade, Vixor came alive in its master's hands. The faint blue glow along the blade let Talo know its powers were now activated granting him unbelievable speed and dexterity. With a diagonally downward arc, the blade hit the first lycanthrope on the right side of the neck, and continued on through to its exit at the left hip. Without slowing, he continued the arc upward while simultaneously closing the distance to the second one. It released its victim to face Talo head on. The lycan lunged forward hoping to rip off his arm before he could finish his swing. That hope now dashed as the blade cut clean through the monster's left arm. Again Talo didn't slow one bit as he put Vixor through his enemies neck, before the arm had even hit the ground. The werewolves reacted just like General Hortus as they twitched and smoked. Just their shriveled corpses remained. Crack, pop, snap, those sounds reminded him of what is was like when Hortus turned. Talo turned to see the two men twisting and contorting as they transformed for the first time.

Astrid without hesitation drove her sword through the man's chest. He fell to the ground motionless. Talo did the same for the remaining soldier and finished him before he fully changed. Both men frozen in a grizzly twisted form as black fluid bubbled from their orifices. The sights and smells on this street would forever be burned into everyone's memories.

Chapter Forty-Three

CULMINATION

S ebastian and Uluck had been spending as much time as they could with the new and improved Seline. "Her body is something new but her voice and mind definitely belong to my sister. I wish I knew why Lucious changed you into this Seraphim. Maybe your human body just couldn't be saved, Seline."

The white glow radiated from the eyeholes in her mask as she looked at both men. "Something tells me that you are correct with the assumption that my body could not be fixed. I believe that I died in my human body so he made me a new one. I must say though that the wings are a great touch." Seline stretched them out as wide as she could. At least twelve feet long, and made of pure white feathers. "I will leave you two later this afternoon, and return to my new home." She looked out towards the approaching island. "I'm sure my new people have a lot of questions."

Sebastian couldn't help but wonder if the part of Seline that liked him still existed. *I know my feelings for her are the same even though I'm not sure if we could ever be together now.* "Seline, how do you feel as a Seraphim?"

Her eyeless gaze turned towards him. "I feel, I feel, strong Sebastian. Strong and at peace with everything around me."

She could tell from his staring that his question had more than one meaning. Seline pulled the glove off of her right hand and touched the side of Sebastian's face. It comforted her knowing that she could still feel the warmth of his flesh. "So how does it feel when I touch you," she queried.

"I can't find the right words to describe it, Seline. Your touch is so warm and comforting that I can't help but smile. It washes away all fatigue and feels like it's cleansing my soul of everything that's negative."

Uluck seeing Sebastian so relieved, couldn't wait for his turn. "Come on sis, it's my turn to try this."

"Very well brother." Seline touched Uluck's face the same way she did the messenger's. The massive warrior's mouth hung open and his eyes closed.

"That's incredible, nothing hurts, nothings tense, and I feel the happiest I think I've ever felt." Seline removed her hand from his cheek and put the glove back on. "Wow, even after you broke the connection I still feel so alive!"

"Good, I'm glad I have that effect on humans." Seline stopped after saying that word, humans like the realization she was no longer one just sank in.

The three of them continued on with more small talk over lunch. Shortly after they finished, Seline said her goodbyes and thrust herself skyward with her angelic wings. She headed for the floating islands and her new home.

A short time before the sun disappeared, Ezra along with his Draconian companions finally arrived at the southern gates of the city. King Elrick made sure he would be the first one to ride out at greet them. "Welcome Ezra, I'm so glad to see you doing well." Elrick's head panned from left to right as he took in the sight of the Draconian army. What they lacked in numbers they more than made up for in size, strength, and presence.

Ezra motioned to the massive Draconian to his left. "King Elrick, it is my honor to introduce the alpha Draconis, Slade."

Elrick held out a hand to greet him. Slade not sure of this custom just followed and did the same. The king grasped his hand with a firm but respectful shake. "It's wonderful to make your acquaintance, I am King Elrick. I humbly welcome you and your warriors to the City of Knowledge." A small army of squires and aids stood by to assist with getting the Draconians settled. "We have an entire section of the city prepared for you to use for housing. The young ones here will show you the way. They will also take your horses to the stables so they can be tended to."

"Thank you for your hospitality King Elrick, but why is our creator not here to meet us?"

Ezra jumped in to the conversation with his own concerns. "Please tell me Ulandra and Piercer are here safe. They never returned last night." He could tell from Elrick's body language that something bad had happened.

Elrick did his best to explain the situation to the mage while fighting back tears. He also informed them of the situation with Seline and Lucious. Slade and Ezra just stood there in a stunned silence.

The mage wiped away the newly formed tears. "Arain Drake hasn't even arrived yet and already our friends perish!"

Slade grabbed his horse packs, slinging them over his shoulder. "I am sorry for the loss of your friend, but I fear she will not be the last before Arain is slain."

Ezra and Elrick both nodded in reluctant agreement. Elrick started heading back into the city. "Come with me you two, there's a very important meeting we must attend." Off the three companions walked towards the council spire, before disappearing inside.

In the council chambers introductions were made followed by a magnificent meal. The meeting started soon after and went on for multiple hours. Updates on all the defensive plans were discussed along with new revisions. The soldiers and people in the city worked in twelve hour rotations so the preparation never stopped. They would be as ready as they could for Arain's arrival with or without Lucious' help. The council finally convened sometime after midnight with sleep being on the minds of most of those in attendance.

Not Ezra, who still hadn't had time to process his friend's death. *I cannot sleep until I say my goodbyes.* With a heavy heart the mage walked into the hospital and went up to the front desk. "Ulandra," is the only thing he needed to say before one of the aid's took him to the room. Ezra walked in, shutting the door behind him. He cried for a moment as he leaned his back against the door. Gathering himself he walked to the side of the box she now laid in. "You were so happy and full of life when we parted the other day. I can't believe you're now laying here dead, and broken." Ezra continued talking to her for a while before succumbing to exhaustion. He borrowed the cot from the next room and fell asleep near his fallen companion.

Morning came with a knock on the king's door. "Come in," he shouted. The door swung open and Talo walked inside. Elrick still sitting at the small dining table in his room put down his breakfast utensils. "Welcome Talo, how goes the hunt?"

Talo walked beside the table. "The hunt goes well, your grace. We stumbled upon a den and some impressive underground tunnels. In total six werewolves were discovered and eliminated."

Elrick sat back in his chair. "What were our casualties?"

Talo cleared his throat. "Between our hunting parties, a total of eight men and women lost their lives, sir."

The king just sat there giving a disappointed head shake. "Thanks to you and your soldiers for taking on such a dangerous task. I hoped we wouldn't loose any but knew we would lose some. Why don't you and your soldiers get some food and rest. I'll meet up with you later."

He gave a bow and left King Elrick to his breakfast.

CHAPTER FORTY-FOUR

THE END

Lucious woke in the same darkness as before. A white light off in the distance, which should be the giant doorway. He picked himself up and walked towards it. The darkness all around him didn't feel so foreign this time, it felt comforting. No sounds just absolute silence as he continued on towards the light.

After a short time walking, Lucious stood in front of the giant doorway. Without hesitation he walked inside. Everything looked exactly the same as the last time he visited. When he entered the throne room Lucious expected to see Pengeren sitting there, but the massive throne now sat empty. Lucious scanned the room looking for a clue that would tell him where he needed to go.

"Lucious, over here," came a man's voice from the other end of the room. Cautiously he walked towards the sound until he could see a tall thin man with long silver hair. "Lucious come, follow me."

Knowing he had little choice in this place, he followed. They walked down a long hallway with green emerald walls. Some of the stones were bigger than Lucious. *This hallway must be worth a fortune.* He ran his left hand along the smooth green surface as he followed. The emeralds were cold to his touch.

The hallway ended giving way to another enormous room. Hundreds of thousands of twinkling balls of light floated overhead. *Reminds me of the clear nights in Addleberry when you could see an infinite number of stars.*

"Pretty, isn't it Lucious?"

He nodded. "It's breath taking. What are they, and who are you?"

"It's just me, Pengeran. I thought you would feel more comfortable if I used this form. I can change into anything you prefer." He changed into an Arabis next and then into a Draconian. "As for what those are, let me show you." Pengeran raised his hand up high. One of the twinkling balls gradually descended into the palm of his hand.

Lucious stepped closer, his curiosity now fully piqued. "I don't know what I'm looking at, but it's so beautiful."

Pengeran held it out towards Lucious. "Hold out your hands."

He did as instructed, cupping his hands to receive the sparkly ball of light. Pengeran gently laid it into his hands. As soon as it touched his skin both of them were transported somewhere entirely new. Lucious and Pengeren both floated in the familiar blackness except this time billions of stars dotted the nothingness. Pengeran pointed behind Lucious. Turning around, the most spectacular view greeted him, a giant sun surrounded by orbiting planets. "Are we inside that sparkling ball you handed to me?"

Pengeran turned to Lucious and smiled. "Indeed we are. This is a completely sterile solar system that has yet to be curated."

Like so many times before, his brain struggled to grasp the enormity of everything around him. "I don't understand, how is all of this inside that ball of light that couldn't have been bigger than an apple?"

Pengeran chuckled out loud. "You and your sister have so much to learn. Thankfully time doesn't concern us. We can continue this next time however as I do believe Arain has just arrived."

Lucious shot up in bed with a gasp, scaring Morgan, and Stormy half to death. Quickly gathering his bearings he jumped out of bed and hurriedly started dressing.

Morgan watched, confused. "What's wrong Lucious?"

He looked at Morgan with fear in his eyes. "My sister's HERE!!!"

To

Be Continued...

AFTERWORD

I would personally like to thank you for joining me on this epic journey, and I hope you have enjoyed it as much as I have. Please feel free to leave a review on Amazon if you have a moment. Also head on over to my website jrgagne.com and signup for my email list where I will be sharing future book updates and free goodies. Thank you again for your time and I can't wait to see you for the third book Gods of Creation.

ACKNOWLEDGEMENTS

A most heartfelt thank you to my wonderful wife Jennifer for the countless hours she has spent making this book as good as it can be. Also, thank you to my daughter Aly for all the support she gives me along the way. Lastly thanks to my dogs, and goats who are always there to play catch or get scratches when I really need a break.

Made in the USA
Columbia, SC
02 September 2022